BRIGHT BURNS THE NIGHT

BRIGHT BURNS THE NIGHT

— BOOK TWO —

SARA B. LARSON

Scholastic Press

New York

Names: Larson, Sara B., author.
Title: Bright burns the night / Sara B. Larson.
Description: First edition. | New York : Scholastic Press, 2018. | Sequel to:
Dark breaks the dawn. | Summary: It is ten years since King Lorcan of the
dark kingdom defeated Queen Evelayn and transformed her into a swan, and
every year he has offered her the chance to resume her human form, provided
she bind herself to him—but this year the kingdoms are threatened by an
ancient power, and Evelayn finds that much of what she once believed was
wrong, and she realizes that she must join Lorcan in a quest to return the
balance of power to their lands before all is lost.
Identifiers: LCCN 2017035312 | ISBN 9781338068788
Subjects: LCSH: Magic—Juvenile fiction. | Shapeshifting—Juvenile fiction. |
Light and darkness—Juvenile fiction. | Kings and rulers—Juvenile fiction. |
Secrecy—Juvenile fiction. | CYAC: Magic—Fiction. | Shapeshifting—Fiction. |
Light and darkness—Fiction. | Kings, queens, rulers, etc.—Fiction. |
Secrets—Fiction.
Classification: LCC PZ7.L323953 Br 2018 | DDC 813.6 [Fic]—dc23 LC record
available at https://lccn.loc.gov/2017035312

ISBN 978-1-338-06878-8

10 9 8 7 6 5 4 3 2 1   18 19 20 21 22

Printed in the U.S.A.   23
First edition, June 2018

Book design by Abby Dening
Map by Tim Paul

For Kerstin, who has always gone above and beyond
and whose generosity knows no bounds.
And for Katie, who has championed me from the start.
Without you, none of this would be.

BRIGHT
BURNS
THE NIGHT

THE SWAN

*S*HE SLID THROUGH THE SILENT, STILL WATER, A GHOST *in the darkness. As white and soundless as snow. She was alone for the moment, but the flock was close behind. She sensed their presence, across the lake they always returned to, no matter how far they flew.*

A chill laced the breeze that ruffled her feathers with a hint of winter. She turned her face toward it, breathing in the telling scents it carried. Wood fire and decay, dying leaves, and the musk of Draíolon. A part of her remembered long legs that carried her through the forest much like her wings carried her across the wind now, and words that passed across lips that could speak, scold . . . kiss . . . But allowing herself to dredge up that part of who she had once been was fraught with pain. And so she retreated into the comfort of the swan.

As time continued its relentless march forward, slowly the burning, aching pain in her breast, the unsettling sense that part of her was gone, missing—she refused to let herself think of the blood, of the pain, of the terror—began to fade. There was the wild, untethered call of the wind and water. The simplicity of hunting for food and staying alert, staying safe. Natural instincts that comforted and erased. There were predators to avoid and a flock to attend to. They looked to her, the newcomer in their midst, suddenly one of them . . . but not quite. Slightly apart, slightly different.

Because once she had been a Draíolon.

Once she had been a queen.

With more time perhaps those memories would fade completely, erased by this new form. Perhaps the love and loss and pain that had made up her other life would someday be replaced entirely by the beating of her wings. And the mournful trumpet she rarely used, the only voice to her despair, would become nothing more than an instrument to warn or call to others of her kind . . .

Perhaps that could *have happened, if it weren't for the one week every year when he came and forced her back. Forced her to remember. Forced the pain and loss back into her heart. And every time she refused him, he sent her back into this body, this shape.*

Keeping her trapped as a swan.

ONE

CEREN'S NIGHTMARES DIDN'T ALWAYS START THE SAME way, but they all ended with Evelayn kneeling on the dais before disappearing into the swirling smoke of Lorcan's power and reemerging as a swan. He'd somehow forced her to shift that terrible night—something Evelayn hadn't been able to do on her own yet—and then he'd torn the conduit stone from her breast, staining the white feathers crimson with her blood.

When Quinlen was there, he knew to wrap his arms around Ceren and hold her silently until the terror and grief subsided once more. But on the nights when he was gone, like this one, she lay in her bed, shivering, desperately trying to force the memories back down so she could claim a bit more sleep from the painfully long hours of darkness. The dawn would only bring another dreary day of pretending to enjoy being a part of the new court King Lorcan had created . . . and fear. Fear of what had truly happened to her dearest friend and the former queen. Fear of how much longer before the power of the Draíolon of Éadrolan—diminished as it was—would disappear entirely. Fear of the gray, seeping cold that spread through their lands a little bit more every year that Lorcan ruled both Dorjhalon and Éadrolan. The murmurs grew louder every season. If they never found Evelayn—if she never regained her full power and position—would winter eventually rule the entire island, and then the world beyond, forever?

Ceren shuddered and rolled to her side, staring into the darkness, toward the wall that divided her and Quinlen's room from the nursery where their daughter slept. With Ceren's acute hearing, she was able to catch Saoirse's breathy sighs even through the stones and mortar. She was almost tempted to go in and pick up her youngling, to bury her face in Saoirse's downy-soft red curls and breathe in the infant scent that barely lingered and would soon be gone completely. But Ceren knew she risked waking Saoirse, and her daughter was sure to make enough noise to then wake up her older brother, Clive. And if *he* woke up . . .

Instead, Ceren closed her eyes and sent up a prayer to the Gods once again, pleading for help in finding and aiding Evelayn, for guidance given to Quinlen and all those who risked their lives trying to find the queen or another way to stop Lorcan, and selfishly for herself, to be able to go back to sleep and for once not be plagued by the blood-soaked dreams.

It was the same prayer she'd recited every night for ten years, since the day Evelayn had disappeared and Lorcan had made himself High King of all Lachalonia.

Though it had gone unanswered for all that time, still Ceren prayed. She prayed and she clung to what little hope remained in her that somehow, someday, her prayers would be answered.

The slight creak of the front door opening jerked Ceren back to complete alertness. Quinlen wasn't expected home until dawn . . . but she recognized his scent moments before he silently strode into their room, his normally perfectly groomed hair disheveled and his color high, as if he'd run home at full speed.

"What is it?" Ceren whispered, sitting up in bed.

Quinlen came to her and tucked a strand of stray hair behind her ear as he sat on the straw-and-feather mattress. "Something has happened at the castle. A message arrived late tonight that has thrown Lorcan's advisers into upheaval."

"Do you know what it is? Or who sent it?"

"No." Quinlen's disappointment was a bitter tang on the chilly night air. "But the rumor is that the message was brought by something . . . *other.*"

"I don't understand." Ceren glanced down at Quinlen's hands, white-knuckled where he gripped his knees.

"It wasn't a Draíolon. They are saying that it was an Ancient's emissary."

Ceren's eyes widened. "An *Ancient?* How is that even possible?" She knew they still existed—Evelayn had bargained with one to get the silk that enabled her to defeat Bain, after all. But it was unheard of for an Ancient to reach out willingly to a Draíolon. Evelayn had risked her life when she'd gone to petition Máthair Damhán.

Rather than responding, Quinlen stood back up and began to pace. "If Lorcan is somehow involved with an Ancient . . ."

Their eyes met in the darkness. He didn't have to finish the sentence. There were few Ancients left alive, and their power was diminished, it was true . . . but they were still capable of great and terrible things. Especially if aided by a king.

"I need eyes and ears in the castle right now." This last line was spoken to the floor. Ceren knew Quinlen hated to even ask, and she quickly threw off the covers, even though exhaustion weighed her body down like lead in her bones.

"Of course I'll go. Will you be able to stay with the younglings?"

"No. I have to get back. But Merryth is almost here to stay with them."

Ceren nodded as she took off her nightdress and began to quickly pull on her clothes. She knew the castle better than almost anyone. Whenever they needed someone to essentially spy on Lorcan and his advisers, it often fell to her to try and sneak through the castle and gather what information she could.

After she wrapped her bright red hair under a dark scarf, Ceren turned to face Quinlen—the male she'd Bound herself to shortly after Evelayn disappeared—and took a deep breath.

"Someday, this will be over," he murmured, the same words he had spoken for so long.

One way or another, she wanted to say. But instead, she nodded and flashed him what she hoped was a confident smile, though he could probably scent her true feelings regardless. "Yes, someday soon."

He stepped toward her, drawing her in for a tight embrace, his entire body tense, the muscles in his back bunched beneath her hands. Ceren felt his kiss against her temple, but before she could lift her face to his, there was a soft knock at the door.

"That will be Merryth." Quinlen stepped back, releasing her. "I'd better go."

"Be careful." His voice was quiet.

"I always am."

Ceren hoped he couldn't scent her fear as easily as she could scent the heavy musk of his worry as she turned and strode to the door, passing Merryth with a silent nod, and then on into the darkness toward the castle.

TWO

THE BRISK BREEZE FROM EARLIER THAT DAY HAD finally quit, leaving the night chilled and still as he strode toward the lake, his footsteps sure, even in the darkness. His sharp eyesight didn't require sunlight to make out the details of the forest around him. The skeletal branches of trees that should have been full of brightly colored leaves bent forward as if reaching for him. The hard ground was carpeted by the leaves that had fallen earlier than ever this year, already brown and trampled into the dormant earth.

Ahead, the sound of water lapping at the rocky shore of the lake was barely audible. He lifted his face and inhaled deeply. She was there. He could scent her. There were times when he'd come to the lake and the flock wasn't anywhere to be seen or scented—but never the week of Athrúfar. They were always there each night that he came.

When he emerged from the forest, the flock of swans that had been serenely floating on the lake began to arch their necks, ducking their heads and flapping their wings in agitation. They moved to encircle the one in the middle who floated on the glassy surface of the lake with preternatural stillness. When she lifted her head enough to meet his gaze with those mournful violet eyes, the stone in Lorcan's forehead flashed hot even as an icy fist clenched his stomach.

"Come to the shore," he spoke loudly enough for Evelayn to hear. "Your stubbornness causes discomfort to no one but yourself." But, as with every other time, she gave no indication that she heard him, and remained unmoving, waiting for the inevitable. Did she understand him? It was hard to know. He'd never stayed in his hawk form longer than a few hours, certainly never weeks, months . . . years. And even in those hours, he processed information differently, he understood language differently. He was himself, but not—a large portion of his mind had to become that of the bird when he shifted.

But the way she *looked* at him, the utter sorrow in the depths of those violet eyes . . .

Lorcan steeled himself. There was no helping her situation—not unless she chose to help herself. And to that end, he finally summoned his power in preparation. It came swiftly, nearly overwhelming in its strength. Little had Bain known that his own son—not Éadrolan—was the biggest threat to his rule. Even before he'd become king, Lorcan had been stronger, faster, better than the other Draíolon he'd trained with—more powerful even than his father. But Lorcan had been *very* careful, and Bain had died never realizing just how strong his son truly was.

That power built inside of him, eager to respond to his call, growing and expanding until, right at the instant the Athrúfar moon broke free of the dark eastern horizon—and moments before it would have consumed him—Lorcan extended his hands toward her and let it burst free.

The familiar cloud rushed across the water, sliced through the flock's futile efforts to guard her, and swirled around Evelayn's swan form. She held his gaze steadily until the last second, when her long, pristine white neck arched back, her beak opened in a silent cry, and then she was gone from view, enveloped by the roiling darkness.

The shadow twisted and elongated as the power surged out of Lorcan. At first it felt the same as it always had. But then . . . something changed. A strand within the power he'd summoned began to push back—to *fight* him. A new thread wove beneath the ones he'd used for the last decade, an unexpected—but incredibly strong—attempt to alter the outcome of changing Evelayn back, as if someone or some*thing* had somehow tapped into his power and was manipulating it to their will. He'd never experienced anything like it.

There was no time to wonder how it was even possible. Lorcan ground his teeth together, straining to regain control. Evelayn was hidden from view, entrapped in the eddying darkness holding her hostage above the lake. But the scar on Lorcan's right hand—the one he'd borne since he'd made his vow to her—flashed with heat, with pain. He *felt* more than heard a cry of agony that could only have come from her.

"Stop it!" He bellowed uselessly at the night sky, even as he

tried to still the trembling in his hands and finish manipulating her body as quickly as possible, despite the escalating pain traveling out of her and into his awareness, threatening to shatter his concentration. A cold sweat had broken out on his forehead; a trickle dripped down his spine as he summoned every ounce of strength he possessed to fight back, to finish the process before he lost control entirely to the dark force that sought for dominance through him—through his power.

And then finally, *finally,* with a sharp exhale, it was done.

The cloud immediately dissipated until there was only Evelayn. Her long, lithe body hung suspended in the air momentarily, her dress more ragged than ever, her head still tilted up to the dark sky above, her lavender-streaked hair hanging lank down her back. But it was *her*—her *true* form. A Draíolon, the queen of Éadrolan. Despite the attempt at interference from the darkness beyond his sight, Lorcan had succeeded. For that brief second he couldn't help the thrill that ran through him—the exultation at what he could do.

But then her sorrowful eyes met his again, for a mere millisecond, and any pride he felt turned as cold as the frigid water she plummeted into.

The water closed over Evelayn's head, cold and suffocating, as it did every time she returned to her Draíolon form. But this time, pain—terrible, burning pain—also assaulted her, and when she tried to swim for the surface, the red-hot agony in her body was so shocking, so intense, it made her cry out, allowing her mouth and throat to fill with water. The change always hurt, but something had gone very, *very* wrong this time. She tried to kick up to the surface, but her legs cramped, and panic began to set in.

Evelayn wasn't even sure she was going up; she was disoriented and her lungs burned from the water she'd inhaled, threatening to steal her consciousness. What a terrible irony if, after everything, *this* was how she died. Refusing to give in, she redoubled her efforts, kicking harder and stretching her arms up, feeling for the other swans' webbed feet, some way to gauge if she was swimming the right way.

When her fingers brushed one swan's leg, she kicked even harder, using the last of her strength to finally burst through the surface of the water into the chilled night air. Evelayn tried to gasp for air, but her lungs spasmed and she merely coughed, gagging on the water she'd inhaled, and then sank again.

She kicked upward once more, but she was weak . . . *too* weak. And then a strong arm encircled her waist, and she was pulled into a large, muscular body. As soon as her head broke through the water's surface, Evelayn inhaled deeply and succeeded in coughing up the water so she could finally draw a deep, ragged gasp of fresh, life-giving air.

Only then did she turn to look at her rescuer and realize it was the very male who had done this to her in the first place.

She shoved at him, trying to break free from his hold, but the male—*Lorcan*, that was his name, she remembered in a rush of deep-rooted memory—tightened his arm.

"What are you doing?" He struggled to keep them both above water without letting her go, and inadvertently knocked a knee into her gut, sending a wave of nauseating pain through her body and forcing her to stop fighting to get free. "Do you *want* to drown?"

"W-what . . . what did you *do* to me?" Evelayn croaked, hating how weak her unused voice always sounded in the first moments after the change, how hard it was to form words when she was so used to the limited noises of the swan.

Lorcan ignored her and began to kick toward shore with powerful strokes. Evelayn finally allowed him, knowing she was too injured to make it on her own. Though she still couldn't pinpoint *what* exactly was wrong—she only knew that something was different, and that she hurt. Badly. Oh, how she missed the power she'd once wielded—power that would have enabled her to heal in mere minutes, perhaps hours. But instead . . .

The moment her feet brushed sand, Evelayn shoved against Lorcan's hold, and this time he released her. She stumbled forward onto the sandy shore, falling to her hands and knees when her legs gave out. Before Lorcan could attempt to help her again, she forced herself to stand, her skin washed out in the moonlight, water pouring off her long, unbound hair and the tattered remains of the dress she'd worn for a decade. The dress she'd worn that fateful night with Tanvir . . . before—

That memory was fraught with pain worse than anything her body was experiencing at that moment, so she viciously cut the thoughts off as she lurched toward the nearest fallen log, her legs still unsteady.

Lorcan followed her but remained standing a few feet away, his clothes plastered to his muscular body, practically melding into the night, except for his frost-white hair, dripping down either side of his face. His silver eyes were fixed on her as if he expected her to bolt at any moment. Even soaking wet he exuded power. He was still the most handsome Draíolon she'd ever seen, and that only made her loathe him more. Especially when her gaze landed on the glowing red stone in his forehead. A reminder of what he had—and what he'd stolen from her, viciously cutting it from her body.

"What did you do to me?" Evelayn repeated, her voice more forceful and angry now that she was growing accustomed to her Draíolon form once more—and was no longer half-drowned.

"What I always do." He lifted one eyebrow above his striking eyes, but she shook her head.

"No. Something is different—something is *wrong*."

Lorcan folded his arms across his chest. "You'll have to be a bit more precise than that."

Her mind struggled as she still thought in terms of the swan, which was agonizingly simple once she was pushed back into this form—her true body. Images and feelings flashed through her mind but words were sluggish to come to her. "I . . . don't . . ."

"Explain what you mean." He was impatient, watching her, his unwavering gaze disconcerting.

But again the words escaped her. "It's . . . pain. It hurts."

"You always say it hurts."

"It's worse." Evelayn clenched her hands into fists, then extended her fingers, over and over, trying to get used to having fingers and thumbs again. A year with only wings and webbed feet made for a rough transition. She wondered if it always felt this unnatural to go back and forth—even if the change was only for a short time. Lorcan had never seemed to struggle like this the few times she'd seen him shift forms. But she refused to give him the satisfaction of asking.

When she didn't elaborate further, a muscle in his jaw tightened, but he didn't push her again.

"There is food and a change of clothes for you in there." Lorcan pointed to the knapsack lying closer to the hunched, spindly trees, specters of their former glory. Her Draíolon senses recognized the scents of food, but she could think of the name of only one—cheese.

"I don't want to change. Nor am I hungry." Which wasn't true—she was cold, miserably so, and her stomach burned with the need to feed this bigger, stronger body. But at least she was finally able to find words more easily. "Let's get this over with."

"Darkness curse me, why are you so insufferably *stubborn*? Do you forget I can scent your lie as easily as I can see it written on your face?"

Evelayn stiffened. "Yes, I *had* forgotten," she bit out. "That seems to be an unfortunate side effect of living as a *bird* for a decade, with only a night here and there when you deign to come and change me back."

His silver eyes darkened to molten ore, but his face was like a mask, completely unreadable. "If you would accept my offer, you wouldn't be forced to live as a *bird*."

Evelayn laughed once, a hard, bitter sound. "You killed my betrothed, carved out my conduit stone, and forced me into my animal form. It's hard to imagine why I haven't accepted your offer, isn't it?"

Lorcan didn't even blink at her accusations. "Lachalonia is suffering, Evelayn. Éadrolan's forests are slowly dying, and Dorjhalon is nearly always ensconced in winter now."

"And whose fault is that?" she broke in angrily. "You speak to me as if *I* should take responsibility for what has happened to Lachalonia."

He ignored her barb and continued, "Your Draíolon are nearly without power. If you won't do it for Éadrolan or for yourself, do it for them."

Evelayn jumped to her feet, the pain and weakness receding in the face of her fury. She felt even more diminished sitting on a log while he towered over her. "How dare you pretend to be concerned about what *your* actions have done to *my* kingdom—to *my* Draíolon. *You* did all of this. I should have killed you when I had the chance."

Lorcan gazed at her coolly, one eyebrow lifted as if he found her amusing, but his hands clenched into fists. There was an odd flare of heat in the scar on her right palm. "Then do it now, my queen," he taunted. "Kill me and end this. Perhaps it would be a relief to be done with it all, instead of continuing to struggle along."

"Don't mock me," Evelayn snapped back. "You know I don't have the power, or I would have long ago. Just as I killed Bain."

His mouth twisted as if he'd tasted something sour. "Oh, yes, your *great* triumph."

"Yes, *my* triumph. Right before my worst failure—giving you the chance to make that vow and believing you'd actually work with me to establish and maintain peace. You're no better than your father."

Lorcan's eyes narrowed and he took a step closer. "Don't pretend to understand me or my choices, especially when you have refused to hear me out for a decade. And *never* compare me to my father *ever* again." The cold fury in his voice and the crackle of the ground around his feet turning to ice was enough to make Evelayn close her mouth and swallow the angry retort she'd nearly spat at him, all too aware of the fact that despite his farce of an offer, he truly held all the power.

They glared at each other in the darkness until Lorcan took a deep breath and turned from her to the shadowed lake where the swans—*her swans*—floated a good distance away, watching them warily, their feathers fluffed out in distress. It could have been her imagination, but it seemed as though his shoulders sagged slightly when he finally spoke again. "You will have to excuse me, Evelayn. I haven't . . ."

He trailed off and her eyes narrowed, wondering what manipulation he was going to pull out next, when he suddenly whirled to face the blackened forest. She heard it a split second after he had—something she hadn't heard in a decade of nights like this one.

Someone was coming toward them.

THREE

EVELAYN SHRANK BACK INTO THE SHADOWS INSTINC-
tively, even though whoever was coming wouldn't know
she was there. The first year that Lorcan changed her
back, he'd taken her to the castle before presenting his offer. But
no one noticed her—no one could *see* her. Somehow, he'd made it
so she was only visible when she was a swan. It had been devastat-
ing to walk the hallways of her former home, to witness the
downfall of her Draíolon but to have no ability to help them. She
hadn't even been able to let them know she was still alive.

After that, she refused to go back, and for whatever reason,
Lorcan had agreed to keep their meetings confined to the shores
of the lake.

When the male came into view, she couldn't remember his
name for a moment, even though his raven-colored hair, glim-
mering bronze skin—more gold than brown—and dark-gray
eyes were familiar to her.

Lorcan burst out angrily, "What are you doing here, Lothar? You know I am never to be disturbed when I visit the lake."

Lothar. Of course. His brother. The prince of Dorjhalon.

A breeze wafted past Evelayn, raising bumps across her still-wet skin, chilling her.

"Of course I'm aware of your ridiculous rule, but there is—"

Whatever he'd been about to say was cut off abruptly as the breeze reached Lothar. His eyes widened, and then he turned toward Evelayn. She froze, not daring even to breathe, though she knew he wouldn't be able to see her—

But then the blood drained from his face, and he exhaled sharply.

"Is *that* . . . ? It can't possibly be—"

"You can *see* her?" Lorcan asked at the same instant Evelayn burst out, "You can *see* me?"

"That's the *queen* of Éadrolan" was Lothar's stunned response. "That's why no one is allowed to come with you— because you're hiding the *queen* down here? The Darkness-cursed *QUEEN*!" His voice grew louder and louder until the last word was a furious shout.

"Silence!" Lorcan commanded. He looked as rattled as Evelayn had ever seen him.

"You can see me," Evelayn whispered.

"What do you mean? Of course I can—you're standing right in front of me."

"Silence!" Lorcan shouted again, this time with a slash of his hand, and suddenly Evelayn *couldn't* speak. Ice coated her lips,

sealing them shut. "You shouldn't be able to see her. No one should." He turned to Evelayn. "Do you accept my offer?"

Evelayn indignantly shook her head, so livid that Lorcan was lucky he'd stolen her power—because the Light only knew what she would have done to him at that moment if she'd still possessed it.

"Then we are done for tonight." He lifted his hands again and she flinched, waiting for the shadows to encircle her, for her arms to be replaced by wings and her words replaced by instinct.

But nothing happened.

Lorcan slashed his hands back down at the ground again; this time twin bolts of ice shot out of his palms to shatter on the soil beneath their feet. A look of thunderous rage darkening his expression preceded the very air turning bitterly cold, and then he roared, *"What have you done?"* to the night sky above them.

"Who are you talking to? What is going on here?" Lothar glanced warily between Evelayn and his brother.

Lorcan ignored him and stalked over to the bag on the ground near Evelayn. She instinctively shrank away from him, farther into the minute protection of the trees. He yanked a bundle of cloth out of the knapsack and thrust it at her. "Put this on and cover up that pathetic excuse for a dress."

She just glared at him, her lips burning from the cold that sealed her mouth shut.

His jaw clenched, and with another gesture the ice was gone. "Cover yourself. Now."

"Excuse me?" Evelayn barely suppressed the urge to leap at him, to try to rip the stone from his forehead with her bare hands and nails.

"We're going to the castle, and I doubt you want to make your big debut in those rags."

Evelayn pushed the dove gray material away. "I'm *never* going there again."

"You don't have a choice." His voice was as cold and unfeeling as the wintry wind that lifted her damp hair, making her shiver.

"Just change me back."

"Not tonight. You're coming with me, one way or another. You can choose if it will be with dignity or . . ." He trailed off and shrugged impassively.

The heat of her rage was her only defense against the chill. "And if I refuse again? What will you do? Cut off my arm this time? Or maybe my tongue so I can never speak back to you again?"

"Don't tempt me," Lorcan growled.

"I hate to interrupt . . . whatever this is"—Lothar gestured between them—"but someone else is coming. I tried to tell you, an urgent message arrived at the castle for you. Apparently, I didn't return with you fast enough."

Sure enough, the sound of more footsteps was heading their way.

"What could possibly be important enough to warrant breaking my *explicit* instructions?"

"Just change me back," Evelayn cut in before Lothar could answer Lorcan's query, her anger tempered by desperation. "I can't go to the castle. You've made me endure so much—don't put me through that again." Evelayn hated how subservient she sounded, but she had no choice. Begging was her only option.

"I can't."

"Yes, you can. *Please*, just do it."

"No." Lorcan cut her off, his eyes flashing in the darkness. "I truly *can't*. I tried and it didn't work. You were right. Something *is* wrong."

Evelayn stared at him, shocked into muteness.

"I'll go try to stall whoever is coming," Lothar finally said into the charged silence. "But I expect you to explain all of this later." He shot his brother a hard glare, then turned and rushed back into the woods.

"I . . . I don't understand."

"There's no time. Put on the cloak, Evelayn. I'll try to sneak you in so you don't have to see anyone." Lorcan held it out once more, and this time, she grudgingly snatched it from his hand and wrapped it around her shoulders, pulling the hood up over her damp hair.

"Let's go. Quickly." He ushered her away from the main path that led to the castle and into the forest, taking a roundabout route, downwind and away from Lothar and whoever else had come searching for the king.

"Your Majesty! You're soaking wet! Should I summon—"

"No. Thank you, Judoc." Lorcan strode quickly away from his adviser, Evelayn disguised at his side.

"But, Your Majesty, there is—"

"Not now," Lorcan snarled, quickly losing patience as they rushed down the dimly lit hallway. Though Evelayn had been silent the entire time they'd hurried back to the castle, beneath the acrid burn of her hatred, he could scent her trepidation—fear, even. He glanced over to see her holding the hood of the cloak tightly around her face, ducking her head down to keep from being recognized.

They'd come in a back entrance and he'd done his best to avoid running into anyone, but the castle was full of Draíolon gathered to celebrate Athrúfar; it was impossible to evade them all.

"But, Sire—there's an urgent—"

"I said not now!" Lorcan roared as he halted and spun to face Judoc. The adviser must have been roaming the halls, searching for the king. "I must attend to my guest before I attend to the message. That is final. I am not to be disturbed until I seek you out."

"As you command, Sire." Judoc bowed, but he shot an anxious look at the female by Lorcan's side, his curiosity and frustration a bitter tang on the air.

Lorcan turned with a swirl of his cloak, reaching out to touch the small of Evelayn's back, to guide her from Judoc, but she flinched away from his touch. He barely held in his growl of irritation.

Who could have possibly sent a message that had caused such an uproar among his Draíolon? He certainly needed to find out as quickly as possible, but he had been serious about needing to attend to his guest first. She was as tightly wound as a bow pulled to the breaking point at his side; he could feel the tension radiating off her so thickly it was impossible to miss. If he wasn't mistaken, she was prepared to flee at the first chance possible.

"This way," he murmured, not daring to risk touching her again.

"But . . . the main quarters are—"

"I said *this way*," he repeated, slightly more forcefully.

She turned from the hallway leading to the wing where her former rooms—and her parents'—had been, and instead followed him up the stairs to their right.

They hurried up the steps and turned the corner toward the rooms he'd taken. There were two Draíolon at the end of the hallway, but he rushed her to his door and flung it open, pushing Evelayn in—her aversion to him be cursed—and then quickly following before they were spotted.

Once the door was firmly shut and locked behind him, Lorcan whirled around—and nearly ran full body into Evelayn. She stood frozen in place only a foot away, staring at the outer room of his quarters. The violet-and-lightning-laced scent that was uniquely hers filled his nose, tempting him closer, but he stayed completely still.

"Ceren." The name was barely more than an unsteady exhale.

Lorcan was silent, so close he could feel the heat from Evelayn's body, despite her cold, damp clothes.

"These were her rooms." This time her voice was slightly louder, though still shaky.

Another black mark against him, then.

When he finally spoke, his voice was low and slightly husky. "I know you think me a monster—"

"I don't *think* it"—she whirled to face him and then stumbled back a step, her shock at how close he was apparent—"I *know* it." Her hood was still pulled up, keeping her face shadowed, but his keen eyesight still caught the flash of fury in her violet eyes.

"I thought you would find it preferable to my taking your quarters—or your mother's."

Her laugh was a bitter sound. "Why bother yourself worrying about how *I* would feel? Perhaps you might have considered that before you stole my power and my kingdom and consigned me to—"

"Do you honestly think I had a choice?" The words burst out of him, spurred by the loathing on her face and the reek of her disgust that overtook the violet and sunshine he'd scented whenever she was with Tanvir—*that coward*—and then he immediately snapped his mouth shut.

Evelayn's eyes widened, her disbelief palpable. "What is *that* supposed to mean?"

"Nothing," Lorcan bit out, pushing past her to stalk over to the dark fireplace. Normally the cold didn't faze him, but in his damp clothes, he found himself chilled, which meant she must have been freezing. And it gave him a chance to compose himself. He wasn't one to lose control, to slip up. *Ever.* If he'd been able to stay composed in the face of his father's relentless cruelty, surely he could do so with Evelayn.

But even as he thought it, his right hand curled into a fist, closing over the scar that bound them together in ways she probably didn't even realize. Had he finally set himself a task that would prove impossible?

Failure wasn't an option. Or they were all doomed.

FOUR

EVELAYN REMAINED FROZEN WHERE SHE WAS, STARING at the changes to the room where she'd spent so many hours of her life. Velvet curtains in exchange for the light, airy ones Ceren's mother had preferred; thick, plush rugs; dark furniture; and oil paintings of mountains encased in snow, in place of the summer scenes that had hung for decades. It was a room that had once brought Evelayn comfort and relief but now turned her cold with dread. If Lorcan was using these rooms, where was Ceren? In the ten years of her entrapment as a swan, she'd rarely let herself think of her dearest friend. Doing so only brought her immeasurable pain and guilt. But now, faced with the changes to the room, she was unable to keep from wondering . . . and fearing the worst.

Once the fire had taken hold of the dry wood, crackling and popping in the weighted silence, Lorcan finally stood. Their eyes met and Evelayn forced herself to lift her chin, refusing to be cowed by the force of his steel-laced gaze as he looked her up and down. When he turned and strode over to the door that joined the outer chamber to the inner, disappearing inside, Evelayn let out the breath she'd been holding. But her relief was short-lived. Moments later he returned, his arms full of clothes. She stiffened, and watched him warily as his long, purposeful strides ate up the distance between them. He moved like a predator, stalking toward her, his very presence exuding power.

"Change your clothes before you become ill." Lorcan thrust the armful of items at her—what looked like a dark-purple dress and an assortment of dry undergarments. Why he had them in his possession she could only guess—and they were all repulsive options.

"No."

"Excuse me?"

Evelayn pushed the clothes away, even as she struggled not to shiver. "I won't wear those."

"And might I ask why not?"

Evelayn looked away, staring at the wall past his shoulder, refusing to answer.

A sharp tang filled her nose, and she realized in a flash of memory that she could scent emotions—and she was fairly certain *that* one was irritation. But his expression in the periphery of her vision was impenetrable, a mask of nothingness.

"If you wish to freeze, be my guest." He tossed the clothes at her feet and turned on his heel. The door to the inner chamber shut, and only then did Evelayn's shoulders sag forward, her heart pounding a drumbeat in her chest.

Despite herself, she bent to lift up the dress and was shocked to realize it looked to be a perfect fit. Did he just happen to have a mistress her exact size? The fabric was heavier than anything she'd possessed before, but was as soft as butter. Evelayn looked down in dismay at the wet, ragged dress that clung to her body. He was all too right—again. She *was* freezing. But taking off the dress she'd worn for Tanvir and changing into something Lorcan had provided for her felt like losing a battle in the war they were waging.

And if she removed the dress, she was afraid she would lose the final connection she had to Tanvir.

A sudden pounding directly behind her made Evelayn jump, and she spun to stare at the shut door, her heart in her throat. The pounding came again, accompanied by a shout.

"Your Majesty! It can wait no longer! You *must* come at once!"

When no one responded, there was another pounding, accompanied by "Sire! Please!"

The bedroom door slammed open, and Lorcan's scent of frost-laced pine mixed with that heavier hint of velvet night preceded the slapping of bare feet against the stone floor as he pushed past Evelayn to open the door, barely more than a crack. She backed up hastily, shocked to see him dressed in a pair of dry breeches and nothing else.

"I will be out momentarily. You may have the message taken to the council room."

Evelayn couldn't tear her eyes from Lorcan's muscular back as he shut the door once more. Dismay churned the acid in her belly. He didn't turn yet, keeping his hand flat against the heavy wooden frame.

"I don't want your pity," he said darkly, his voice low.

"I don't pity you." The words came out brusque, but it was a lie, and she knew he knew it. Even after all he'd done, and all the pain he'd caused, she couldn't help it. Would she ever be able to erase the sight of all those scars? A veritable maze of angry red and ghostlike white lines, some long and thin, others wide and blunt. A map of torture and abuse she couldn't even begin to fathom.

Lorcan spun to face her, his silver eyes flashing in the firelight. Her own eyes widened at the sight of even more scars across his sculpted chest and abdomen. Even his shoulders and biceps bore marks.

"Who did this to you?" The question was barely more than a whisper.

"My father's method of training was perhaps more brutal than those employed to train you." Lorcan bent and scooped up the undergarments off the floor. "But apparently far more effective."

Evelayn belatedly realized she still held the dress, clutching it with white knuckles. He moved past her to lay the undergarments on the chair closest to the fire and went on into his room, only to emerge moments later fully dressed. Without another word, he exited his quarters.

She was left standing alone in the center of the room as the scrape of the lock clicking into place dashed her hopes of escape.

The castle was in chaos, servants rushing to and fro, gossip flying as fast as the feet that carried it. It suited Ceren perfectly. She was able to slip in unnoticed, her ears perked and her eyes keen as she made her way through the corridors. She'd worn a drab dress, and her hair was covered in a white kerchief. The outfit of a lower member of court, far enough above the servants not to warrant their suspicion, but low enough not to garner the interest of the nobility who still resided at the castle or who had come for Athrúfar. She'd mastered the art of slumping just enough, of acting meek, to make her veritably invisible.

It was why Quinlen had asked her to come, much as he hated it. She was one of the best spies they had, and he knew it. Evelayn had always told her she was a consummate actress when she wanted to be. *If only she could see me now,* Ceren thought. What would the queen think of her former friend? She was certainly not the laughing, carefree youngling Evelayn had known a decade ago, before . . .

"It was a beast of some sort, I'm sure of it. My cousin is friends with the doormale, and he swears the messenger was at least eight feet tall."

"My sister said she couldn't sleep and was standing at her window when the messenger came. At first she thought it merely some kind of animal, it wasn't *that* big after all. But then it looked up at her, as if it *knew* she was looking down from her window, and she swears its eyes burned red as fire."

"I didn't see it, but I overheard Lady Devroux speaking about the whole ordeal. She was taking a walk around the grounds when the messenger came. She didn't see it either, but she heard the voice and she said it was like ice, so cold it burned her ears!"

Ceren wandered through the halls, sifting through the rumors for any threads of similarity or truth. Very few of the stories matched up, which led her to believe none of them had truly seen or heard the messenger. And whoever *had* must have been taken immediately to be questioned—or silenced. But where? She'd caught no sight of the king, his brother or mother, or any of his council.

It was easier—safer—to keep to the wings of the castle frequented by servants or the lower nobility, but if she wanted answers, Ceren realized she would have to venture closer to the main parts of the castle. It increased the risk of being recognized if any of the Light Draíolon were up and about, but if she had to think of an excuse quickly, so be it. Quinlen needed information.

The talk was quieter in the more lavish wings of the castle, the gossip more subdued, but no less sensational. Ceren pretended to inspect statues, to admire paintings, but never paused for too long. She did nothing to garner notice.

She scented King Lorcan moments before he strode down the hallway, his adviser Judoc hurrying to keep pace with him. Ceren's instinct was to quickly turn away, before he could see her face, but nothing caught attention more than sudden movement. Instead, she forced herself to slowly turn to face the tapestry behind her, as if she hadn't noticed the king coming.

"But, Sire, it is unheard of for you to leave a guest unattended in your personal quarters!" Judoc protested as they sped past Ceren, his voice lowered, but not enough to escape a Draíolon's keen hearing.

"Leave it to me to decide what to do with my personal guests. It is none of your concern—nor anyone else's. Do I make myself clear?" Lorcan's words grew harder to decipher the farther away they got, but Ceren dared not follow—at least not right away.

"Oh, Your Majesty! We were just speaking of you!" One of the Dark Draíolon standing nearby with a friend called out after her king, but he ignored her, turning the corner that would lead to the council room Evelayn had once used—and which Lorcan now utilized for his own meetings.

"Come. Perhaps if we hurry, we can catch him." The two females rushed after Lorcan, which left Ceren by herself in the hallway for the moment.

A guest? Alone in his rooms?

Ceren's heart pounded life-sustaining blood through her body, but her hands went cold with trepidation. Did she dare even attempt something so risky? They had been her rooms for most of her life, after all. She knew them better than anyone.

There was no chance she would be able to listen to the meeting Lorcan was no doubt assembling. The council room was heavily guarded and there were no hidden doors, entrances, or passageways she could use to spy on the king.

But there *was* a way to get into his quarters.

The rumors had been ridiculously unhelpful. If she could find out who his guest was, at least she would have something substantial to take back to Quinlen. Unless Lorcan caught her, and then she would likely never return to Quinlen again. Or Saoirse and Clive.

Ceren stood undecided for a long moment, thinking of her

younglings, of her Mate. Was it worth the risk? There was a chance the "guest" was merely a distraction . . . for Lorcan's baser wants. But it was common knowledge among all the nobility *and* servants that Lorcan had never once taken a female to his rooms before, for any reason, so there was little reason to believe he would start tonight—and it was even more baffling why he would leave such a person alone, unguarded, in his private quarters. No, there was someone important up there, she was sure of it.

Ceren took a deep breath and turned to trace a path that was as familiar as breathing to her. For the first time since Lorcan had taken control of her former rooms, she was going back.

FIVE

T HE PARCHMENT SAT ON THE TABLE IN FRONT OF HIM, the candelabras nearly burned down to their nubs in the now silent room. Lorcan held his head in his hands and stared down at the words, scrawled in blood-red ink. For all he knew, it *was* blood.

To send a demand like this, to the castle . . . it was too blatant. The rumors were surely flying out of control by now. And on the same night that changing Evelayn had no longer worked. It wasn't a coincidence, he was sure of it.

But what could it possibly mean?

He couldn't leave her alone in his quarters much longer, he knew. Either she would grow desperate enough to try something dangerous, or someone would hear about his guest and become curious.

As if in response to his thoughts, the door behind him opened.

"Begging your pardon, Your Majesty, but Lord Crenwheal

sent me to see if you or your guest would be needing anything tonight?"

Of course he did. Lorcan took a long, slow breath to calm his frayed temper before he snapped at the servant.

Without turning to look, he answered, "How solicitous of Judoc. But no, thank you. My guest has already been taken care of and is no longer with us. And I wish only for solitude."

"Of course, Sire. I will relay the message and beg your pardon, once more."

Lorcan lifted a hand in dismissal and waited until he heard the door shut before he glanced over his shoulder to make sure he was truly alone again and then slammed his fist down against the table with a dull thud. "Darkness curse you," Lorcan swore at Judoc. Now the entire castle would be abuzz with news of his "guest."

The heavy chair scraped across the stone floor when Lorcan pushed it back and stood. Most Draíolon feared him and wouldn't dare go to his quarters without his express permission or his summons. But with all the events of the night stirring them up into a flurry of agitation, he didn't dare take chances with the queen of Éadrolan alone in his rooms.

He picked up the parchment and folded it back into a square, staring down at the seam where he'd sliced through the hardened sealing wax. Thankfully, the seal hadn't been tampered with when he finally came into possession of the message. As it was, just the news of *who* had delivered the message had sent the Draíolon into a frenzy of gossip and speculation, from what his advisers had told him. If anyone had read its contents, he could only imagine what chaos and panic would have ensued. It was fortunate he was well practiced in the art of keeping his expression blank when under scrutiny, no matter how shocked or upset he truly was. He had his father to thank for that. And tonight it had served him well, as a handful of his advisers had been present when he opened the parchment and read the contents of the message.

One week. That's all she'd given him. A *week* to return with her stipulations completed. After a decade of little to no success.

Lorcan shoved the parchment into the pocket of his vest and finally quit the shadowed room where he'd once stood before the council of Éadrolan and told Evelayn he would make a vow. His right hand closed into a fist over the scar on his palm as he shut the door, ignoring the sentinels standing guard, and strode down the darkened hallway back toward his quarters and the very female who had forced him to make that fateful cut.

Evelayn sat on the floor in front of the fire, no longer cold, as her dress and hair had finally dried. She'd managed to resist the temptation of changing her clothes—but only just. Even now, she held the dark-purple gown in her lap, fingering the plush material absently as she stared into the flames.

She was a stranger in her own home—*trapped* in her own home. And to what end? What game was Lorcan playing now? He'd seemed angry when he'd claimed he couldn't change her back, which led her to believe that he was in earnest. But he was also a flawless actor, and could just be playing yet another part.

Why, though? Why keep her in this form now—why make her visible after all this time?

Evelayn tried to keep her mind focused on those questions, but the longer she was left alone, and in her true form, the harder it was to keep her memories and pain at bay. She couldn't help thinking of the night everything had exploded in her face—the night she'd gone from supreme happiness to horror in the space of a few hours. Too many years had passed to hold on to the details of his face, but with effort, she could summon the memory of Tanvir's amber eyes and his smile. The feel of his hands on her back . . . and his lips on hers.

She still wore his ring on her hand.

The fire blurred in front of her. Evelayn lifted the dress and pressed it against her mouth, trying to force the sobs that threatened to escape back down into the depths of her shattered heart. She couldn't bear the thought of Lorcan walking in on her crying, to scent the triumph he would no doubt experience at her suffering.

A soft click in the lock sent Evelayn scrambling to her feet, dropping the gown and swiping at her face to erase evidence of her weakness. She searched frantically for a weapon of some sort—anything with which to defend herself from whatever Lorcan intended to do to her. Not that it would be any use against his power, but she had to at least *try*. He hadn't made a violent move yet, but there had been the message to occupy him. Now that he'd been gone some time, surely he had taken care of whatever it was, and was ready to come back and deal with her.

Before she could find anything, the lock scraped and Evelayn froze. The door cracked open, only a sliver at first, and then wide enough to permit a body to enter. Not Lorcan, Evelayn realized with simultaneous relief and terror. It was a female, backing in slowly, as if making sure she wasn't being watched. Someone from the lower nobility, based on the clothes she wore, and someone nearly the same size as her. Was this the female he entertained here, whose dress he'd tried to give her?

Evelayn glanced wildly about the room, searching for somewhere to hide, but the door clicked shut softly, the lock sliding back into place. The female turned to face her.

And then she screamed.

SIX

THE STRENGTH WENT OUT OF CEREN'S LEGS, AND IT
was all she could do not to fall to her knees.

"Evelayn?" The name was a whisper of sound, slipping across her lips. The other female stayed frozen in place,
staring back at her. Her lavender-streaked hair hung limp down
her back, her dress was in tatters, and she was rail thin, her violet
eyes two round wells of despair. But . . . *it was her.*

Ceren shook her head, her mind refusing to accept the evidence her eyes presented. It couldn't be . . . it *couldn't.* Here?
In Lorcan's quarters, after all this time—after all the years of
searching and praying? Perhaps she wasn't real. A spirit, come to
torture her.

But then the specter spoke. *"Ceren?"*

Ceren needed no more incentive—she rushed forward and
threw her arms around Evelayn, who had always been more sister than friend to her. Ceren had never felt her so frail, so

diminished. Evelayn's shoulders shook with sobs as she hesitantly put her arms around Ceren, returning the embrace.

"How is this possible? What happened to you—where have you been? We've searched *everywhere* and—"

"What a touching reunion." A voice as smooth as velvet interrupted.

Ceren gasped and whirled to see Lorcan standing by the door, his handsome face set in his usual indecipherable mask.

"How did you get in here?" When his cold silver eyes landed on hers, Ceren had to suppress a shiver.

"These were once my rooms. And I often had need of getting in or out through . . . unorthodox methods."

"Ah, yes, that's right. The elusive Lady Ceren." He sketched her a mocking bow.

Evelayn still hadn't said a word; she stood frozen at Ceren's side. Her fear was a bitter tang to Lorcan's wintry ire.

"You do realize I will have to punish you for this. Severely. Sneaking about my castle, breaking into my rooms? Whatever will others think?"

"*My* castle," Evelayn finally spoke, her voice quiet but made of steel.

Lorcan's gaze slid to hers, and Ceren detected an odd note in his voice, an unfamiliar undertone to his scent when he lifted one brow and responded, "As you say. But, unfortunately, in *my* control at this time. If word got out that a Draíolon had broken into my rooms and left unpunished, what kind of chaos do you think that would inspire?"

"No one need find out that she came in here."

"True," Lorcan conceded with a tip of his head, "but . . ."

Evelayn stiffened beside Ceren, who just listened, watching their exchange in baffled silence.

"What do you want, Lorcan? What must I do to ensure her safe return to . . ."

"Quinlen," Ceren supplied. "And our younglings."

Evelayn spun to face her, eyes wide. "You and Quinlen? You . . . you have . . ."

Ceren nodded, the thought of Clive and Saoirse sleeping peacefully, innocently, at home—their fates now in the king's hands—sent a shock of terror through her, turning her body cold.

"What do you want?" Evelayn repeated, turning to Lorcan once more, who was watching them silently, his expression unreadable.

He didn't respond for a long, terrible space of time in which Ceren could hear only the pounding of her own heart and the crackle and hiss of the fire in the hearth.

"You wish to bargain for her safety and freedom," he said at last, a stony statement.

Evelayn lifted her chin, her jaw set. Ceren hadn't seen her for a decade, but she remembered *this*—the queen's indomitable strength. It bolstered her own flagging courage.

Lorcan leaned back against the wall, crossing one ankle over the other. Despite his nonchalance, power still emanated from him, a beacon of tension in the room. "And so desperation shall drive yet another hasty decision, spinning the web of regret ever larger."

Ceren glanced to Evelayn to see if that odd pronouncement made sense to her, but she looked just as confused as Ceren. Before she could think on it further, Lorcan continued.

"You know what I wish, my lady queen. As I have wished it for ten long years."

The scent of Evelayn's distress flared into lightning-charged anger in the blink of an eye, but rather than lashing out as Ceren had expected, she merely said, "If that is your price," through gritted teeth.

Lorcan nodded once, a brief, severe movement. "Then it shall be done. When you keep your word, I'll see to it that she is returned home safely." He gave two quick jerks on a bell pull before looking Evelayn up and down once again. "And you will change so that you don't look so pathetic when I announce our impending Binding."

Ceren gasped. *"What?"*

Lorcan ignored her and continued, "I will give you five minutes of privacy to put on that dress before I come out and do it for you." He turned on his heel and strode toward the adjoining room.

Ceren whirled to face Evelayn, grabbing her hand. "You can't do this. It's not worth it!"

But Evelayn remained standing as stiff as a statue until the slamming of the bedroom door made her flinch.

"It's already done." She stared down at their clenched hands. "I couldn't bear it if he . . . if you . . . You have *younglings*."

Despite the fissure of fear in her heart that threatened to crack open at the thought of her family, Ceren repeated, "You can't do this. Sometimes you have to sacrifice the few for the many. We're not worth this."

The flames in the hearth reflected in Evelayn's eyes, a flash of firelight burning in her violet irises. "*Never* say that again. I've made my decision. We're not discussing it further. Now help me change before he comes back out."

Ceren bit back her retort at the command in Evelayn's voice and merely nodded, her stomach clenched in horror as she thought of what Lorcan was requiring of her queen.

SEVEN

T HE DRESS WAS LUXURIOUS, DRAPING OVER HER BODY as though it had been made for her. And Evelayn hated it as much as the male who had given it to her.

"There's no time to really do anything with your hair," Ceren said as she finished tying the bodice.

"It doesn't matter." Evelayn ran her fingers through the tangles, trying to keep her trembling under control. *I am strong, I am not afraid,* she coached herself silently, even though the words rang false. She *had* to figure out a way to save her friend, and if this was what was required, then so be it.

If Tanvir had survived, she would have—but he hadn't, so there was no use thinking of what might have been. Ceren's future and safety rested in her hands; she would Bind herself to Lorcan to ensure whatever punishment he'd intended to dole out be rescinded. And despite her friend's protests, it *was* worth it.

A knock at the door startled Evelayn. She'd forgotten Lorcan had summoned a servant. Lorcan emerged from the adjoining room and paused for a moment to look her over, his gaze traveling from the top of the dress to her bare feet and then back up again. Without a word, he turned and cracked open the door, shielding them from view.

"You summoned, Your Majesty?"

"Yes. I require two guards to escort a female to the prison."

"What?" Evelayn burst out, but Ceren grabbed her arm, yanking her back when she moved to storm toward the king.

If the messenger was shocked at his king's request or the outburst from inside his quarters, his voice didn't reveal it when he coolly replied, "Yes, Sire."

"And one more thing." Lorcan leaned forward, murmuring so quietly to the servant that not even Evelayn's acute hearing could catch his words.

"Yes, Sire," the servant repeated, and then Lorcan shut the door and faced the two females once more.

"You will not take her away." Evelayn stepped in front of Ceren, hoping she looked braver than the trembling in her knees suggested.

Lorcan's eyes narrowed. "Consider carefully what you do in the next few minutes, my lady queen. I have not said I will *keep* her there—yet. But I must do what is necessary to help you realize the gravity of the situation so you don't do anything rash, such as change your mind."

"Evelayn, don't," Ceren whispered, her voice so quiet Evelayn barely heard her warning.

"I refuse to let you put her down there!"

"Why ever not? It was good enough for me and my family, wasn't it?"

Heat rose up Evelayn's neck. "You were a threat to my kingdom—to the entire island of Lachalonia!"

"How can you be sure? What had I ever done to give you that impression?"

Images flashed through her mind: her mother's enshrouded body lying on the ground before Evelayn called down the sun to consume her, Bain chasing her through the forest intent on killing her, Tanvir falling to the ground in front of Lorcan—*dead*.

Evelayn flung her hands out at Lorcan, reaching for a well of power that had long been empty. When nothing happened, she instead balled her fingers into fists and launched herself at him, pummeling his chest and shoulders over and over again. He withstood the abuse silently, not even flinching.

"You are a . . . a *monster*!" she shouted, beating her fists against his body uselessly, no more effective at hurting him than a mouse nipping at a jaguar's heels. Or a swan attempting to fight a hawk.

"A monster, am I?" he repeated coldly. Faster than the blink of an eye he snatched her wrists, halting her attack. She struggled against him, twisting and pulling, but to no avail. He was all sinewy muscle and unadulterated power—far her superior in physical strength. He held her captive.

"I *loathe* you," she spat, having nothing left to fight him with except her words.

"A fact of which I am fully aware," he said in that same stony tone. "And yet, if you wish to have your friend returned home safely, I still must require you to break your vow to Tanvir and Bind yourself to me. Perhaps with time, you can learn to see past the *monster* to the king inside."

Rage bubbled up through her belly, burning hot in her hollow heart. There was a time when anger overcoming her in such a way was a warning to calm down or risk causing irreparable harm by losing control, but those memories were a hazy thing of the past. She was entirely powerless now, which made her even more furious, because *he* was the reason she could do nothing to protect any of her Draíolon, least of all Ceren.

Nothing except Bind herself to him.

"You and I both know there is nothing you can do to stop me." Lorcan's voice was as soft as velvet, his gaze never wavering from hers. Evelayn's breaths came faster despite her attempts to maintain a mien of control. "You have agreed to Bind yourself to me. If you change your mind, you will leave me with no choice but to punish your friend for her crimes."

"There is always a choice," Evelayn said, trying to ignore the branding heat of his hands around her wrists and his body so close to hers.

"Yes," Lorcan agreed, "and right now, that choice is *yours*."

Ceren spoke from behind her. "Do not worry for me."

"You say that perhaps someday I will realize you are not the monster I say you are—and yet you keep acting like one." Evelayn continued to ignore her friend. "Why don't you prove what you claim to be true? Prove you aren't a monster, and let her go without punishment because it's the right thing to do."

"But *is* it the right thing to do? Who are you to say what is right or wrong? You know so very little of what has happened—or what *is* happening—in our kingdoms at this time." Lorcan's hands tightened around her wrists, to the point of pain. He towered over her, his eyes flashing as he stared down at her. But still she lifted her chin and clenched her teeth in challenge. They glared at each other, locked in a silent battle of wills.

And then as suddenly as he'd grabbed her wrists in the first place, Lorcan released her with a push, sending her stumbling toward Ceren. He sauntered over to sit in one of the massive, oversize chairs near the fire, lounging back as he regarded her, the picture of insouciance. "You, above all, should recognize that as royals we don't have the luxury of rash decisions. Everything has consequences, and I fear that you are not quite in possession of enough facts to know whether or not this particular situation warrants the leniency you suggest." He lifted a hand and idly summoned a flickering black flame to hover above his palm.

Evelayn forced herself to stand tall as she gazed at the shadowflame he wielded—the casual reminder of just how helpless she was, and how pointless her attempt to defy him. "And yet, the consequences that would follow the exercise of your *leniency* can be bought with my heart. How convenient for you."

Lorcan leaned forward, his silver gaze unrelenting on hers. "Have you ever made a bargain, Evelayn? Taken a gamble because you felt the possible reward was great enough to warrant the risk?"

Evelayn barely managed to keep control of her expression, hoping she still possessed the skill to hide her true emotions—which at the moment warred between shock and fear. He couldn't possibly know about what had happened with Máthair Damhán, could he?

"How is that relevant to this conversation?" She disregarded the warning squeeze of Ceren's hand on her arm.

"It has *everything* to do with this conversation," he fired back.

A sudden thunderous boom echoed through the castle, making the very floor shudder beneath her feet. Lorcan shot up from the chair, all pretense of nonchalance erased.

"What was *that?*"

He ignored her, his head cocked, listening. Evelayn's keen hearing caught the sound of someone running down the hall at the same moment Lorcan turned and rushed toward the door. He was already halfway across the room when someone pounded on the thick wood and then flung it open.

"What is the meaning—"

Lorcan's imperious exclamation cut off when Lothar stumbled into the room, his tunic soaked in blood.

"I tried . . . to stop her . . . I tried . . ." The words came out with a gurgle, and then he collapsed on the floor.

EIGHT

L OTHAR!"

His name came out a hoarse cry as Lorcan rushed to his brother's side. Lorcan's hands felt like stone, clumsy and useless, as he ripped away the tunic to reveal two gaping wounds in Lothar's abdomen. It looked as though he'd been impaled by massive, jagged swords.

Lorcan barely registered the sound of fighting in the castle as he wadded up the now ruined material and pressed it to one of the wounds to stanch the flow of blood. Suddenly, someone else was there, pressing another bundle of cloth against the other cavernous tear in his brother's flesh. Lorcan risked a quick glance and was shocked to see Evelayn on her knees beside him, her expression drawn.

"He's lost so much blood . . ." The words were soft, but he heard them as though she'd shouted. Light and Dark Draíolon were capable of healing fast enough to stave off death from most injuries, and royals healed even faster than any others. But these wounds were so large, so terrible . . .

"*Dammit*, Lothar! What happened?" Lorcan pressed even harder, willing his brother's flesh to knit together, to repair itself before he bled out right in front of him. After all the years of trying to keep Lothar from receiving the brunt of their father's wrath and wildly violent mood swings, was *this* how his life would end?

"*Sire!* Bar the door! Sire!" The warning shout echoed down the hallway as yet another boom shook the stone walls and floor.

"Who could possibly attack you and do this?" Evelayn asked.

Lorcan looked up at Evelayn, at the concern on her beautiful face, and the hold she already had on him squeezed ever tighter. "I am afraid we're about to find out."

Their gazes remained locked for one breathless moment, and then she said, "You must go. Go and stop them." Evelayn shouldered him back, placing her hand over Lorcan's to keep pressure on his compress. "Ceren—come help me!"

Lorcan stared down at her hand on top of his night-black one and then at Lothar's still, bloodless face, his copper skin paled to fawn. Ice and darkness rose through his body, a massive wave of power summoned by his fear and fury.

Another boom rattled the castle, and Evelayn practically shouted, "*Go!*"

He loathed the necessity of it but knew she was right. With a growl, Lorcan pulled his hand out from under hers and jumped to his feet. Without a word, he strode out into the hallway, shutting the door behind him in hopes of protecting those inside from whatever terror had entered the castle.

This late at night the hallway was dark, but that was to his advantage. His eyesight was as keen as any nocturnal creature's. Ahead, a handful of Dark Draíolon barricaded the top of the stairs, wielding shadow-swords and hurtling great blasts of shadowflame at whatever intruder had penetrated the castle defenses to this point.

Lorcan moved silently toward the sentries, all of his senses trained on what lay ahead. The air was full of the rank stench of spilled blood, the acrid musk of burnt upholstery, along with a heavy dose of fear and adrenaline mixed together like lightning traveling through snow. But *there*, beneath it all, was a faint scent that stopped him in his tracks.

He took a deep, steadying breath and summoned his own twin swords made of writhing darkness and shadowflame.

Then he plunged into the fray.

Evelayn's hands shook from the effort of pressing down so hard, but she was afraid to let up even a tiny bit, sure Lothar had very little—if any—blood left to spare.

"I don't understand. Not only does he have full access to his power, but he's a *royal*. Who could have possibly done this?" she whispered to Ceren, who was likewise pressing down on his torso.

"And during Athrúfar, when they are coming into the height of their power," Ceren added, just as quietly. With the door shut, the sounds of the fight were muffled slightly, but they could still hear it—along with cries of dismay and fear as Draíolon in the rooms all around them were awoken by the commotion.

Evelayn gazed down at the still, too-pale face of Lorcan's brother. The brothers shared similar bone structure but very few other likenesses. Lothar had the same copper skin as his father, rather than the obsidian-black tone Lorcan had inherited from their mother.

"Where is Abarrane?" she asked at the thought of the other queen. "Is she here as well?"

"Sometimes," Ceren answered without looking up. "Lorcan regularly sends her back to Dorjhalon to be his eyes and ears in their kingdom."

Another boom shuddered through the castle, accompanied by screams of pain that were suddenly silenced. Evelayn's hands trembled against the blood-soaked compress.

"Is his tissue regenerating at all?"

"I don't dare release the pressure to look."

Evelayn shut her eyes and offered up a brief prayer to spare the prince of Dorjhalon. Lothar had never shown any inclination to take after his father, mother, or brother. She'd made the wrong choice when she'd allowed Lorcan to live and let him claim the power back for his people. And if Lothar died now, there was no hope of ever replacing Lorcan as king without destroying the balance in Lachalonia in the other direction . . . at least until he had a son who was of age.

Realizing the futile direction of her thoughts, a tiny burst of laughter slipped out.

"What could possibly be funny about this situation?" Ceren finally looked up, her eyebrows raised.

"I was thinking we can't let Lothar die, because if he dies, then I can't kill Lorcan without permanently destroying the balance in our world. Which is quite funny actually, when one remembers the fact that I am completely powerless. Oh—and the minor detail of having now promised to Bind myself to him." Evelayn laughed again, a hollow, almost hysterical sound.

"You're not powerless. There are other types of power—other ways to win this battle." But the despair reflected back to her in Ceren's eyes when their gazes met over Lothar's prone body spoke a different story than her words.

"Perhaps you are right," Evelayn said, even though she was certain neither of them believed it.

The door suddenly banged open, making them jump. Evelayn's body went cold as she twisted to see who was coming for them—they had no weapons, no shields, no power. No hope of defending themselves and protecting the prince.

But no one entered. The sounds of fighting were louder than ever. There was a thud and a dull bang, the sound of a fist slamming into flesh and something crashing into the wall. Lorcan's voice was audible but distant; she couldn't even make out his words. She tensed, though she had no idea what she could do.

Another thud—a body hitting the floor?—and then a tall, disheveled Draíolon walked through the doorway.

Evelayn rose to a crouch, preparing to do something, *anything*, to at least *try* to defend herself, and then froze. Her heart lurched, as though an invisible hand reached beneath her rib cage and was squeezing it, stealing her strength and her ability to breathe at the same time.

"Oh, thank the Light, it's you. *Ev*—the blood! You need to keep pressure on the wound . . ."

But Ceren's words were a dull echo beneath the roar of Evelayn's blood in her ears. Her hand slipped off of Lothar's body as she unsteadily rose to her feet, her legs feeling as though they would collapse beneath her at any moment.

Because the male she faced—the one who stared back at her with wide amber eyes, his usually golden skin unnaturally pale—was Tanvir.

NINE

LORCAN PUSHED THE SHADOW-SHIELD FORWARD AND stalked down the rest of the stairs, forcing the intruder farther back into the main hall, away from the rest of the nobility upstairs—and the queen in his quarters.

One female had done all this? One measly female. Anger burned icy hot in his veins, along with the flow of his power. But there was something . . . *off* about her, beyond her unnatural amount of power. The smell of decay, for one, and a sense that all was not as it should be. She appeared to be a normal Draíolon, but there was something about her pitch-black eyes, her inky lips, and the occasional jerking movement that didn't seem quite right.

There was no way a Draíolon this powerful wouldn't have been known to him before this moment. If he weren't in the middle of trying to keep her from killing any more of his subjects, Lorcan would have had the ability to concentrate on deciphering what exactly it was that struck him as wrong. But instead, he was busy maintaining the shadow-shield that kept her at bay while still wielding his shadow-swords.

She summoned another blast of flame—a strange bluish purple, of neither Light nor Dark power—and blasted it at his shield. The dark shadows shuddered, but held.

"I don't know what you hoped to accomplish tonight, but unfortunately what you *will* find is your death." He addressed her for the first time.

"I've come to deliver a message, King of Darkness." The words were a raspy threat.

A sudden terrible theory began to form, one that explained the attack and the unnatural power . . . but was far worse than a rogue Draíolon.

Lorcan drew some of his power back to sharpen his sight—to focus all his senses on the female on the other side of the shadow wall between them. Sure enough, the Draíolon form she'd taken wavered and faded slightly, turning him cold with fury.

"I know what you are, messenger. You can tell your master I already received her *note*." He sneered on the last word.

"That was only the first half of her message, King of Draíolon. I am the second."

With a sudden shriek, she shed her glamour to launch herself into the air, using her sticky legs to cling to the ceiling and scuttle toward him, over the defensive wall he'd created. Lorcan jumped back, swinging his shadow-sword at her. The daughter of Máthair Damhán dodged, moving at blinding speed. Where had she come upon such power? To glamour herself, to wield magic she wasn't supposed to have access to? It shouldn't have been possible.

She took advantage of his slight lapse in concentration and lashed out. Lorcan whirled out of reach in the blink of an eye, but she somehow still caught his left bicep with a sharpened pincer, slicing through his flesh and muscle. Large, lethal weapons that easily could have caused those gaping wounds in Lothar's abdomen were attached to her arachnid body. Wrath like he'd never known summoned an even stronger flow of power into his body, nearly consuming him. She'd injured and killed so many of his Draíolon, filling the air with the fetid scent of death and blood.

"Your master should have realized who she is dealing with. You will both regret this night's work," Lorcan snarled. And then he let his power loose and flew at her, swords flashing with black lightning—a raging fury of shadow and ice that left no mercy in its wake.

Tanvir was . . . *alive*. Evelayn stared at him, incapable of believing the evidence of her eyes—reality unable to penetrate her numb grief. She'd *watched* him die. Seen him swallowed up by Lorcan's power and then fallen to the ground, still—silent—*gone*.

But . . . she hadn't checked to make absolutely certain. She'd rushed to his side but just as quickly leapt forward to attack Lorcan, leaving Tanvir lying there without having felt his skin for warmth, or checking for a heartbeat. Was it even *possible*? Was he truly standing mere feet away from her after all this time? His bark-brown hair was longer than she remembered, hastily pulled back as if he'd been woken up, his sunshine-gold skin more pallid than it had been, but it was *him*.

Tanvir. Evelayn tried to speak his name, but her throat was suddenly so dry, no sound would come out.

He stared openly at her, visibly stunned. His scent filled her nostrils, but there was a strange hint of something rancid—something *off*—beneath the citrus and spice that had once been so familiar to her.

"Tanvir." This time a whisper came out, a hoarse cry that was half sob. Evelayn lurched forward, toward him, but he flinched and she froze again, stunned to realize the look in his eyes wasn't truly shock—it was *dismay.*

"Tanvir?"

"Why are you here?" When he finally spoke, it sounded like an accusation, and he still didn't make any move to come to her.

Not *You're alive* or *Is it really you?* but *Why are you here?* Evelayn reeled back as though he'd slapped her.

"You shouldn't be here. You have to go. *Now.*"

"I . . . I don't understand."

She was shaking, her whole body humming with the need to rush into his arms, but he didn't want her. *He didn't want her.*

Evelayn somehow made herself face Ceren, who was very busy inspecting Lothar's torso, pushing down hard on both wounds since Evelayn had abandoned her post. But Evelayn knew her well enough, even after all the years apart, to recognize her unease.

"What are you even doing here—in Lorcan's quarters of all places?" The words were flung like daggers, accusation in his every inflection.

Evelayn clenched her jaw against the rise of emotions that threatened to pull her under. Tanvir was *alive*—and standing in this very room. But in the last decade, he had apparently come to loathe her.

Don't let him see how much he's hurting you, she coached herself. *You are a queen. His* queen. *Act like it.*

Evelayn took a deep breath, donned her most imperious mask, and turned to face him with her chin lifted. Her voice was flinty when she said, "How is it that *you* are here in the king's quarters? How is it that you are even *alive*?"

Before he could answer, an unearthly scream echoed through the castle—a shriek of agony that sent a ripple of dread down Evelayn's spine. No Draíolon could have made that noise.

"Someone should go help him."

Tanvir's lip curled. "Don't tell me you care about the king's welfare? After what he did to you? What he *continues* to do?"

"And what do you know of that?" Evelayn shot back. "You, who apparently have lived here all this time, and never come to find me—to *help* me."

For some reason, everything was upside down, *wrong*. This wasn't their reunion, was it? It couldn't be. After all these years she was back in her Draíolon body, visible to all, and he was alive and in the same room—they should have been deliriously happy and relieved. He was supposed to help her figure out how to stop Lorcan and get out of the mess they were in. He was supposed to rush to her side and take her in his arms.

He was supposed to still love her.

Tanvir finally moved, but it was to turn away and shove the door shut, cutting off the sounds of whatever was happening outside Lorcan's rooms.

"I never said I cared about his welfare," Evelayn finally said evenly to his back, drawing upon decades-old lessons from Aunt Rylese on concealing her true emotions. "But if he dies out there, and Lothar dies in here, then Lachalonia itself may die. *All* the power would be gone. Better to have it out of balance than destroyed entirely."

Ceren flashed her a look of concern and confusion. She seemed to be just as unnerved by Tanvir's response at seeing her alive as Evelayn was.

"You forget that you could go reclaim your power with the Dark Draíolon out of the picture." He spoke to the wall, apparently refusing to face her.

Evelayn tried not to let the sting spread any further than her bruised heart. "I don't have my stone. There is no way for me to claim the power."

"Perhaps you could find it?" Ceren suggested hesitantly, glancing quickly at Tanvir, then back again, as if she were nervous to speak and remind him of her presence. "It's probably hidden in here somewhere."

"He doesn't have it," Tanvir said.

Evelayn saw her own surprise mirrored in Ceren's wide eyes. "How would you know that?"

"I just do" was his cold response. Then he finally whirled to face them, his expression a nearly unrecognizable mask of stone.

"If you're determined to save one of them, I'd rather it be this one. But we'll need a needle and thread. Sometimes Draíolon on the battlefield survive if we give their body a little bit of help."

"I highly doubt Lorcan has a sewing kit lying around in his personal quarters."

"I suppose you would know better than I."

Evelayn barely managed to swallow her angry retort. What had happened to the Draíolon she had fallen in love with? What had the last decade brought him that made him so hardened? She was still reeling from the shock of finding out he'd somehow survived Lorcan's initial attack. But perhaps a part of him *had* died that night, after all.

Ignoring Tanvir, she knelt beside Lothar once more to help Ceren, whose arms were visibly trembling from the effort of keeping pressure on both wounds.

She heard the footfalls heading their way and caught the now familiar scent a moment before the door flung open and Lorcan himself stalked in, disheveled and bloody but alive.

And angry.

"Well, well." He took in the scene in one sweeping glance. "It appears that while I was occupied with saving all of your lives, I missed the grand reunion. Was it everything you dreamed of, my queen?"

"Do you have a sewing kit?"

Lorcan blinked, obviously thrown by her unexpected response. "I can't say that I do."

"Well, if you wish for your brother to have a chance of living, it would seem that we are in dire need of one. Immediately."

Lorcan's gaze dropped to where his brother still lay, his lips nearly white and his entire torso drenched with blood despite their best efforts. Evelayn felt a flash of heat in the palm of her right hand, along the scar from the oath Lorcan had made to her, accompanied by a sudden dismay that was so strong it nearly overwhelmed her. But as quickly as it came, it dissipated once more.

It took a conscious effort to not jerk her hand away from Lothar's body, to not let her eyes fly to Lorcan's to see if he'd experienced what she just had. What *was* that?

"Well, why are you just standing there? Go and find one at once!" Lorcan thundered. Tanvir shrugged and sauntered toward the door. "I suggest you hurry or else I'll finish what I started ten years ago."

"Be my guest," Tanvir said, and then walked out into the hallway.

Evelayn stared after him, unable to reconcile this saturnine being with the male she had been ready to Bind herself to for eternity.

"I regret that you probably find him changed . . . or revealed, as the case may be." Lorcan strode forward and dropped to his knees beside her. "Little good that it may do, you have my condolences."

"You regret that I find him *changed*? How about you explain how I find him *alive*?" Evelayn twisted to him, but her gaze was drawn to his arm. She'd assumed the blood had been from whoever—or whatever—he'd fought and apparently defeated. But his bicep had a deep slice in it and was still bleeding rather profusely.

"You're injured."

"It's nothing. What can I do for him while we wait?" Lorcan shrugged off her concern and bent toward his brother, hesitantly reaching out as if he would cover her hand with his and add more pressure, and then withdrawing once again.

Evelayn refused to acknowledge the lurch deep in her body, the tug of empathy that threatened to undermine her fury at the male beside her. So he actually seemed to care for his brother—he wasn't entirely made of ice. Just mostly.

"There's nothing to be done, unless Tanvir returns and shows us what he learned on the battlefield," Ceren responded when Evelayn remained silent.

"He'll return. If anyone knows what it is to wish to save a sibling, it's Tanvir."

If Ceren was as surprised as Evelayn to hear how well Lorcan seemed to know some of the more intimate details of Tanvir's life, she hid it well. But why *did* he know about Tanvir's sister?

"You never had a brother or sister. But imagine if you had . . . What would you be willing to do for her? How far would you go to keep her safe?"

Evelayn glanced at him, but he still stared down at Lothar's unmoving form.

"I imagine I would do nearly anything for a sister. Or a brother. Or anyone that I truly loved."

Lorcan looked up at her, his eyes two unfathomable pools of silver. When he didn't turn away, but held her gaze, her mouth went dry. Evelayn finally broke away to look to the door, hoping

Tanvir returned quickly—and that Lorcan didn't notice the heat rising up her neck.

She hated that he had any effect on her, but especially right now. He'd done some terrible, despicable things, and for that she should loathe him—and she did. She *hated* him. Just . . . not as completely as she had before this night. Draíolon were complicated, and it was unfair and unrealistic to label anyone as all bad or all good—she knew that. To be a just ruler, she'd spent hours upon hours studying all about the complexities of their natures. But to find those complexities in the male she'd considered her greatest enemy for a decade was unnerving at best, and terrifying if she was truly honest with herself.

"He has to make it."

The words were so quiet, she almost wondered if Lorcan realized he'd spoken out loud at all.

Regardless, she responded, "He will. We won't let him die."

Their gazes met again, and this time there was a brief moment when his pain was unmasked, when she caught a glimpse of truth behind the facade he presented. The unexpectedness of it stole her breath. That and the realization that she *did* want Lothar to live—and not just because she wished for him to take Lorcan's place. It was because she didn't want to see that kind of pain in anyone's eyes ever again.

Not even Lorcan's.

TEN

DAWN WAS STILL A WAYS OFF WHEN CEREN STEPPED out into the courtyard where she'd once taken nightly walks with Quinlen. She glanced back at the castle, half expecting Lorcan's Dark Guard to burst out after her, claim she'd tried to escape justice, and haul her off to prison after all.

But no one came.

She wrapped her arms around herself, chilled by the cold night air, and hurried away from the castle back toward Solas, where Quinlen was no doubt half frantic with worry. As soon as the forest enveloped the castle, taking it from view, Ceren stumbled and fell to her knees, no longer able to hold inside everything she'd spent hours hiding. Hot, fat tears splashed down her frozen cheeks, quickly turning into sobs that racked her body. Evelayn was *alive*—and at the castle. But it was not the triumphant return of a queen. Instead, she had slipped back with the silent stealth of a fugitive.

Ceren had been reluctant to leave Evelayn, but after Tanvir

returned and they'd sewn up Lothar, Lorcan had told her to get out of his sight, to go home. *Don't you dare tell a soul what—or whom—you have seen tonight. I know where you live if I need to arrest you,* he'd said. Still, she'd hesitated, until Evelayn's eyes widened and she'd gestured for her to leave as if she couldn't believe Ceren hadn't immediately taken the opportunity to go free and run from that place—that room full of blood and tension.

She huddled on the half-frozen ground, unable to regain control of herself now that the immediate danger had passed. *Evelayn was alive.* Quinlen and so many others had dedicated the past ten years of their lives to finding her, and now she was here. But what good did it do any of them with her trapped in the castle with the king?

The king, who had acted in ways she'd never seen before. The king, with whom, even though she would probably never admit it, possibly even to herself, Evelayn had . . . *something.* Ceren still didn't know what to make of their interactions, of the way he looked at her, or the way Evelayn responded to him. She'd promised to Bind herself to him to ensure Ceren's safety—but she obviously hadn't known Tanvir was alive when she'd agreed to his demand. Now that Lorcan had let Ceren go and Evelayn knew the truth about Tanvir, would she still go through with it?

Tanvir . . . Ceren had heard rumors of what he'd become ever since that fateful night, but she'd barely seen him. It was said he was practically a recluse, holed up in his quarters in the castle, neglecting his lands and people, choosing to sequester himself. Ceren thought seeing Evelayn again would have given him cause to celebrate, that it would have rejuvenated him.

Nothing was as it should have been.

"Ceren?"

She jerked up to see Quinlen rushing toward her.

"Are you hurt? What happened? I've been searching for you—"

"It's Evelayn." She cut him off, climbing unsteadily to her feet. He stopped short, grabbing her arms in both of his hands to steady her.

"I don't understand."

Ceren looked into Quinlen's familiar face, into the eyes that had anchored her for so long, and said, "She's alive. I saw her. Queen Evelayn is *alive*."

Lorcan stalked back and forth across the room, the strain making him restless. "How long before we know if he'll survive?"

"Only time will tell. In the next few hours he'll either begin to improve . . . or he won't." Tanvir leaned back in the armchair close to the hearth where he'd taken a seat after helping them transfer Lothar to the massive four-poster bed in Lorcan's inner chamber.

Lothar lay on the bed, unmoving. Thick black thread bound his wounds shut, but the normally metallic skin was still a livid red. Evelayn stood on the other side of the room silently watching, her arms folded, but Lorcan refused to look to her. There were too many questions in her eyes. Questions he wouldn't— *couldn't*—answer.

By all accounts, he should have been exhausted from the immense amount of power he'd been forced to draw upon to defeat Máthair Damhán's daughter. But it hadn't hit him yet. No doubt a crash was in his near future, but he was grateful for the reprieve, however long it lasted. Lorcan rarely felt the effects of using his power; yet something was different ever since he'd changed Evelayn and been unable to turn her back into a swan. There was an extra draw that made it more difficult for him to fully access his power. Still, he'd managed to summon enough and had left the creature that attacked them helpless to do any more damage to him or any of his Draíolon. He could have killed her, but instead had left her alive—just enough for her to return to her master with a message of his own. One that he would have to deliver upon very soon.

First, he had to ascertain whether Lothar would live or die. Then, Lorcan knew, he had to figure out a way to subdue the damage and hysteria that was doubtless spreading faster than daylight at dawn. But how to explain what had happened so as not to rouse even more suspicion or fear than was doubtlessly already circling the castle and beyond?

As if he could read the king's mind, Tanvir spoke up yet again. "Such unique wounds. And so slow to heal, at that."

Lorcan stopped and shot Tanvir a warning look. But the other male continued, undeterred.

"I have fought in many battles and have seen just about every possible variation of how a Draíolon can hurt another Draíolon. And yet, I've never come across anything like *this* before."

"Then it would seem you obviously are not as experienced as you supposed." Lorcan faced Tanvir fully, the icy burn of his wrath building in his veins once more.

"Am I not? Well, you fought the foul beast—I mean, *Draíolon*—that did this. I bow to your superior knowledge and experience." Tanvir inclined his head, a challenge in his eyes.

Lorcan regarded Tanvir steadily, but the fool didn't back down. After all these years of sulking, he'd finally found a will to fight again. Unfortunately, he had chosen a very unwise time and way to go about it. Lorcan shot a thin cord of darkness at him, winding around his torso and the chair, trapping him, and threatening to snake up toward his neck.

"I suggest you take your leave and return to Letha before your misplaced courage rewards you with a consequence you may regret."

There was a gasp from behind him.

Tanvir bared his teeth and lunged forward, as if he would attack Lorcan, but the cord held him in place.

"*What* did you just say?" Evelayn's question was deadly quiet, but it ricocheted through the room as if she'd shouted.

"Don't listen to him." Tanvir looked past Lorcan to where he could hear Evelayn storming forward across the room. A volatile mix of fury and confusion burned Lorcan's nose. "You know he's a liar, Ev."

"*What did you just say,*" she repeated from beside Lorcan—a command now rather than a question.

"I told him he should leave before he lives to regret speaking so freely—and incorrectly."

"No. You said to return to *Letha.*"

Lorcan glanced down at Evelayn, but she wasn't looking at him. She was staring straight at Tanvir, every taut line of her face and body limned with barely contained wrath. "Yes, I did."

"His *sister*, Letha."

"Yes, his sister, and only living relative. Did he tell you of her, then? I find myself surprised to hear that." Lorcan also looked to Tanvir, who snarled at him with such unmasked hatred in his eyes it reminded him of the way he had once had to disguise his true feelings toward his father. The difference being that Lorcan had done nothing to warrant such intense loathing from Tanvir—in fact, quite the opposite.

"He told me of her *death*." Evelayn's voice was cold.

Sudden understanding dawned on Lorcan, along with the realization that he had, yet again—though unwittingly—been the means of delivering her a terrible blow. "It is unfortunate that he sought to deceive you, seeing as she is very much alive and living here, at this very castle, as we speak."

"He's a liar, Ev," Tanvir repeated, finally meeting her gaze, his expression softening into one of pleading. The way he moved so easily from one face to another reminded Lorcan of himself. It filled him with disgust, knowing what it was to manipulate, and be manipulated—disgust that Evelayn had been the victim of such manipulation for so long.

"Don't call me that." She stepped toward Tanvir, but she hadn't softened one bit—if anything, she sounded more furious than ever. "I wondered what could have made you act the way you have tonight—why you are so changed toward me. But I believe I begin to see."

"Ev—Evelayn," he corrected himself quickly, "you have to understand my shock when I saw you standing there, alive. It had been so long, and I believed you to be—"

"I have only one question for you. Is your sister truly dead, as you told me?" She squared her shoulders, facing him with all the authority and aplomb of his queen. Not a female speaking to the male she loved. It would have made him proud, had Lorcan not also scented the bitter scorch of betrayal that ran beneath her superficial rage. "Or does she live?"

Tanvir remained silent, a muscle in his jaw ticking.

Evelayn whirled to face Lorcan, her violet eyes flashing. "What do you know of Letha?"

Lothar suddenly moaned from the bed behind them. Evelayn and Lorcan turned simultaneously to see his brother's hands clench and unclench, his head thrashing first to one side and then the other.

"If he's alive enough to be in pain, he's alive enough to survive," Tanvir commented dully from behind them, the fight gone out of him—for now. "Congratulations."

Lorcan wove his hand through the air at the same time that he stepped toward his brother, releasing the cord that bound Tanvir.

"I suggest you leave. Now," he added without facing the other male or even giving him a backward glance.

There was nothing but silence for a long moment, then he heard Tanvir move, rising from the chair.

"Evelayn . . . please . . ."

But she resolutely continued to face Lothar, her shoulders stiffly thrown back, her chin lifted.

The door clicked shut as Tanvir left.

ELEVEN

TANVIR STORMED INTO THE OUTER ROOM OF HIS QUARTERS only to stop short when he spotted Letha sitting at the table near the window, wrapped in a dressing gown, nursing a mug of something that wafted steam into the chilly night air. He caught the scent of chamomile and lavender.

"I take it whatever has kept you this long while did not go well?"

"Why are you up?" Tanvir asked, unable to keep the hostile edge from his voice.

"I heard them summon you and couldn't go back to sleep." She set the mug down with a dull thunk on the table. Her bark-brown hair—the same shade as his—hung in a thick braid down her back, and her skin was luminescent. But Tanvir could still remember how she'd looked the first time he'd seen her after that fateful day when he'd lost track of her on the battlefield. Hair raggedly shorn to just below her chin, her skin sallow, her eyes lackluster.

Until she'd seen him standing there, alive, saving her from the fate she'd thought never to be released from. Her face had lit up with shock and relief; he'd never forget the fragrance of her gratitude as he'd embraced her for the first time in so very long.

But now he had a new memory that tarnished the other: the burn of Evelayn's anger, the pain of her betrayal. After so long, he'd nearly convinced himself that he'd never see her again. But of course he'd been mistaken—as he had been so often before.

"Sit down, brother, and tell me what has happened." Letha gestured to the chair on the other side of the small table.

Tanvir sat heavily on the plush cushion and propped his elbows on the table, to drop his head into his hands.

"Let me get you something to drink," Letha offered, as gracious as ever. Once, they had fought and groused at one another. Once, she had been as invincible as he on the battlefield. But her time as a prisoner had changed her. Before, Tanvir had felt as though he needed to constantly watch his back lest she take him by surprise with an attack of some sort; now she seemed as fragile as porcelain. Yes, he'd saved his sister from death, but not from the consequences of what had happened to her. This female was nothing like the one he'd lost that day on the battlefield.

"There's no need. Not unless you think to offer me something much stronger than that tea in your mug."

Letha was quiet for a moment, and then, "I heard sounds of fighting. Was the castle under attack?"

"It would seem so."

"But that's not what has upset you."

"No," he confirmed.

"Tanvir." He flinched when she touched his arm gently. "Look at me. Tell me what has happened. For once, let *me* help *you*."

He did as she bid, looking up to meet her butter-yellow eyes that had always seemed to glow, even in the faint, flickering light of the few candles she had lit during her apparent vigil, waiting for him to return. "There is nothing you can do, I'm sorry. It is merely . . ." *The price I had to pay to rescue you.* But he couldn't say the words—he couldn't bear to add to her guilt. "The reminder of an old hurt. Don't think on it."

Letha's fingers wrapped around his arm. "Tanv, I'm not as fragile as you think. And I can tell when something has upset you far more than just a memory."

He shook his head but didn't respond.

They were quiet for a long moment, and then Letha said, "I fear you made a bad bargain, all those years ago."

Tanvir's head jerked up. "You cannot possibly think that to be true. You're here and alive, are you not? That's all I ever wanted."

Letha eyed him speculatively, her fingers flexing against his arms. "All? I think not, brother. I think you've learned to want more . . . though you've tried to hide it all these years."

He yanked away from her, forcing himself to ignore the flash of hurt that crossed her face. "You don't know what you are talking about. And there truly is nothing you can do. Especially not tonight. The castle is safe for now, and I have returned, so go back to bed. You need to get your rest."

Tanvir pushed back the chair and headed for his room, refusing to look at her sitting there, surely watching him walk away.

The scent of her dismay was enough; he didn't need to see it on her face.

Only once the door was shut and the lock shoved firmly into place did he let his shoulders sag, and the pain hit him as if he'd been blasted in the chest by shadowflame. He'd known the potential cost of his choices when he'd made them but . . .

Tanvir lifted his right arm and rubbed it, remembering the feel of the cord that had been wound around it when he made his vow to be Bound to Evelayn. He squeezed his eyes shut but couldn't block the memory of that night. Of the way she'd looked at him—the way she'd kissed him. So much trust, so much love.

And tonight, he'd finally received his reward for what he'd done all those years before—he'd watched that light in her eyes die.

He'd watched her love for him shatter.

Tanvir dropped to his knees on the hard floor and let his head fall into his hands.

"What do we do now?"

"What does this mean?"

"I have to see her—I must get to her at once!"

This last was from Rylese, Evelayn's aunt, who had jumped to her feet when Quinlen made the announcement, the blood leaving her lips, her eyes so wide the whites were visible all around her earth-brown irises.

All those who they had been able to reach in time had gathered in their home, making the normally spacious dining room feel cramped and close. Though it was bitterly cold outside, a frigid wind beating a constant barrage against the drawn shutters and sturdy walls of the house, it was miserably hot in the room full of males and females who had dedicated their lives to finding Evelayn and somehow restoring her power. Ceren wished to open a window but didn't dare for fear of being seen and questioned. If Lorcan found out that she had told not only Quinlen but an entire group of Draíolon that she'd seen Evelayn in his quarters this past night, he was sure to do far worse than imprison her.

"As much as we'd all like to rush to her side," Quinlen called out over the other voices, "we must wait. For now," he added when many protested—loudly.

"It is a very precarious situation." Ceren spoke up from where she stood beside Quinlen.

"Are we not *all* in a precarious situation? Every year, our kingdom weakens and dies a little more. If our queen has finally returned, we must go to her—we must fight for her!"

"And be cut down in the process? We are nearly powerless, especially against the power of King Lorcan and his Draíolon. Which is why that is precisely what we shouldn't do." Quinlen's deep voice cut through the rising din of the restless group. "If we tried to storm the castle, it would be tantamount to a suicide mission, leaving Queen Evelayn completely without allies."

"Lord Quinlen is right. We must be cautious—more now than ever," General Kelwyn said from where he stood near the wall, observing silently until that moment. "King Lorcan will be watching closer than before, not only because the queen has returned, but because Ceren knows."

"Then what are you suggesting?" Rylese spoke again, her

sharp gaze slicing to Ceren before returning to Quinlen. "That I
leave my niece there in the hands of that . . . that *monster*?"

"He won't hurt her."

There was an immediate outcry of disagreement.

"I speak truthfully!" Ceren was as shocked to hear herself say
the words as anyone in the room—or at least she would have
been before the few hours she'd spent in the castle. But though it
defied logic and experience, she knew it to be accurate. After wit-
nessing the way he'd treated Evelayn that night, she knew her
friend was safe. For now, at least.

"How dare you defend him!" The shout came from the back
of the room. "She was supposedly your closest friend—you saw
him transform her and then tear the stone from her breast. Who's
to say he wasn't waiting for you to leave to finish the job?"

More shouts and cries.

"He hasn't done it yet—why now?" Ceren yelled to be heard
over them all, but she wasn't loud enough.

"SILENCE!" General Kelwyn roared, and immediately the
room went quiet. "Let her speak—and no more interruptions."

All faces turned to Ceren, begrudging and impatient.

"I don't know why he did what he did that night . . . but he
hasn't hurt her since," Ceren tried again, ignoring the tension that
had built in the crowd. "He has done nothing this night that gave
me concern, either. His brother was gravely injured during the
attack on the castle, and he was wholly absorbed in tending him."

"What attack?"

"What is she talking about?"

"Is Prince Lothar *dying*?"

The new outburst hit Ceren like a tidal wave, threatening to pull her under. Her adrenaline had kept her going up, but suddenly it drained away entirely, leaving her exhausted to the point she could barely summon the energy to remain standing before them all. These were her friends and allies, her most trusted confidants. But right now, they felt like more like strangers on the verge of riot. So much had happened that night, so much that she still had to process—and so much more to try and figure out. Like where Evelayn had been, and why she'd suddenly returned.

But for now, there was *this* to deal with.

"I will return to the castle later this morning, to make certain she is unharmed." *After I rest for at least an hour or two,* Ceren added silently to her offer.

"And why would he allow you to see her again? How can you be sure you could even get an audience with *him*?"

"If I show up and send a note that Lady Ceren has come about important business, I guarantee he will see me." Ceren lifted her chin, attempting the pose she'd seen Evelayn employ so many times, daring anyone to argue with her.

Though the other Draíolon didn't seem very happy about her proposal, General Kelwyn and Quinlen readily agreed, and soon were making plans while she only half listened, her thoughts turning to the castle and to her closest friend.

There was a crack in the shutters that allowed her to peek outside if she squinted, only to see downy white fluff swirling slowly toward the brown, half-dead earth. The first snow of the year during *Athrúfar* in *Éadrolan*?

Even though it was true she didn't believe Lorcan would harm Evelayn, Ceren knew she had to help her queen escape his grasp and regain her power as soon as possible.

Or they were all lost.

TWELVE

B
Y THE TIME LOTHAR FINALLY STOPPED THRASHING ON
the bed, the sun had risen, breaking through the clouds of
a storm that had left a fine dusting of snow across the
castle grounds. Evelayn's eyes burned with fatigue—and with
the assault on her senses. She hadn't seen sunlight as a Draíolon
in a decade. She'd forgotten just how *bright* it was, how many lay-
ers there could be to light. Whenever she looked toward the
window, she had to fight the urge to squint.

"When I've been in my hawk form too long, it takes some
time to readjust to my Draíolon senses, too."

Evelayn glanced at Lorcan in the chair where he'd spent the
majority of the night, leaning toward his brother. "Is that supposed to be comforting?"

Lorcan rubbed at his eyes wearily. "Of course not. Why
would *I* wish to comfort *you*?"

The hard edge to his voice was at odds with the apa-
thetic words.

"I don't understand you." Evelayn had spent the night examining him, trying to come to terms with the many different sides she'd seen of the powerful male. "You made a vow of peace, and then turned around and did this to me." She gestured to the scar on her breastbone where her conduit stone had once been embedded in her skin. "You leave me for a year at a time on that lake as a swan—but *not* a swan, not truly. Only to force me back into my Draíolon form every night of Athrúfar and ask me to *Bind* myself to you. And now I'm here. And you . . ."

"And I *what*, exactly?" Lorcan bit out when she trailed off.

Evelayn didn't like the way the intensity of his scrutiny made her feel. "You . . . you don't make sense. I don't know you—I don't *understand* you. At all."

Lorcan pushed his chair back with a loud scrape and stood, facing her across the bed and Lothar's sleeping form. "You are not alone in that sentiment. No one truly does, though some may believe to."

"No one? Not even your mother? Your brother?" She couldn't help but remember the scars on his body—scars inflicted by his own father.

"No one." The burning force of his gaze was so strong it nearly felt like he was touching her, though he wasn't close enough to do so. The scar on her hand flared hot for a moment, and she closed her fingers over it. "Though perhaps you might know me better than any other."

"If that were true, it would be a terrible comment on your life, for I don't know you at all—as I just said."

"Are you quite sure about that? What if I were to tell you

that I have shown you more of my true self than to anyone else in my life?"

Though she desperately wished to tear her eyes from his, she could no sooner force her power back into her body. Everything in her felt taut—stretched too tight. "I would say then you must truly lead a sad and lonely existence."

"The lot of a king. Or a queen."

Evelayn shook her head. "I refuse to believe that. My mother had my father. And I have Ceren and—"

"Tanvir," he finished for her.

The sudden silence was heavy with unspoken accusations.

"Tell me how Tanvir is alive—how *Letha* is alive."

Lorcan finally looked away, breaking the hold he had over her. "I don't think that is my story to tell."

"Then tell me this—why did you make me think you'd killed him? Can you answer *that*?" Anger rose up again and Evelayn clung to it. Anger was good—it was much safer than . . . whatever she'd been feeling moments earlier.

Lothar moaned on the bed, and they both turned to him. When he didn't move again, she felt Lorcan's gaze return to her, but she ignored him, busying herself by lifting the sheet to check on Lothar's wounds. He, just like Lorcan, had a map of old scars on his torso, though his had healed differently, turning almost yellow against the metallic copper of his skin. But the new wounds were far worse than anything he'd previously sustained. Thankfully, the skin appeared to be knitting itself back together—at last.

He would bear some new, truly horrific scars, but it looked like the prince would live after all.

Lorcan moved as Evelayn tucked the sheet back up around Lothar's bare shoulders once more. Her sensitive ears picked up the whisper-soft brush of his feet on the floor, but she refused to look. It took her completely off guard when she sensed him on the same side of the bed as her. His scent of frost-laced evergreen mingled with the smoldering ash and smoke of shadowflame grew stronger, as did the tension in the room.

"Tanvir was supposed to get close to you. To help . . ." Lorcan trailed off, his voice disconcertingly near. "But he took it too far."

Evelayn stared at her hands clenched on the sheet. "He was *supposed* to get close to me," she repeated coldly.

"Evelayn, look at me."

She wanted to ignore him but knew that made her seem weak. So she willed her expression to give away nothing of her inner turmoil—though the Light only knew what he could ascertain through her scent—and turned to face him. In the early morning glow his disconcerting silver eyes stood out even more starkly.

"Why was he supposed to get close to me—and why would *you* know that?"

He studied her intently, his scrutiny so completely unwavering, it was all she could do to remain still and not back away. The full force of the king of Dorjhalon's focus was a formidable—and unnerving—thing indeed. "I know you well enough to know if you hear it from me, it will do no good."

"Don't pretend to know me." She refused to let him see that he—or his claims about Tanvir, which struck her as if he'd sliced her as deeply as whatever had attacked Lothar—had any effect on her. Evelayn pressed the emotion down and lifted her chin, meeting his gaze squarely.

"You still believe I don't know you?" Lorcan reached up suddenly to touch her raised chin, letting his fingers move across her skin toward her neck. She inhaled sharply. "You do this when you are hurting inside but refuse to let anyone see. You utilize self-possession the way I use insolence. We are more alike than you know."

Warmth rose in her body, a response that shocked and dismayed Evelayn. "Stop it." She tried to make the words sound like a command, but they came out more like a plea.

Lorcan stared into her eyes, his fingertips a brand on her skin. A building ache deep within made her heart thud against her lungs. She could see the desire in his eyes, scent the musk of it rising from his taut, muscular body. His gaze dropped to her mouth and he let his thumb brush across her lips, parting them slightly . . .

Evelayn suddenly jerked her head away, backing up until she hit the table beside Lorcan's bed. "I said *stop it*." She spat the words this time, clinging to the shreds of her anger and dignity, which had almost been entirely erased by the look in his eyes and his touch on her skin. "You will never do that again. Do you understand me? *Never*."

Lorcan's face had turned to stone, unreadable. "Never is a long time, my lady queen."

A knock at the outer chamber was one of the most welcome

intrusions Evelayn had ever experienced. Lorcan studied her for a moment longer, then turned on his heel and strode out of the inner chamber to the door beyond.

Evelayn spun to face the table, clutching it with both hands to hold herself up, as her legs began to tremble and threatened to give out entirely. A humiliating sign of weakness. *It's the exhaustion. And I'm starving.* But the excuses rang hollow as she unwittingly thought of the rough skin of Lorcan's thumb brushing across her lips. She couldn't deny the way it made her belly tighten and the heat rise in her body. How could he possibly affect her like that? After everything he'd done . . .

But more and more she was beginning to realize that perhaps she didn't really understand what he'd done at all—or why.

"I must go," Lorcan spoke from the doorway, startling her, but she didn't turn. "There is much to be done to . . . control the damage last night's catastrophe could very well cause."

She knew he meant far more than just the physical damage to the castle. Evelayn nodded but refused to face him.

"Will you join me?"

"So you may keep an eye on me?"

He was silent, but she sensed him stiffen.

"I will stay here with your brother. I have no wish for anyone to know I am here . . . yet." Evelayn was proud of how firmly her words came out, no matter how she shook inside.

"If that is your wish." This time he didn't wait for her to respond before shutting the door, leaving her alone at last. She exhaled slowly, lifting one hand to press to her chest, trying to calm her racing heart.

A plan. She needed to make a plan.

Her fingers brushed the empty scar on her breastbone, and a sudden idea took form.

"*Evelayn?* Is that really you?"

She gasped and whirled to see Lothar blinking blearily at her in the morning light.

THIRTEEN

Lothar felt as though he was sinking through quicksand—again.

As a youngling his father had taken him for a walk, just the two of them—a rare show of interest in his younger son. Or so he'd thought. When the king paused and waved him farther down the trail, Lothar didn't think anything of it. It had been an unusual day of sunshine during the dark months of winter in Dorjhalon. Though most Dark Draíolon preferred the night to the day, the cold and snow to the heat and rain of summer, Lothar found himself lifting his face to the warmth, inhaling deeply to absorb the crisp, piney aroma of the evergreens surrounding them. A scent that reminded him of his older brother. When the ground grew soft beneath his feet, he'd assumed it was merely from the moisture of melted snow. That was his first mistake.

Trusting his father was the second.

Or perhaps it was the other way around.

It had taken only a few seconds to realize he was stuck, the shifting ground sucking him in—*down*. In moments, he had already sunk to his knees. Lothar's heart thudded and his breathing grew short, but he tried to keep his voice level when he called out to his father to help him.

Help never came.

He should have known better, but he was still young then. He'd still possessed hope in the years before Bain beat it out of him entirely. The only response had been these words:

Use your abilities to escape. Prove you are worthy to be called my son.

Lothar would never forget the terror, the sheer panic, as he continued to sink into the bowels of Lachalonia. How every movement made it worse, the ground falling away beneath any attempt to lift his legs, to grasp at the earth, to pull himself up, to escape a terrible, slow death.

Some part of him recognized he was fighting death again, in the castle where he now lived, even in the depths of his darkened mind. Lothar knew he needed to escape the grasping, pulling oblivion, but it was so difficult. Especially because every inch of him hurt; even there in the darkness, he could feel it. He'd experienced many degrees of pain throughout his life, but nothing came close to this bone-deep agony that penetrated even unconsciousness. And he was so tired . . . exhausted in a way he'd also never experienced before. Every time he forced himself to reach for cognizance, it fell away, out of his grasp, causing him to sink further into the abyss. The temptation to give in, to quit struggling and release himself to the comfort of oblivion, was strong.

Almost too strong. But Lothar knew that was tantamount to giving up, and a deep, visceral part of him recognized that if he slipped back into the blackness again, he might never resurface.

There were voices somewhere nearby, vague and indistinct. But they tugged at him, refusing to let him slip beneath the surface entirely. Just as Bain's goading, his anger at his son's incompetence, had eventually spurred Lothar to lose control of his recently unblocked power with a blast of shadowflame that had launched him out of the quicksand to land on his face at his father's feet, panting, upset, but alive—now the voices provoked the part of him that refused to be an utter failure, and somehow he found the strength to claw his way to the surface.

His eyelids peeled open, as gritty as if he truly had been buried in sand, to find himself lying in Lorcan's bed, the room full of early morning light. The pain that had been agony while he was unconscious became unbearably excruciating upon waking. He felt as though he'd been split asunder and only raggedly pieced back together. A glance down revealed that was perhaps closer to the truth than he wanted to believe. Vague memories of what happened were just out of reach, hazy and ill-defined. But before they could fully solidify, he scented violets and lightning—and quite a bit more.

With some effort, he turned his head—and there she was. After a decade, the queen of Éadrolan stood beside the bed, gripping the table with one hand, her other fingers pressed against the scarred indentation on her breastbone. Her sheet of tangled hair partially obscured her face, but there was no mistaking her.

"*Evelayn?* Is that really you?" he rasped out of his raw throat.

She jerked toward him, her violet eyes wide. "You're awake!" she announced unnecessarily.

"So it would seem," he managed to respond, though every word cost him.

"Lie still," she instructed, again needlessly—he had no intention of moving more than absolutely necessary when it hurt this much to merely turn his head and breathe. "It's a miracle you're alive. I don't know what attacked you, but I've never seen wounds like that before in my life."

Flashes of memory rose unbidden at her words:

The summons, pulling him from the Athrúfar feast, where he'd been trying to keep the rumors about the messenger from spreading while his brother dealt with the queen somewhere else. Another Draíolon waiting with an urgent message, but since the king had commanded he not be disturbed, they came to him instead . . .

The strange scent surrounding the female in the receiving room that had set him on his guard . . .

The moment she'd morphed, shedding her Draíolon form and turning into something he'd never seen before, except in drawings . . .

The attack when he refused to call for Lorcan—swift and violent . . .

"Here, drink this." Evelayn was watching him, her eyebrows pulled together in concern over her eyes, as she held out a cup with a pungent liquid inside.

"I'm afraid you'll have to help me." The words were halting, laced with pain though he tried to conceal it.

"Of course, I apologize. Here." She bent forward to slip her hand beneath his head and help lift it off the pillow. Even with her assistance the movement shot a fresh wave of agony through his body. Lothar quickly drank from the cup, hoping she couldn't see or scent his weakness.

"I can't even fathom how much pain you must be in," she commented quietly as she gently set his head back down on the pillow, somehow reading his thoughts.

"If Lorcan had been wounded to this degree, he would still be on his feet, no doubt." Lothar stared up at the canopy, feeling his uselessness acutely. He had to assume Máthair Damhán's daughter had been beaten, as there was no urgency or fear in Evelayn's movements or voice. But still, he wished his body would heal faster. A slight warmth spread from his belly throughout his body, particularly his wounds. The tea was taking effect, dulling the pain ever so slightly.

"No one would be standing after the injuries you sustained. Not even Lorcan. I was not exaggerating when I said it is a miracle you are alive." Evelayn still held the cup of bitter tea, fiddling with the silver handle.

"Where is my brother? Is he . . . ?"

"He went to see to the damages left after the attack. But he was here by your side for most of the night."

Lothar glanced down at the bandages on his torso. "Was anyone else . . . ? Did he stop her?"

"Her?" Evelayn's eyes snapped to his. "The Draíolon who did this was a female?"

"A female—yes. But she was no Draíolon. It was one of

Máthair Damhán's daughters. She claimed to have another message for Lorcan." Lothar shifted slightly, hoping his ability to heal had perhaps made some progress now that he was awake, but the fresh wave of agony spoke otherwise. "He must have angered her thoroughly to warrant this kind of message."

"*Máthair Damhán?*" she repeated, her voice sounding a bit off. Shock—perhaps even alarm—tainted her scent. "What dealings could he possibly have with her?"

Lothar had spent the better part of his life being ignored, and therefore had learned to observe silently, catching the tiny details that escaped most. He didn't miss the way Evelayn's fingers tightened on the mug she still held, or the sudden stiffness in her shoulders. *Interesting.* "Honestly, I don't know the full extent of their dealings. But I do know one thing for certain."

Evelayn set the mug down, slightly harder perhaps than she intended, because she flinched when it clanged against the marble top of the table. "And what is that?" She kept her voice admirably even, betraying very little of the urgency simmering beneath her cool exterior. What were *her* dealings with Máthair Damhán?

"She is the one who wanted your conduit stone."

Evelayn jerked as if she'd been physically struck. "H-how . . . could you possibly know that?"

"Because Máthair Damhán is the one who has it. After you disappeared, my brother took it to her himself."

FOURTEEN

THE SUN HAD BROKEN THROUGH THE CLOUDS WHEN Lorcan finally walked into his bedroom, casting the room in bright, white light. His shocked relief to see Lothar awake was short-lived, as a wall of animosity hit him with such strength he nearly stopped short. Evelayn sat beside the bed, glowering at him with fresh fury burning in her eyes, darkening them to mulberry. Even without her power, the room was filled with an acrid tang, as if her lightning was still there, simmering beneath the surface.

"Can I at least sit down before you tell me what I've done wrong now?" Lorcan hated the weariness that seeped into his voice, but he felt barely capable of remaining on his feet after the horrors of the last many hours and the sleepless night.

He sank onto the nearest plush, high-backed chair, and Evelayn immediately jumped to her feet.

"You took my conduit stone to *Máthair Damhán?*"

Despite himself, he flinched, shooting a look at Lothar, who was busy staring into his mug, but he quickly recovered. "Excuse me? Where did you hear such a claim?"

"Don't even *think* about lying to me." She jabbed a finger at him, longing to blast him out of his chair, no doubt.

"I wouldn't dream of it."

Her teeth snapped together with an audible click, as if she wished for the ability to bite his throat out. Which she probably did. She stalked toward him, her hands balling into fists.

"And we're back to this," he murmured.

She stopped a few feet away, her hot anger a spice on the charged air that burned at his nose. But when she spoke, her question came out an agonized plea. *"Why?* Why would you take it to *her?"*

Lorcan sank back in the chair, too exhausted—too undone by the grief and hopelessness on her face—to try and maintain the guise of insouciance. "I can't tell you."

"No more games," she bit out, visibly attempting to hold on to her anger, even though it had already fled from her grasp.

"This is no game." He sighed heavily. "I literally *can't* tell you, Evelayn. I am bound by an oath."

She reeled back. *"You* have an oath with Máthair Damhán? That involves carving my stone from my body and taking it to her? But . . . how? *Why?"*

Lorcan remained silent, unable to explain further.

It took her all of a few moments to lift her chin, to plaster determination on her face. "It doesn't matter. We simply have to go get it back."

"There is nothing *simple* about that." Lorcan pinched the

bridge of his nose, trying to ward off the pounding in his head that threatened to become a full headache.

She began to pace, wringing the skirt of her dress in her hands. Though she was already pale, her face had gone completely white during their exchange. But now, when she finally stopped and faced him again, two bright spots of color rose to burn in her cheeks. "I know the way to her lair . . . I've . . . I've been there before."

"I know."

"Let me go. Let me try to retrieve my stone, and I will—" She cut herself off as his words sank past her fevered scheming. "Wait—*what?*"

Lorcan hated the words that came next, but they had to be said. "You promised to Bind yourself to me. I can't let you leave until you keep your promise."

"Is it because of the silk? You know I bargained with her because of the silk I used to trap your father."

"No." Lorcan held her gaze steadily, hoping the risk he was about to take wasn't the worst mistake he'd yet made. "I know you took Tanvir and that general, and visited Máthair Damhán to bargain for a skein of her silk . . . because it was my idea."

"*No.*" Evelayn shook her head. "You're lying. *Again.*"

"You know I'm not. You'd be able to scent my dishonesty if I were." She'd never seen him look so worn down. Lorcan pushed himself out of the chair to stand, facing her, his hands palm up as if offering himself as evidence.

She whirled away from him—from the proof of his scent. Evergreen and ice, power and weariness, but . . . no dishonesty. He was telling the truth.

"*How?* How could it possibly have been *your* idea?" Evelayn couldn't bear to face him, staring straight ahead to the bed where Lothar had finally given in to the soporific effects of the healing tea and dozed off, despite the heated exchange.

She felt Lorcan draw closer to her, sensed his body directly behind hers. A whisper of heat brushed her arms but was gone as quickly as it came—as though he'd lifted his hands to touch her and then thought better of it.

"I told you I wished for you to hear it from him . . . but circumstances have forced my hand and there isn't time." He was close enough that his breath stirred her hair as he spoke and Evelayn had to suppress a shiver, but she remained silent— inhaling deeply, waiting for any hint of dishonesty to color the air foul.

"You seemed shocked to hear that Lord Tanvir's sister, Letha, was alive. That, at least, was not my idea, but his. I can only assume he didn't want to arouse suspicions that might cause you to question him, or his motives.

"My father's generals recognized the fire in Letha and Tanvir—and also their loyalty to each other when they fought side by side at the warfront. He commanded us to separate them in battle and take her captive. For his many faults, my father was an excellent student of Draíolon nature. Bain wasn't making headway, the war had dragged on for too long. He needed a stunning victory—and quickly. So he took a chance, and it paid off. Tanvir was the perfect opportunity. His parents had recently died, making him a lord—a feasible reason for him to travel to this castle under the guise of putting his holdings in order. Bain blackmailed Tanvir by holding his sister captive and threatening her with horrific abuses unless he complied with my father's demands."

Evelayn's fingers were white where she clutched her dress. She tried to keep her breathing steady, but her lungs disobeyed, rising and falling faster and faster as he spoke, until she felt as though she could hardly draw breath as Tanvir's treachery was laid out bare—and the last whole piece of her heart was shredded beyond repair. "A spy. He was a spy," she gasped, the words barely above a whisper.

"Yes. He fed information to my father, gleaning what he could from castle gossip, the meetings he was able to gain admittance to . . ."

"And his relationship with me," Evelayn finished, the words like ash in her mouth, as the initial anxiety from Lorcan's revelations turned her whole body cold. "How did he do it without getting caught? The wards at the border—"

"Don't affect animals, such as hawks. Like the ones my father had trained and used to send and receive messages."

Evelayn's head reeled, her entire reality spinning on its axis, twisting truth into lies and lies into . . . what? "What does this have to do with you? How did the idea to bargain for the silk come from you?"

"I also saw an opportunity in Tanvir and seized it. As you may know, my animal form is a hawk. I went to him in bird form and delivered a message—an offer of my own. Protection for Letha—as much as I possibly could ensure without arousing my father's suspicions—and her eventual freedom if he did what *I* asked."

"Which was what?" Evelayn asked faintly, still staring straight ahead, almost unseeingly.

"To get the kingdom of Éadrolan to aid me in defeating my father."

FIFTEEN

CEREN TRIED TO CALM THE POUNDING OF HER HEART as she slipped into the servants' entrance to the castle. When she had finally admitted to Quinlen that Lorcan had nearly had her thrown into prison, he'd refused to let her return to the castle to see the king with a message as she'd offered. Instead, this time she had disguised herself as a chambermaid, the lowliest of the servants and the least likely to warrant notice. The trick was not drawing the attention of the other servants, who would easily recognize an interloper in their midst. Lorcan had long since dismissed the Light servants, replacing them all with Dark Draíolon from his kingdom. Well, nearly all of them—he'd kept on a few who helped run the castle.

Gestra was one of those. She was waiting at their appointed spot when Ceren quickly strode down the hallway, keeping her head ducked, her face obscured by the large white dust cap covering her hair entirely.

"You got my message," Ceren breathed in relief.

"Here. Take these to clean the fireplaces in the sitting and dining rooms." Gestra spoke quickly and quietly as she pushed a bucket and other cleaning supplies into Ceren's hands. "The normal maid has taken ill. It's the best I could do."

"Thank you. I know the risk you take to help us," Ceren murmured back.

"To help us all," Gestra corrected her.

Ceren nodded, and they silently parted ways as two other maids rounded the corner, rushing to complete their work.

She took the servants' hallways to the dining room first, since it was nearly time for luncheon and more Draíolon were likely to be there than in the sitting room. Many other servants passed by, but luckily they were all absorbed in their tasks—hefting trays laden with food and drinks, or carrying cleaning supplies like her. Most of them were silent, but a few spoke to one another in hushed tones. Ceren caught a few snippets of gossip, about the attack on the castle, the efforts to hide the evidence of how bad it really was, and even how the king himself had joined in the cleanup efforts . . . but nothing about the queen. And surely if anyone had discovered Evelayn's presence in the castle, the servants would be the first to spread the news.

Her heart sank, but Ceren had no choice except to continue with her disguise and do the jobs Gestra had found for her.

She wedged her way through the dining room servants' entrance, which was concealed as part of the wall when not pushed open for use, and narrowly avoided knocking into a male with an empty tray rushing back to the kitchen for more food.

"Watch yourself," he snapped, and she lowered her head

submissively, remaining silent as she hurried toward the fireplace and the filthy job of cleaning out the soot from the previous night's fire.

She'd been on her hands and knees long enough for her fingers to feel raw from scrubbing the brick, her nails crusted with black soot, and her knees aching, when she heard a familiar voice directly behind her.

"Well, if you can't make him listen to reason, *someone* has to. What happens in Lachalonia does not merely affect us. It stretches beyond our shores—to the rest of this world where the magicless dwell."

It was High Priestess Teca—the female Light Draíolon who had run the temple before the loss of their power. She still lived there, guarding their precious tomes and practices, and so far—at least as far as Ceren knew—Lorcan hadn't pillaged the sacred building, despite the priestesses' lack of power to truly protect it.

Ceren didn't recognize the male voice that responded—but she did know what the scent of freezing winds and the forest at night meant: a Dark Draíolon.

"And what possible proof can you provide for this claim? You've never traveled beyond the protection of this island, so how could you know about the world beyond our shores, as you put it?"

"We have not wasted the past decade bemoaning our loss of power. We have been studying our ancient tomes, particularly the accounts of Drystan and the consequences of his heinous acts." Teca was insistent, but the male laughed loudly.

"*That* is the basis of your concern? An ancient myth—a *nursery rhyme?*"

"It is no more myth than the Ancients who have apparently decided to come out of hiding and attack Draíolon as well. Something that was unheard of before now, I might add."

The male laughed again. "The Ancients aren't attacking us. That is nothing more than sensationalized gossip."

"What do you find so humorous, my dear High Priest?"

Ceren stiffened, her blood running like ice in her veins. There was no mistaking *that* voice. Dowager Queen Abarrane—Lorcan's mother—had joined the conversation and stood mere feet from where she knelt, continuing to scrub the grime with trembling hands.

"This *priestess*"—she could hear his sneer—"has been attempting to convince me that the imbalances caused by the Light Draíolon's lack of power extend past Lachalonia to the world beyond."

Abarrane tsked. "Sounds like the mewling of one bemoaning her loss of position and power. It must be quite difficult to have fallen so very far."

"I am standing right here—you're welcome to speak to me directly."

Ceren had to admire Teca's courage, even as she flinched in anticipation of Abarrane's response.

"And if this pompous excuse for a priest were capable of seeing past his obsession with *his* position and power, perhaps he would be willing to admit what he knows in his gut to be true."

"Enough." Abarrane's voice had turned cold. "Don't think that I'm not willing to go against my son's edict. If you anger me enough, I will have you . . . *removed* . . . from your precious temple. Permanently."

The threat was unmistakable. Ceren could only pray that none of these Draíolon noticed her working away practically beneath their feet, so close she wasn't able to *not* overhear the heated conversation.

"You may do as you wish, but nothing will erase the truth. Not even silencing me."

The ringing of the luncheon bell cut across Abarrane's response, and to Ceren's great relief, the Draíolon moved away from the fireplace.

Teca's warning was concerning, as was Abarrane's threat. But none of it helped Ceren ascertain if Evelayn was still inside the castle—and unharmed. Now that no other Draíolon were nearby, she hurried to finish the job, then rose to toss out the filthy water and to concoct a plan to find out where Evelayn was and if she was still all right.

Evelayn whirled to face Lorcan. "You expect me to believe you *wanted* me to defeat your father? That you wanted him *dead*?"

He was only an arm's length away from her, his eyes burning like molten silver. "Of course I did. *He* was the true monster, not me."

The memory of the scars that covered his body rose unbidden, the vicious marks she'd seen lancing across his well-defined muscles. She looked down at his torso, as if the shirt he wore would fall away, revealing the damages he'd sustained. "You father did all of that to you."

"If not personally, then by command. Yes."

Evelayn had the sudden irrational urge to reach up and place her hands on his chest, to try to absorb some of the pain in his voice. She forced them to stay still at her sides.

Commanding herself to remember he didn't deserve her concern, she said, "Tanvir is the one who had the idea to get the silk."

"Yes. Because I wrote to him and told him to suggest it."

She shook her head. "No. I . . . I can't believe it."

But then another memory surfaced, of Bain chasing her through the forest, of how he'd had her trapped on the ground and she'd been moments from death . . . until a blast hit the king from behind—a blast that she had been certain was shadow not light, a fact that she had forgotten until now. And then, when the king had been gaining on her again, Lorcan had sent that blast at her . . . but it had hit *between* her and Bain, indicating a terrible lack of aim.

Unless it had been on purpose.

"The day I . . . The day your father died . . . that was *you*." She realized numbly. "You . . . *helped* me."

Lorcan stared down at her silently, letting the truth sink in.

Evelayn pressed the tips of her fingers against her temples, hardly able to comprehend how wrong she'd been about so many things. "I still don't understand what any of this has to do with my conduit stone or why you gave it to *her*."

"I had to ensure your success. I couldn't risk her refusing your request—or worse." He still held her gaze, the enticing scent that was entirely his remaining free of dishonesty.

"What *exactly* did you do?" Her heart was in her throat, awaiting his response.

"I made a bargain. It came with a price."

"A *price*?" Evelayn choked out, touching the empty spot above the neckline of the dress. "For who? Certainly not for you!"

"It was a steep price for you," he admitted quietly. "But it was not without its price for me, too—everyone believes me to be a monster. Because I am, because she forced me to be one. But it was the only way. The other alternative was your death. He would have killed you. And you know it."

"And it never occurred to you to, oh, I don't know, tell me that you used me as a bargaining chip? To warn me what the price of my victory would be?" Evelayn struggled to keep from shouting and disturbing Lothar, who was softly snoring behind them now. Lorcan's mocking words whenever she spoke of "her victory" made sense now. He'd known she never would have succeeded without him, which irrationally only made her angrier. "Why wait so long to tell me this? Why did you wait to take my stone from me? Why let me grow complacent, believing true peace to be within reach? Why did you make that oath when you had no intention of keeping it? Is this all just a big, elaborate game to you?"

"A game?" Lorcan laughed bitterly. "She held me captive, Evelayn. *For months.* She refused to let me reclaim my power and return until Athrúfar, because she taught me that it was the only time I would have the power necessary to do . . . what I had to do."

But his words couldn't penetrate her anger—her grief and fury. Evelayn stalked forward, closing the gap to shove at his chest. He didn't so much as flinch.

"Because of you, my entire kingdom is suffering. You hurt those around you heedlessly. You toyed with me, let me believe

Tanvir truly loved me, waited until what should have been the most joyous night of my life to make your 'grand entrance' and do your evil deed. Instead of revealing the truth, you let me believe Tanvir had died. You stole my power and *destroyed* my life." Despite herself, as the words spilled out, they grew louder and sharper, her hands balling into fists that she pummeled against him, helpless to hurt him in any other way. "Why? Why the theatrics? Why the cruelty? If you are so noble, then *why*?" The last came out a broken cry, her eyes suddenly burning. All at once she was sobbing, her entire body shaking with the force of her tears.

"I'm sorry, Evelayn." His voice was hoarse, his cool, minty breath washing over her heated face. "I know you will never believe me, but I truly am. I did what I had to do."

She shook her head, unable to speak. But for some reason, despite everything she'd just spat at him, she didn't back away. Instead, her fists slowly relaxed, until her hands lay flat on his chest.

And when he gingerly lifted his arms and falteringly placed them around her, for some reason she didn't protest. Slowly, hesitantly, he gathered her to his body, holding her tighter when she didn't pull away, as she tried to regain control of herself. Little by little the crying began to abate, but still she didn't move. Lorcan had done so many terrible things . . . but he had also saved her and helped her defeat his own father. His words from earlier that morning ran through her mind—his claim to know her better than she thought. And the way he'd touched her face, letting his finger trail across her mouth . . . her lips . . .

She could feel his heart begin to beat faster beneath her

hands, which were still trapped between them, and her belly tightened in response.

What are you doing? she accused herself, and yet she remained completely still, waiting.

Until the door slammed open behind them, and they jumped apart, spinning to face the intruders.

"Well, that didn't take long," Tanvir said from the doorway. Ceren stood directly behind him, wearing a chambermaid's outfit covered in soot and staring at them with her mouth hanging partially open.

SIXTEEN

HOW DARE YOU ENTER MY QUARTERS WITHOUT PER-mission," Lorcan thundered, whirling to face Tanvir, whatever had been happening between him and Evelayn forgotten. Two black cords of shadow chain shot out from his hands and quickly wound around both Tanvir and Ceren, trapping their arms at their sides.

"What are you *doing*? Why did you come back?" Evelayn swiped at the remaining moisture on her burning cheeks, staring aghast at Ceren, who should have been home with her younglings.

"Ceren unwisely returned to make sure you were unharmed. When she couldn't find you, she came to me for help," Tanvir answered, anger apparent in every rigid line of his body.

"And you thought it best to barge into my personal quarters uninvited." Lorcan's face, in comparison, was a mask, betraying no emotion whatsoever. "I daresay she is not the only unwise one."

"I succeeded in finding Evelayn for her, did I not? Whether she is unharmed remains to be seen."

"Ceren, I'm fine—" Evelayn began, but Lorcan cut in before she could continue.

"Tread lightly, Lord Tanvir," he warned coldly. "You do not wish to anger me."

"What have I to lose? You've already taken everything from me."

"*I* am the one who *saved* your sister. Anything you've lost, you lost yourself through your own deceit and pride."

"I have no pride left. You and your father made sure of that."

Lorcan stepped toward him menacingly. "I don't think you wish to endanger your sister again through your foolishness."

"Is that a threat?"

"I am not my father, but I have my limits on how much insubordination I will tolerate."

"Enough!" Evelayn shouted, stepping forward between the two males. Even though Tanvir was basically incapacitated, she half expected him to slam his head into Lorcan's if provoked any further. And there was no telling what Lorcan would do if Tanvir didn't close his mouth. Tanvir was so belligerent—as if he *wanted* the king to hurt him. She'd been watching him, all the things Lorcan had told her running through her mind, their history taking on a whole new light. His reluctance to get close to her at first, his lies about his sister, many of the comments he'd made or things he'd done. She'd thought it was because he felt himself unworthy to Bind himself to a queen . . . but that hadn't been it at all. He'd been suffering from guilt, because he'd been lying to her. As much as she wished it weren't true—that Lorcan was the one lying—she knew deep down that he'd been the one to speak the truth.

"You lied to me. About *everything*," she said to Tanvir now, proud of herself for keeping her tone even, letting none of her pain and betrayal bleed into her words.

Tanvir wouldn't meet her eyes. "I didn't have a choice."

"*There is always a choice.*"

"It was my *sister*," he tried to explain, voice beseeching. "I had to save her."

"You could have told me the truth. You could have *trusted* me."

Once, the misery on his face would have broken her defenses and enticed her to step toward him, to try to comfort him. Now it only dug the pain he'd caused her even deeper into her body. Ceren watched the entire exchange silently, her eyebrows pulled together in concern and confusion. Evelayn couldn't bear to look at Tanvir any longer and whirled to face Lorcan instead.

"Take me to her. I have to get my stone back."

Lorcan gazed at her steadily. "Bind yourself to me and we can leave today."

Everything felt wrong, twisted into knots. Part of her longed to return to her swan form, to the freedom from the worries of this body and this life. To retreat to the safety of the lake and the flock that had become hers. "Don't ask that of me right now."

His expression was still masked, but she could see the regret in his eyes, smell it weaving through his scent. "Please, Evelayn, Queen of Éadrolan. Bind yourself to me."

"*Why?* Why do you insist on this?" She could barely contain her agitation. Why did he continue to push for her if he felt remorse about doing it? And then a sudden realization hit her. "That's the bargain, isn't it? This is part of your oath to her?"

He remained silent, but she saw the truth of it in his eyes.

"What are you talking about?" Tanvir spoke up from behind. "Don't tell me you are actually considering this, Ev. I know I've made mistakes—that I've hurt you. But I never lied about how I feel. I do love you. Don't do this. Don't—"

"*Stop,*" she commanded without turning, and he immediately fell silent.

Lorcan's gaze was unwavering as she deliberated. The way he'd treated her and the things he'd done were reprehensible—cause for her to loathe him. And she *had*. She'd hated him for ten long years. She'd spent so much of her life believing his heart was as cold as ice . . . yet he had never been anything but honest with her, even when she didn't want to hear it. Except for those things he was bound to keep secret.

Could she do it?

Yes, there had been a moment, before Tanvir and Ceren burst in, when she'd felt . . . something . . . other than hatred for him. But to Bind herself to him—*forever*?

It's the only way. You are the queen, she coached herself. *It's time to stop being selfish and do what you must for your kingdom.* Lorcan had helped her kill his own father to free them from war, and he'd promised to help her get her stone back.

She needed her power—her kingdom needed it.

"I will." She forced the words out before she could change her mind.

"You will?" Ceren burst out from behind her in shock.

"You will?" Tanvir spoke at the same time.

Lorcan stared at her; the most painful ghost of hope she'd ever seen crossed his face. "You will?" His question was soft, barely more than a whisper.

Being a queen means doing what you must for your kingdom. Even this.

"I will. I will Bind myself to you, Lorcan."

SEVENTEEN

THEY GATHERED IN THE SOLARIUM, A ROOM EVELAYN had rarely visited before but which had now become indispensable to the Draíolon, Ceren had explained as they'd hurried through the castle. Lorcan's sentries cleared the hallways for them so no one saw the queen. She wasn't ready for that—not yet.

With the change in the seasons and weather patterns because of the imbalance of power, what had once been mostly composed of flowers and bushes meant to bring peace and happiness to Light Draíolon in the winter had now been turned into a garden where much of the castle's vegetables and fruits were grown.

When Evelayn had asked Lorcan why he'd picked this particular room for the Binding, he hadn't looked up from the cravat he was tying when he quietly said, "I thought you would like it." A sentiment that had baffled her. Why should he care what she would like? He never had before. She was merely a pawn to him. Wasn't she?

The solarium was humid, as warm as a balmy summer day. They were greeted by the loamy scent of rich soil and thriving plants, interlaced with the perfume of the few flowers that still grew there. She could almost believe it *was* summer in here, not a world chilled by the early arrival of winter. Condensation smeared the view to the grounds beyond the glass walls, turning the outside—the reality of what her kingdom had become—into something hazy and not quite real.

Much like the fact that she was truly going through with this.

She still wore the velvet dress Lorcan had given her, the heavy material stifling in the warm room. Once she had agreed to Bind herself to him, Lorcan had allowed Ceren to take her and spend a few minutes to try to at least get a brush through her tangled hair. They'd simply braided it down her back, not wanting anything elaborate. She'd never dressed with more care than the night she'd made her Oath of Binding, promising herself to Tanvir in the spring. And all for nothing. He'd lied to her; he'd been willing to let her join their lives and hearts for eternity without admitting his true role in the war—and in her mother's death. Evelayn had looked down at the ring on her right hand—the one that had brought her so much happiness and hope, but now only reminded her of Tanvir's betrayal. In one quick movement, she'd pulled it off and set it down on the table-top with a clang.

"You don't have to do this," Ceren had whispered as she worked out the tangles as gently as possible.

Evelayn had simply said, "Yes, I do," and Ceren hadn't pushed her again. They'd remained silent for the next couple of minutes. But then, as she set down the brush and placed the diadem Evelayn hadn't worn in a decade over the queen's hair, Ceren spoke once more.

"Ev . . . I'm so sorry about Tanvir."

Evelayn had stared at herself in the mirror, at the changes since that fateful night ten years earlier, and had to take a deep breath to keep her emotions in check. "Me too." Then she'd turned away from the reflection that merely revealed all she'd lost, and stood. "Let's go. The sooner I do this, the sooner I get my stone back."

Now Ceren stood behind her, an unseen but comforting presence as Evelayn watched Lorcan. He was quietly speaking with Patryk, his High Priest. Patryk kept looking at her, his initial expression, that of unadulterated shock at seeing the queen of Éadrolan alive and standing in the solarium, diminished only slightly.

When Lorcan turned and gestured for her, Evelayn had to force her legs to move, to propel herself toward him—and an eternity of being Bound to the king of Dorjhalon. She couldn't read his expression, and even the nuances of his scent were difficult to sort out from the rich, nearly overpowering fragrance of growing tomatoes, cucumbers, zucchinis, and many other vegetables. His eyes were shadowed in the fading light, which turned them to iron as the sun slowly sank toward the earth through the west-facing windows.

This male was her future now—the one who had hurt her and manipulated her, mind and body. But Tanvir had done the same . . . Was it any better that Lorcan hadn't been secretive about it? Was there any hope of being able to trust this king who was to be by her side forever? A sudden terror overcame her as they faced each other. Her stomach clenched, making her feel as though she might vomit, at the same time that her heart began to race. She struggled not to gasp, even though her lungs weren't working properly and tears were humiliatingly close to the surface. The heat of the room couldn't penetrate the sudden chill that made her legs tremble and threaten to give out. *You are stronger than this. Just breathe.*

"Evelayn." Lorcan spoke, but it sounded like he was standing across the room from her, not an arm's length away.

Warm hands suddenly gripped hers, and she looked down in surprise to realize they were his. Strength and determination, grief but also hope, rippled through her with a flash of heat from the scar in her palm. Pure emotions, untainted by deceit or manipulation. An unexpected balm to the wild frenzy within her. The panic lessened and she glanced up at Lorcan, her eyes wide. He nodded slightly, a barely perceptible movement of his head.

Those emotions . . . they were *his*. Somehow she could feel what he was feeling. And they were not the emotions of a tyrant.

He was the true monster, not me. Lorcan's words about his father—whom he had helped her kill—returned to her. *Perhaps you can learn to see past the* monster *to the king inside.* By making this choice, she was forever entwining her life with his. Evelayn stared into his eyes for a long moment and was shocked to realize her panic had receded entirely. It had been replaced by a strange sense of calm.

"Are you ready?" he murmured for her ears only.

Evelayn took a deep breath, wondering at the change within her and her sudden certainty. "Yes. I am."

Lorcan stared into her eyes, his expression softening, which oddly had the opposite effect on her heart, which began to pound once more, but in an entirely different way this time.

"Shall we proceed?"

Lorcan startled as if surprised to realize they were not alone, and released her to turn to the High Priest. "Yes, you may begin."

High Priest Patryk looked to her. "Queen Evelayn of Éadrolan, you have previously made an Oath of Intent to Bind yourself to Lord Tanvir of the Delsachts. In order to proceed, you must rescind your oath. Do you wish to do so?"

She tried not to let her mind go to the ceremony when she'd been so sublimely—and naïvely—happy. But images from that fateful Athrúfar night surfaced regardless. She knew mentally that it had been ten years ago, but she'd spent most of that time as the swan . . . To her heart, the oath she'd made to Tanvir still felt fresh—the wound of his betrayal was a raw, bleeding thing deep inside her. She forced herself to focus on the strange certainty she'd felt moments earlier when Lorcan had gripped her hands and brought her out of her panic.

"Yes, I wish to proceed." The words came out like a poison being expelled from her body.

"Very well. Stretch forth your right hand."

Evelayn did as instructed. Patryk produced a Binding rope and wrapped it around her arm. "You may speak the words to cancel your oath."

She took a deep breath, and the words she'd said to Tanvir that night, before all those Draíolon gathered to feast and celebrate what should have been a joyous occasion, surged up. At least this was being done in private, with only a few Draíolon in attendance.

"I, Evelayn, High Queen of Éadrolan, rescind my Oath of Intent to Bind myself to Tanvir, Lord of the Delsachts. He shall forthwith be cut from my body and my heart, cast away and removed from my future. This I do, by the Light." As she spoke, a chill began at the top of her skull and slowly cascaded down her body, until she felt as if she were coated in ice.

"So it shall be." Patryk produced a silver knife and used it to slice the rope so that it fell to the ground, symbolizing the severed oath. The moment the rope was cut, the cold sensation released her, expelled with the oath she'd broken and cast away.

"It is done." High Priest Patryk intoned, bending to pick up the ruined rope and casting it aside to be burned later. A pang of regret hit Evelayn—she wished it could be Teca here performing the ceremonies. But as she was powerless, the High Priestess was unable to do it. She wasn't even aware that her queen had returned.

"King Lorcan and Queen Evelayn, please face each other and take each other's wrists with your right hands," Patryk instructed.

They turned to each other. When Lorcan wrapped his long fingers around her narrow wrist, Evelayn's scar flashed hot once more, which oddly made her shiver.

The High Priest produced two beautiful chains made of

polished silver links. Where the Oath of Intent to Bind was made with ropes, the actual Binding was performed with silver chains—symbolizing the unbreakable nature of the Binding, as opposed to the oath. The poorer families would borrow the temple's chains, but the nobility often had their own, made with family crests engraved into the silver and passed down through generations. Such was the case with these—one was from her family, and one from his.

Evelayn stared down as Patryk wrapped the chains around their right arms, but she could feel Lorcan's unwavering focus completely on her. A strange, tingling heat began in her hand and slowly rose up her arm as the priest finished twining the chains. She remembered feeling warmth when she had made her oath to Tanvir, but this sensation was far more intense.

"Evelayn, High Queen of Éadrolan, in the presence of these witnesses and the ancestors who watch over us from the Final Light, do you stand ready to Bind yourself to Lorcan, High King of Dorjhalon?"

Ceren made a small noise from behind her, but Evelayn ignored her. Instead, she finally made herself look up at the male who held her arm in his hand. She could feel the rough striation of his scar against the smooth skin on the inside of her wrist. When their eyes met, her breath suddenly caught in her throat. "Yes," she managed to say.

"Lorcan, High King of Dorjhalon, in the presence of these witnesses and the ancestors who watch over us from the Final Light, do you stand ready to Bind yourself to Evelayn, High Queen of Éadrolan?"

He didn't hesitate before replying, "Yes."

The longer she looked into his silvery eyes, the faster her heart beat.

"Then you may proceed."

Evelayn took a deep breath and spoke the sacred words that had been used since before memory to Bind Draíolon to one another. "By these chains unbreakable, forged through flame and iron, do I Bind myself to thee, Lorcan, High King of Dorjhalon. We are now one, never to be torn asunder, our lives welded together from this time forth. My Eternal Mate shall you be, and I yours. I so swear, by the Light of Day and the Dark of Night." As she spoke, the warmth intensified, growing stronger; by the time she finished, her entire body burned with heat.

Lorcan's fingers tightened around her wrist slightly, almost unconsciously as he repeated the words. She noticed for the first time that his skin had turned cold, while her heat continued to spread through her body, feeling as though living fire raced beneath her skin. She stared up at Lorcan, trapped in the power of his gaze, drawn into a spell she didn't understand and in which she feared to lose herself entirely. When he finished, his hand on her wrist was freezing. Evelayn was shocked to realize she wished for him to take her in his arms—for his ice to cool the heat that raged within her.

"It is done," the High Priest intoned, reaching out to place his hand on top of theirs and the chains. "I seal this Binding upon you both, never to be broken or severed, except upon death. Forthwith, you are of one heart and one soul. What is Bound this day be not torn asunder."

"What is Bound this day be not torn asunder," they all murmured, even Ceren.

"I pronounce you Eternal Mates."

But Evelayn was hardly aware of anything beyond the depths of Lorcan's eyes and the heat raging through her.

"I will not fail you," Lorcan whispered, lifting his free hand to brush his cold fingers against her burning cheek. Despite herself, Evelayn turned her face into his touch, her eyes closing in relief.

"Is that steam?" Ceren gasped from behind her, and Evelayn jerked back, shocked to realize her friend was right. Steam had risen from where he touched her, as if they truly were made of fire and ice.

"I've never seen anything like it," the priest murmured.

Evelayn backed away hastily from Lorcan until the chains wrapped around their arms stopped her. Patryk hurried to unwind and remove them. The moment her arm was free, the heat drained from her body, until she was left chilled, even in the humidity of the solarium. Shaken, Evelayn turned her back to Lorcan, willing herself to regain control over her body and mind.

Ceren stood a few feet away, watching with her eyebrows knit together in concern—and disapproval.

Her earlier certainty wavered at the look on her dearest friend's face, as what the priest had said rang through her head— the finality of his words. *It is done.*

She was now Bound to Lorcan.

EIGHTEEN

H E KNEW THE MOMENT THE OATH WAS BROKEN. Tanvir was stoking the fire when his right hand turned as frigid as the ice that had coated the outer edges of their windows that morning. The sensation traveled up his arm, spreading throughout his body, until he was practically shaking from the cold. And then, as suddenly as it had come, it was gone, leaving him utterly gutted.

Letha's bedroom door opened and closed. When he didn't acknowledge her, Letha asked, "What's wrong?"

"Nothing." Tanvir's hands tightened into fists as he moved to the window, staring out unseeingly at the straggly trees where there once was a thriving forest. Her scowl was easily discernible, even in her reflection on the glass panes.

"If you wish to keep secrets from me, at least have the decency to be honest about it."

"Fine." He turned to face her. "I don't wish to talk about it."

She nodded curtly. "I understand. But it might help if you did."

Tanvir threw his hands up in the air. "And that's exactly why I usually just say 'nothing.'"

"Who else are you going to talk to? You stay holed up in here, in these three little rooms all the time."

"As do you," he reminded her curtly.

"Where would I go? You are the High Lord and haven't visited our holdings in over five years. The house must be in ruins by now; surely the staff abandoned it long ago. I have no desire to converse with anyone about my . . . about what happened in Dorjhalon, and that's all I am ever asked about here. So, yes, I stay in these rooms. With you."

"I am in contact with the lesser lords and the overseers, who assure me that the house and the holdings are all in tolerable condition—as well as can be expected with our power gone and such dismal weather that only continues to worsen every year." Tanvir couldn't help the anger that seeped into his words, but her unspoken accusations cut deep. "I am not as inept as you clearly think me to be."

"I never said you were inept. I know you're perfectly capable—if you choose to be."

"I can't have this conversation right now," Tanvir bit out before she could continue, turning to the window once more. Mercifully, she stayed silent.

Somewhere in the castle at that very moment, Evelayn was making the most horrific mistake imaginable. He'd been a fool to think he really could save his sister *and* end up with the queen. But for her to do *this?* Merely to spite him. That had to be the reason—she couldn't honestly believe Lorcan was telling the truth about giving her stone back in exchange for her Binding. As if he kept it hidden in a drawer somewhere, just waiting to return it to her.

But of course she didn't think that, he remembered suddenly. Lorcan had said they would *leave* to retrieve her stone as soon as she Bound herself to him. She knew it wasn't here. And soon they wouldn't be, either.

Tanvir whirled around and rushed past Letha into his room.

When he emerged holding a knapsack and wearing his heavy winter cloak, her eyes widened. "What do you think you're doing? I didn't mean for you to inspect our holdings right now."

Tanvir ignored Letha and continued to rush around their quarters, grabbing items he might need and stuffing them into his pack.

She waited, but he didn't volunteer any other information.

"After all these years, holed up here, hiding from the world . . . *now* you're suddenly leaving? Because of what I said? Truly, Tanv, I don't think—"

"This has nothing to do with you."

He felt her bewilderment at his boorishness but ignored it as she moved to stand near the fireplace, her thin arms crossed in front of her narrow body. Arms that had once been strong, capable. Bain and Lorcan had much to answer for; but only Lorcan remained to receive his deserved punishment for his part in the war, and in hurting Letha. For hurting Evelayn, as well, and somehow still manipulating her into Binding herself to him.

Tanvir was done with letting the Dark King shape his destiny—
or anyone else's. "I have something I must do."

Letha watched him silently, but he could scent her concern,
the sharp tang of it beneath her normal honey and freesia.

It took only a few minutes to gather what he thought he'd
need. All except the last few items—the ones that were sure to
arouse her concern about something far worse. There was no
helping it, though. He had to leave quickly; he couldn't wait for
her to retire to her rooms again, which probably wouldn't be for
hours. They spent most afternoons reading, besting each other in
chess, or engaging in other more trivial games to pass the time.
She was right, they had become pathetically depressing. They'd
both survived the war, but to do what? To live half lives, hiding
from what was left of the world they'd once known?

Well, he was done with such an existence. Tanvir strode over
to the chest and lifted the lid. He felt Letha's sharp gaze on him
but ignored her as he knelt and pushed aside the dust-ridden
material that protected what lay beneath.

"What *exactly* are you doing?" Just as he'd predicted, her concern turned into cold disbelief as he withdrew the scabbard with
the sword's hilt sticking out from the chest, then the daggers, and
finally the Scíath, a shield that could not only deflect a blade but
also a blast of power from another Draíolon.

"I told you, this has nothing to do with you." He shoved the
daggers into his boots.

"By the Light, Tanvir, you look as though you're going to war
again—except I can't think of who you intend to fight." Letha

walked over and knelt in front of him. "At least tell me this: Does it have anything to do with Evelayn . . . and Lorcan?"

Tanvir clenched his teeth together, unreasonably irritated by her intuition. "He's forced her into a horrible decision." Even with the fire burning steadily in the hearth, the cold air from outside seeped in through the cracks around the window, causing a noticeable chill in the room. But that wasn't why his hands trembled as he pulled the sword partway out of the scabbard, checking the condition of the blade.

Letha hesitantly reached out and placed a soothing hand on his arm. "I haven't seen you this angry in . . . quite a while. What could he possibly have—"

"She's *Binding* herself to him." Tanvir yanked his arm away, cutting her off. "Rather than forgive me, she's agreed to Bind herself to that foul Dorjhalon king."

Letha's expression softened. "Oh, Tanvir."

He shoved the sword back in the scabbard and stood up, turning his back on her. "Spare me your pity."

She was quiet as he quickly strapped the sword around his waist, but he sensed her moving.

"Here. You don't want to forget this."

Tanvir twisted to see her holding out the shield as if it was a peace offering. But when he tried to take it, she didn't let go.

"I hope you don't think you're leaving me here."

He stared at her in horror. "That's *exactly* what I'm doing." Tanvir's fingers tightened on the edge of the shield.

The look on her face was one he'd seen many times

throughout his life—the fierce determination that had helped her become one of the most formidable Draíolon in Éadrolan's army. But he hadn't seen it for over a decade, since before Bain and Lorcan destroyed her.

"I won't let you leave without me."

While he was glad to see some of that old spark back in his sister, she couldn't have picked a worse time. "You don't even know where I'm going—or what I'm going to do."

Letha bent over and drew her own sword and scabbard out of the trunk. "Then tell me." She strapped the scabbard around her hips.

Once, they could have summoned weapons with barely even a thought, drawing upon their power and training. But thanks to Lorcan, they were left to use steel rather than Light. Still, Tanvir had never been more determined to wield a weapon than he was in that moment. He gripped the hilt of the sword tightly as he looked his sister square in the eye and said:

"I am going to kill the king of Dorjhalon."

NINETEEN

WHAT HAPPENS AT THE END OF ATHRÚFAR? IF WE haven't reclaimed my stone and my power before then, will you . . . ? Will I be forced to turn back into a swan?" Evelayn broke the uncomfortable silence that had held them in its grip ever since they'd left the castle and begun the trek to the White Peak and Máthair Damhán's lair. She'd changed into breeches and soft, fur-lined boots, with a fur-lined cape to match. All courtesy of Lorcan, of course. Evelayn had tried to refuse, to convince him that she didn't like such heavy, animalistic clothing. But he'd insisted, reminding her that they were going to be traveling for days in the cold wind and snow.

"Not by my hand." Lorcan spoke quietly but vehemently. He was directly ahead of her, his frost-white hair a beacon in the falling darkness. He'd pulled his cloak over his head when they'd first left the castle, and Evelayn had done the same, hoping to avoid notice as they meandered down one of the paths that led to Solas. To the casual observer, they would have appeared to be two ordinary Draíolon, heading back to the city for the night. But once they'd moved into the protection of the trees, they'd veered off the path, heading northeast through the woods toward Diasla, and he'd pulled his hood down. "I am doing everything I can to uphold my portion of the oath, and by so doing, I should be freed from her stipulations."

"Now that we're Bound"—the word nearly stuck in her throat, she still couldn't quite believe what she'd done—"will you tell me what exactly you promised Máthair Damhán?"

Lorcan glanced back at her, over his shoulder, his expression inscrutable in the darkness. "Can you run? We need to cover as much distance as possible."

"Of course I can run." Contrary to her words, Evelayn halted, crossing her arms in front of her chest. "But why won't you answer my question?"

Lorcan sighed and turned to face her. "I'm not sure what will happen at the end of Athrúfar. We need to reach her lair before then, which means we must hurry, since you are incapable of shifting and I can no longer do it for you."

"I don't see how shifting would help—I'm much faster at running than I am at flying as a swan."

"As a royal, in your animal form, you can access your power in different ways. One being the ability to direct the power to substantially increase your strength and speed. How do you think I made the flight from the White Peak to your castle in just a few hours rather than days?"

Evelayn scowled at the reminder of that horrific night and the realization that she was the only thing keeping him from taking to the skies and reaching their goal before sunrise. "As I have no access to my power, it hardly matters that I can't shift."

Lorcan took a step toward her, but she backed away and he stopped. "If you can run, let's see how far we get. When we stop to rest, I will tell you what I can."

A cold wind whipped through the dying trees, tearing more browned leaves off the gnarled branches and blowing them across the snow-dusted ground. "Fine," she agreed at last.

Lorcan nodded curtly. "Ready?"

Once she had lived for her runs, for the freedom and speed of sprinting through Éadrolan. Even though it was very long ago, the familiar eagerness—the way her muscles twitched in readiness, and her heart rate picked up as adrenaline released into her system—surged as if she hadn't missed a day. "Always," she said, and then she took off at a dead sprint, leaving Lorcan behind her.

Ceren pulled her wrap more tightly around her body and prepared to step out of the warmth of the castle into the cold, dark night. She'd watched Evelayn and Lorcan leave some time earlier with a hard knot in her stomach that had only grown worse when they'd disappeared into the embrace of the forest surrounding the castle. She'd tried to convince them to let her come, but Lorcan had been adamant that she would slow them down. Even Evelayn had gently told her to go back to her younglings. *You don't want to go to her lair, trust me. I would never go back if I didn't have to,* she'd said. Ceren still vividly remembered what Evelayn had been like when she'd returned from Máthair Damhán's cave the first time with the silk. It had been a harrowing experience, one she'd barely even been willing to speak about. Ceren's fear of what could have made the queen—the strongest Draíolon she knew—so traumatized led her to agree to stay behind, letting the two of them leave. But once they were out of sight, she immediately regretted her decision.

"Where did they go?"

Ceren barely managed to smother her scream as she whirled to see Lothar directly behind her. He still looked weak, but he was dressed and on his feet.

"What are you doing out of bed—and in the servants' quarters?" Ceren hissed.

Lothar lifted one shoulder. "Whatever Evelayn gave me to knock me out did its job. My body finished healing. When I got up to change, I noticed two Draíolon hurrying away from the castle—two Draíolon who looked suspiciously similar to my brother and the queen. I kept waiting for them to come back, and when they never did, I came to investigate." He moved to block her exit when Ceren began to inch her way toward the door.

"It's nothing for you to worry about. There's a missive with instructions waiting for you in your room—where you should be right now, resting." She tried to push past him. When he winced, she paused with eyebrows raised. "All the way healed, are you?"

"Mostly healed," he conceded.

"Go back to your room, Prince Lothar. Read the letter from your brother and do what he needs you to do."

Lothar finally backed away enough for her to pull the door

open. Ceren had just turned to step outside when Lothar grabbed her arm and yanked her back.

"What in the—"

He clamped one hand over her mouth and pointed with the other.

Her initial anger at his manhandling sank into confusion and then concern as they silently watched two more Draíolon head in the same direction as the queen and king. Only these two were armed to the teeth—one even carried a Scíath, as if expecting a battle.

"Is that Lord Tanvir?" Lothar whispered as a brisk wind pushed the hood off the other male's head, exposing his golden hair for a moment before he yanked it back up again.

"I think it is," Ceren agreed, her stomach sinking.

They watched as the pair moved swiftly toward the forest, only pausing for a moment to inspect the ground. As if they were tracking something—or some*one*.

"He's going after the king," Ceren breathed in horror.

"My brother? Why would he do that? Lorcan is the one who saved his sister!"

Ceren glanced at the prince and shook her head. If he hadn't read the letter yet, he didn't know what Lorcan and Evelayn had done. And she wasn't sure she wanted to be the one to tell him. He saved her having to answer when he turned on his heel and said, "I'm going to stop them."

"Prince Lothar—you're in no condition to go after them. You need to rest and finish healing." Ceren hurried to follow the prince as he rushed into the kitchens, shocking the harried cook and her attendants when he grabbed a knapsack and began to shove items into it. "Please, if you would just read the letter your brother left for you . . ."

"There's no time," Lothar said, determined. "If I leave now, they will be easy to track with the snow on the ground. But I'm going to have to hurry if I wish to intercept them before they reach my brother."

Ceren sighed. "If you refuse to stay here, then I am coming with you."

"I don't need help," Lothar bit out, affronted.

"No. Right now you don't. But if you aren't quite as healed as you claim, you might in an hour or two—or three. Especially if this storm gets worse."

He glared at her for a long moment but then threw his hands up in the air. "Do as you wish. But I am leaving as soon as I get my cloak."

Ceren tried to quell the rush of nerves that set her stomach twisting. This was what Evelayn would have done in her shoes . . . wasn't it? If she let Lothar go out there alone and he collapsed and died after all that Lorcan and Evelayn and even Tanvir had done to keep him alive, it would be a terrible blow. And considering Evelayn had only just Bound herself to Lorcan and was already going to face Máthair Damhán, Ceren didn't want to let Lothar's foolish bullheadedness lead to more tragedy for them.

She quickly found a quill, ink, and parchment.

Dearest Quinlen,

I had hoped to be back in your arms today, but
circumstances at the castle have become such that
I must follow after our queen to help protect her.
Much has happened that I wished to speak to you
about in person, rather than through a letter. But
I can't leave Evelayn alone, to fend for herself
against the forces conspiring all around her. She
has Bound herself to Lorcan (yes, you read that
correctly), and they have gone to retrieve her stone.
But though she seems to have decided to trust him
for reasons unfathomable to me, I still don't. And
now others are trailing them with ill intent, I fear.
I must hurry if I wish to intercept any of those
who might wish her harm. I may be gone for
some time. Please give kisses from Mama to
Saoirse and Clive and tell them I love them and
will be home soon.

I love you.

Ceren

She folded up the letter and sealed it, gave it to Gestra to deliver, and hurried to find Lothar before he left without her.

TWENTY

THEY HAD ONLY BEEN RUNNING FOR AN HOUR, PERHAPS a little more, when Evelayn began to tire. At first she was able to push through the burning in her legs and lungs, to ignore the creeping exhaustion, but it didn't take long before she began to slow, much to her humiliation. She'd never let *any-one* outrun her before and she couldn't bear the thought of Lorcan being the one to see her weakness.

When he suddenly halted, she skidded to a stop as well.

"What is it? Is something wrong?" She inhaled deeply, trying to scent anything unusual, her ears perked to listen for a warning sound of some sort.

"Nothing is wrong. I merely thought we should pause for a moment."

"I don't need to rest." Her neck grew hot.

He lifted one eyebrow. "*I* wanted to get a drink and a bite to eat."

"Oh."

Lorcan sat down on a fallen log and unslung the knapsack from around his shoulders, loosening it to pull out a piece of some sort of dried meat. He offered her some, but she shook her head. She felt too sick from pushing herself so hard to stomach meat, particularly salted, dried hunks of it.

"Ah, yes, you prefer lighter fare. I forgot." He shrugged and put the second piece back. Then he unhooked the waterskin from his waistband and took a deep draft.

Evelayn pulled out a slice of cheese and a roll from her bag and forced herself to eat. Even though it was the last thing she felt like doing, she knew she needed the energy it would provide.

As he sat there, eating and drinking, Lorcan seemed so . . . *normal.* Completely un-Lorcan-like as he stood and re-slung the bag over his shoulders to hang down his back. There was almost no hint of the cocksure, acerbic royal she'd known evident at the moment. He was being solicitous . . . almost *kind.* He, too, wore heavier clothing than normal, but none of it was fur-lined. When she'd complained about *that,* he'd reminded her that he was a Dark Draíolon and actually enjoyed the cold. That enjoyment was evident as he tilted his face toward the chilled breeze that promised more snow.

The clouds broke apart above them at that exact moment, letting a glimpse of the moon shine down on their little clearing, washing him in iridescent light. His skin was so dark, he practically blended into the night—all except his white hair and the flash of his silver eyes reflecting the moonlight when he turned and met her bold assessment of him.

How had so much changed so quickly? She was now stuck in

her Draíolon form rather than the swan, going to Máthair Damhán again, and Bound to this mercurial, powerful male.

When he spoke, it almost made her jump. "You were a swan for the better part of ten years, Evelayn."

"Excuse me?"

"You can't expect to be in the condition you once were. You haven't run in a decade." He hooked the waterskin back onto his waistband.

"I told you I didn't need to rest. I was fine. I *am* fine."

"No"—he stepped toward her and held out a hand—"you're lying. And we don't have time for your pride."

She stared at his hand as if he were trying to hand her a snake. "Are you planning on dragging me behind you?"

When he barked out a laugh, it seemed to take *him* by surprise as much as it did her.

"No, my lady queen, I am offering to siphon some of my power into you so that you can run faster without tiring."

Evelayn's eyes shot up to meet his amused expression. "You can *do* that?"

"Take my hand, and I will show you."

His silver eyes seemed unnaturally bright for such a dark night, as if they attracted and refracted any ounce of light available, making him seem almost predatory as he took another step toward her. A rush of fear took her off guard and she had to swallow back a sudden panic. She was powerless and alone in the darkened forest with the king of Dorjhalon. The most powerful being on land at the moment. What was she thinking Binding herself to him? To this male who had hurt and manipulated and killed . . .

"What caused it?" He spoke softly, his voice hardly louder than the whisper of the breeze.

"Caused what?" she forced herself to respond, managing to keep her voice from betraying her.

"Your fear."

"I'm not afraid."

"I can smell it on you, I can see it in your eyes. You can't lie— not to me." Lorcan closed the gap between them so that he stood less than an arm's length away. "There's no reason to be frightened. I will protect you."

Evelayn took a deep breath to steady herself. His now familiar evergreen-and-frost scent filled her nose; and beneath that, the heavier fragrance of the Darkness he wielded was a constant reminder of the power simmering in his blood, woven through every muscle and sinew in his body. "And if *you* are the reason . . . how will you protect me from yourself?"

He looked taken aback. "Why would you be frightened of me *now*? After everything else . . . After Binding yourself to me?" The wind picked up a bit, blowing strands of his hair out of the leather band, pulling it back and across his face. The night had grown bitterly cold, making Evelayn grateful for the fur-lined clothing he'd insisted she wear. "We are going to retrieve your stone and reclaim your power. What else must I do to prove to you that I am not your enemy?"

"I don't know," she answered honestly. "A few seemingly good deeds can't immediately erase a decade of cruelty and deception."

Lorcan studied her face for a long moment. The intensity of

his scrutiny made her belly tighten—partly in fear, but not entirely. "My whole life, I have been surrounded by those who feared me or hated me, or both. Some merely for the fact that I was my father's son, without ever knowing me at all. And I lived with that, as I had to. Even my own brother came to loathe me. But now . . . I have a chance to change all of that. With you." Slowly he lifted his hand toward her, giving Evelayn time to pull away. Instead, she stood frozen, waiting. When his fingers brushed her cold cheek, it sent a jolt through her that launched her heart into her throat. "My life was bound to yours even before today, Evelayn. I made a Blood Vow that tied our fates together ten years ago." His voice was a husky murmur as his fingers curled to cup her jaw. "I will never harm you—nor let anyone or any*thing* else harm you. If you die, I die, remember?"

She stared up into his quicksilver eyes, hardly able to breathe. A flare of heat blossomed in her right hand, where her scar bisected the formerly perfect skin.

"I know you feel that," he whispered, so close that his breath was warm on her icy lips. He took her right hand in his left and ran his thumb across the scar, sending a shiver up her arm. "When we made that Blood Vow, something happened. For some reason, it created a connection far beyond just the stipulations of the vow. We can sense each other, feel one another's emotions."

Her heartbeat had become a beacon in her body, pounding at the arch of her throat where his fingers brushed against her skin, in the hand that he held, and in her belly that tightened as she realized she was staring at his mouth.

"Please, my lady queen, don't be afraid."

Evelayn didn't dare move, didn't dare speak. But not from fear, not anymore. If she was afraid of anything, it was of the urge to close the gap between them. To give in to the sudden madness that made heat pool in her abdomen and her head buzz with the desire to lean forward, to feel his mouth on hers.

A gust of wind whipped through the clearing, blowing directly in her face and breaking the spell of Lorcan's gaze and his heated touch in a world turned cold. She abruptly stumbled away a step, pulling out of his reach.

They stared at each other, the silence drawing out as the clouds gathered above them. The scar on her hand twinged and a sensation of uncertainty washed over her. *His* uncertainty.

If you die, I die, remember?

She was Bound to him. She'd made her choice. Finally she took a deep breath and then held out her hand. "I told you, I'm not afraid."

He gazed at her for a moment longer, then a hint of a smile broke out across his face. Lorcan took her hand in his and turned back to the path.

"Ready?" he asked once more.

"Ready." She smiled back at him as warmth and strength surged into her hand, up her arm, and throughout her body.

He squeezed her a little bit tighter, and then they took off at a sprint just as the first flakes began to spiral to the ground.

TWENTY-ONE

DAWN WAS RAPIDLY APPROACHING, WHICH MEANT they had run for the majority of the night. It had not begun to grow lighter, but Lorcan could scent the coming sun on the crystalline air. Even though he had helped sustain her throughout the night, he knew Evelayn needed to rest. And truth be told, he did as well. It took an immense amount of concentration and energy to siphon some of his power into her, especially while running full speed through a snowstorm. There was at least a couple inches of accumulation on the ground, soaking through their boots and making the trails treacherous. If they veered off to where the trees grew thicker, there was less snow, but their speed was hampered by the branches that reached for them like bark-crusted claws, tearing at their cloaks, hair, and skin.

He slowed and then pulled her to a stop. "We need to rest. At least for a couple of hours."

Evelayn didn't argue, merely nodded. Her nose was red and her hair had little bits of snow and frost clinging to it. Her fingers were like ice on his, so frozen into his grip that he had to help pry them off of his hand so he could set about making a shelter and starting a fire.

Once the fire burned brightly beneath the makeshift shelter he'd created with his cloak and some tree branches, he sat down beside her on the hard ground.

"Won't you freeze?" Evelayn glanced up at his cloak above them, blocking the little bit of snow still falling and helping to trap some of the warmth from the fire.

"I told you, the cold doesn't bother me. Just as the heat of summer doesn't cause you discomfort, but I can't stand it." He opened his pack and took out more food.

"It might not bother me as much as you, but if it is extremely hot, it does make me uncomfortable." Despite the fire, she was still shivering when he glanced over at her.

"Why don't you lie down and try to rest." He brushed off her concern. The snow gave the night air an icy bite, but the fire created enough heat to keep him from getting chilled. "I can sit up and take the first watch."

"I'm not going to sleep while you stay up. You need to rest also. What would we even need to watch for? We're not at war . . . are we?" The cold wind blew a gust of smoke into her face, making her blink rapidly.

"I don't know what Máthair Damhán is doing, or why she is suddenly pushing so hard to have me fulfill my vow. Something has changed. She's sent messages before, but not like this. And she's never attacked us until now. I refuse to be taken off guard again." He shifted on the hard ground. "How about you sleep for an hour and then you let me sleep for an hour. Then we can continue on."

Evelayn looked at him steadily for a moment, doing her best to hide her unease, but he could still see it in her violet eyes. "All right," she finally agreed. When she lay down on the ground and rolled over so her back was to him, Lorcan allowed himself to look away out into the dark night. Already the blackness had melted into a deep gray, hinting at the sun that would be rising in mere minutes.

"Will your mother be angry?"

He didn't have to ask what she meant. There was a reason he hadn't informed his mother about the Binding ceremony or his plan to leave with Evelayn to reclaim her power. "Don't concern yourself with how she'll react. We have to focus on surviving this first."

"That wasn't very comforting."

Lorcan sighed. "My mother is . . . complicated. But she will accept you with time, I believe."

"Still not very comforting." Evelayn spoke to the flames, so Lorcan couldn't see her face or read her expression, but he scented her trepidation. "Did you tell her about . . . any of this? Does she even know you're gone?"

"No." Lorcan shifted on the cold, hard ground. "There wasn't time to explain it all to her, and she might have interfered if she knew what I intended to do."

"You mean, if she knew you were helping me to reclaim my power."

One of the branches had burned through so that it collapsed

into the heart of the fire, sending a burst of flames into the darkness—a shower of light that momentarily blinded him. "You have to understand, she was Bound to a royal who became obsessed with power, ruled by violence, and forbade her to show love toward her sons. She wanted us to be free—free of him, and free of any other Draíolon, male or female, who could ever become like him. She supported me, helped me even, to overthrow him. Her own Mate." Sometimes he still woke at night drenched in a cold sweat from nightmares where his father was alive and found out that Abarrane and Lorcan had been working together and forced Lorcan to watch while he tortured his mother to death.

"*Abarrane* helped me, too? *She* wanted me to kill Bain? But she loathes me."

"My mother knew the only way to escape his abuse was for him to die. But she also wanted me to be king in his stead, which meant *I* couldn't do it—and neither of us dared risk Lothar."

"Which meant I was the only one who could."

"Precisely." Lorcan hesitated to admit the rest but decided it was better she knew. When they returned, Evelayn would be walking into a beehive of trouble with the other queen. "But I explicitly chose not to inform her about our Binding or helping you reclaim your power because she would try to stop me if she did."

"Why? All I've ever wanted was peace. Can't she see what the imbalance of power is doing to our world?"

"I believe she would rather risk that than allow another royal to exist who could threaten her—or me."

"So she will let Lachalonia shrivel and die rather than let me reclaim what is rightfully mine—the very power that enabled your 'escape' from Bain?" She finally rolled over, her violet eyes flashing in the firelight, her cheeks stained red—from the heat of the flames or her anger, Lorcan wasn't quite sure.

"*She* isn't letting anything happen or not happen, because she is not choosing for me *or* you. Which is exactly why I sent an urgent summons to her this morning, to keep her from finding out about any of this. She is on her way back to Dorjhalon even now. By the time she returns to Éadrolan, this will all be long behind us and she will have to learn to live with my decisions."

Evelayn opened her mouth but then shut it again, as if thinking better of whatever she'd been about to say. Finally, she lay back down, turning to the fire once more. She'd been silent for so long, Lorcan began to wonder if she'd given in and begun to doze off, but then she spoke once more, a soft question that took him completely off guard.

"Do you ever miss him?"

When he didn't respond right away, she pressed. "Even though he did terrible things to you, he was still your father."

Lorcan clenched his teeth together, a surge of memory rising up, carried on a wave of pain.

"I honestly don't know how to describe what I feel when I think of him." He struggled against the instinct to push her away, to deflect her question, especially after the heated exchange about his mother. However, he knew if he wished to gain her trust or ever hope that she could come to care for him, he had to open himself up to her more than he had to anyone else before. "Even though he was cruel, I suppose there was always a part of me that wished to please him. At least when I was a youngling. You are right—as much as I hated him, he was still my father. Perhaps I don't mourn *him* so much as the death of the dream that he would someday become a better father. The death of any hope that he could have been a better king, rather than leaving me a world torn apart by his greed and machinations."

The pop and hiss of the fire consuming the wood he'd gathered was the only sound for several moments. When she spoke again, her voice was heavy with sorrow.

"I miss my mother and father every day." She rolled over once more, her eyes luminous in the darkness. "We have a complicated web between us. Your father is the reason my parents were taken from me. And, no matter that you and your mother helped orchestrate it, *I* am the one who took him from you. I'm not sorry for that, because there was no other way to stop him. But I *am* sorry for what he did to you. For what he has thrust upon you as the king who must take his place."

Lorcan shrugged, not trusting himself to speak without betraying the full depth of his volatile emotions. Hesitantly, she reached out and gently placed her hand on top of his. Her touch felt like a brand, searing not only his cold skin but also his ice-filled heart.

"Perhaps you were right after all," she murmured, her voice barely audible over the hiss of the fire. "Maybe with time I will be able to see past the monster I believed you to be to the king that you are trying to be instead."

Their eyes met, and he found himself struggling to stay where he was, to not follow the compulsion to pull her toward him and finish what they had nearly started hours ago, when they'd almost kissed. Her gaze dropped to his mouth, her scent warming with the fragrance of her sudden desire, and it was almost more than Lorcan could stand.

"Go to sleep, Evelayn," he said roughly, forcing himself to turn and stare at the flames, ignoring the fire raging in his own blood.

Lorcan heard her move but didn't look up. In his peripheral vision he could tell she'd lain back down.

"You'll wake me in an hour?" she finally asked.

"I promise."

Mercifully, within a few minutes her exhaustion beat out her willpower, and Evelayn's breathing slowed and deepened. Only then did he let himself breathe freely, inhaling her scent more deeply. Only then did he allow himself the freedom to look at her—to *really* look at this fierce yet unsettlingly intuitive queen he'd Bound himself to—studying the planes and angles of her face, the brush of her eyelashes on her skin, the beating of her pulse in her throat, the curve of her lips as they parted slightly in sleep.

Just as the Blood Vow he'd made with Evelayn bound him to her in unexpected ways, so, too, did his vow with Máthair Damhán. And he could sense the Ancient's impatience growing ever stronger, a distant but nagging burn in his veins.

He'd told Evelayn the truth—something had to have changed. Something drastic.

Lorcan wasn't sure he wanted to find out what, but they had no choice. He looked northeast, to where, far beyond his sight, the

White Peak stood a stark sentinel—and where, deep within its bowels, Máthair Damhán waited for them.

"Where are they going—and in this storm?" Ceren pulled her wrap more tightly around her face as they trudged forward into the blowing snow, but it couldn't block the biting cold from stinging her cheeks and nose. It even hurt to talk because her lips were frozen.

Lothar paused, staring down at the ground, and then pointed. "They're still tracking Lorcan and the queen."

Ceren squinted to see through the blizzard, but then she saw it. Multiple footprints, nearly obscured by the falling snow but still discernible when one looked closely.

"You were right, then: They're not stopping, even in this weather." A heavy pit of dread lodged in her belly, like she'd swallowed a stone. There was no good reason why Tanvir would set off into the woods in a blizzard with his sister, both of them armed to the extreme, chasing after the newly Bound king and queen.

"And they're in a hurry. We're going to have to move much faster if we want to catch them." Lothar had moved forward, following the trail of footprints, which were spread far enough apart to indicate that all four Draíolon were running full speed despite the storm. "Can you run?"

"Can *you*?" Ceren retorted testily. "I'm not the one who was on my deathbed half a day ago."

Lothar scowled at her. "I'll take the lead."

"Why shouldn't I? I'm more capable than you seem to think."

"Because I am a Dark Draíolon—I'm comfortable in the snow and darkness. I can see better than you in these conditions."

Ceren couldn't argue those points, but it didn't keep irritation from unfurling in her chest, making her breathe faster. "Fine. Take the lead."

Lothar nodded and took off at a sprint.

"For now," she added in a low mutter, then hurried to follow him.

TWENTY-TWO

E VELAYN TRIED TO CONCEAL HOW HARD SHE WAS BREATH-
ing, but she knew Lorcan was aware of her struggle.
Another surge of warmth, accompanied by a fresh wave
of energy, rose up her arm from the hand he clutched as they ran
through the forest and the melting snow.

"You're going . . . to wear . . . yourself out," she panted
between strides.

"I'm fine," he replied without glancing at her.

But she could see the sweat dampening his hairline and creat-
ing a V down his back, causing his tunic to stick to his skin. The
clouds had parted early in the day and now the sun was shining
brightly down on them as they rushed toward the border, and to
Máthair Damhán's distant lair beyond that.

"You didn't . . . even rest . . ." she pointed out, but this time
he didn't respond, just increased his speed so much that she
couldn't catch her breath to speak anymore.

When she'd woken, the sun had already risen, and Lorcan

had claimed he'd dozed while she slept. He'd insisted they leave right away, and the scathing look he'd given her when she'd accused him of lying had been enough to make her snap her mouth shut and climb to her feet.

Evelayn panted as they raced through the forest toward Ristra. She wasn't used to being the one who couldn't keep up—and she didn't like the feeling one bit. It took all of her concentration and strength just to follow where Lorcan led, tugging her this way and that to avoid branches and boulders in their path.

Finally, when the sun slipped below the western horizon, Lorcan slowed and halted, letting go of her hand to grasp his knees. Evelayn leaned against a tree, her lungs burning and her side cramped. She couldn't imagine what it had cost him to sustain her for so long. He bent over to catch his breath; she'd never seen him so physically vulnerable. If she'd wished to try and attack him, now was her chance. Beyond the fact that she didn't have a weapon and was even more exhausted than he, the realization that she didn't *want* to hurt him anymore hit her like a blast of the icy wind that had kicked up again in the past hour, erasing the warmth of the sunny day.

Evelayn didn't want to let herself think too much about what that meant.

After a moment, Lorcan straightened and glanced over at her. "I'll go find some dry kindling and get a fire started. It's going to be a cold night again. We can rest for a few hours and then keep going."

"I'm not helpless, you know," she said. "I can go look for kindling. You stay here and set up the shelter."

He paused in removing his cloak from where he'd stowed it in his pack to shoot her a patronizing look. "I just siphoned my power into you for the better part of an entire day so you could keep up with me. The only thing you need to do right now is eat and rest so you can hopefully run without my help for as long as possible later tonight."

Evelayn glared at him. "If it's such a burden, then keep your power to yourself," she snapped.

"It has been a while since you lived in your Draíolon form, it's true, but surely you can't think you're going to regain all your former strength and speed after only one day of running?"

"And whose fault is that?" Her neck and cheeks grew warm with her rising temper. "I don't recall choosing to tear my own stone out of my chest and to go hide as a swan for a decade."

Lorcan's expression darkened. He tossed his pack on the ground beside her. "We don't have time to argue about this— again. We agreed that there is limited time to make it to the White Peak. I left my kingdom without a king the day after a major attack to help you get your stone back. And the only way we're going to make it before Athrúfar ends is with my help. Those are the facts, no matter how angry they make you."

"We left *my* kingdom without a king," she muttered as she grudgingly sat down on a semidry boulder to pull out some of the food she'd brought. "But I daresay they'll survive, considering they've been without their queen far longer than just a few days."

A muscle ticked in Lorcan's jaw, but instead of responding, he turned on his heel and strode away from her into the forest, ostensibly to gather the kindling. At least she hoped that's all he was doing. Angering the king of Dorjhalon when they were alone in the woods with yet another blizzard approaching probably wasn't one of her better ideas.

Without his presence to fill her senses, everything else took greater shape and form around her. The sounds of the forest swelled up in place of the cadence of his stride and the timbre of his voice, and the musk of decayed leaves and wet soil replaced the crisp balsam, ice, and velvet night scent that she'd become so attuned to in the past couple of days. Why was she so aware of him? She tried to convince herself it was a defense mechanism— staying on her guard in case he turned on her. Just because she was physically attracted to him didn't mean anything—she'd always felt *something* around him, even when she was in love with Tanvir. He was, after all, incredibly handsome and powerful. And true, she'd seen some very different sides to him, facets to his personality that enticed her to want to believe him—to *want* to trust him. But that didn't mean she *should*.

Evelayn hadn't been completely alone since she'd returned to the castle, and the sudden solitude gave rise to thoughts and worries she hadn't let herself consider until that moment. The night before had brought up the grief she'd never fully been able to work through after her mother's death. Lying there on the hard, cold ground in the darkness, alone with Lorcan—the male she'd abhorred for so long and was suddenly Bound to—she'd missed her parents so terribly, the ache had been as sharp as a blade driving into the hollowed cavity of her chest. She'd wondered what they must think of her, watching from the Final Light, so beaten down, so useless as the queen for their Draíolon. Bound to a male they'd long considered their enemy. Were they disgusted with the turn their only daughter's life had taken?

Evelayn took a bite of the day-old bread she'd packed, forcing herself to chew and swallow, even though her mouth was even drier than the roll and her stomach had clenched into a tight ball of anxiety once more. As much as she hated to admit it, Lorcan was right. She wasn't going to regain her former strength and speed tomorrow, or even the next day. It would take weeks of conditioning, if not more, to be able to run the way she had years ago. And for some reason, *that* fact, the indignation of having him drag her through the forest, of the many things that had happened to her in the past few days, was the one that made her eyes sting and her lungs constrict, as if the air had suddenly grown thin. She clenched her teeth on the lingering bits of stale bread in her mouth and inhaled deeply through her nose, determined not to add to her humiliation by letting Lorcan return to find her crying.

A loud shout from the direction he'd stormed off in made her jump to her feet and spin toward it. Before she could charge after him, though, she scented another Draíolon rushing toward her from the other direction.

There was no time to find a weapon, and without her power, she was completely helpless. Rather than try to hide, Evelayn squared her shoulders, prepared to meet her attacker with dignity, if nothing else.

A female Draíolon burst out of the trees, a sword drawn and a Scíath in her other hand. Though she'd never met her before, Evelayn instantly knew who it was.

"Letha?"

Tanvir's sister drew up short, surprised, perhaps, to hear her name. But Evelayn couldn't have mistaken her—she looked so much like her brother. Their scents were even similar, except there was freesia mixed in with the honey, and Letha's hair was a lighter brown with streaks of burnt orange, just like the flower in her scent.

"Don't move," Letha commanded, leveling the sword at her.

There was another shout, followed by a cry of pain from somewhere behind them.

"That was Tanvir . . . wasn't it?"

Letha just stared at her coldly, deadly intent evident in every tense line of her body.

"He isn't stupid enough to attack Lorcan . . . is he?" Evelayn glanced over her shoulder, adrenaline racing through her body, when the sound of an explosion boomed through the trees.

"I said don't move!" Letha shouted, but her voice trembled slightly this time.

"He could *kill* him, Letha. You have to let me try to stop him!"

"Why would I believe that you care?" Letha stepped closer, so that the tip of the sword brushed the base of Evelayn's throat, an unmistakable threat.

Evelayn slowly lifted her hands in supplication, keeping every other part of her body still. "I don't know what he told you, but regardless of how he hurt and manipulated me, I have no desire for him to die."

Another boom shook the ground beneath their feet, much closer this time. Honestly, Evelayn couldn't believe Tanvir was still alive and fighting. He was powerless—what had he been thinking? Regardless, they were running out of time to save him, of that she was certain.

Evelayn summoned every last bit of training she'd endured as a youngling and stared the other female down. "Letha, I am your queen, and I command you to step back."

The sword wavered slightly, but then she stiffened her hold once more. "You *Bound* yourself to that . . . that *demon*." Letha's lip curled in disgust.

"I did what I had to do," Evelayn echoed what Lorcan himself had said to her many times over the past couple of days.

She caught the sound of a Draíolon sprinting toward them moments before a tree suddenly exploded so close that Evelayn instinctively ducked, just as Letha stumbled forward. The sword sliced through the side of Evelayn's neck in a blinding burst of agony. Hot blood rushed down her throat and onto her tunic as she collapsed to her knees.

"Evelayn!"

She dimly heard a male's shout but couldn't recognize the voice over the pounding of her pulse in her ears as her vision tunneled to black.

TWENTY-THREE

LORCAN LEAPT OVER THE BURNING TREE, HIS HEART IN his throat as Evelayn crumpled to the ground. Tanvir, who had barely managed to avoid him by using trees to block his blasts, made it to her first and dropped to his knees at her side, leaving himself unprotected.

"What did you *do?*" he cried out at his sister. It was that complete disregard for his own safety in the face of Evelayn's injury that disarmed Lorcan and stayed his hand. Tanvir was many things, and he'd done much to deceive Evelayn, but it had been for his sister's sake. And his love for the female who now lay in a puddle of her own blood because of that selfsame sister was undeniable.

Rather than finishing what Tanvir had started when he burst out from behind Lorcan in the woods, slicing a vicious blade through the air toward his exposed back, Lorcan rushed over and knelt across from Tanvir to assess Evelayn's wound. The fur-lined cloak he'd given her was already soaked—ruined.

"There's too much blood. We need to put pressure on it with something clean." He looked up at Tanvir, and Letha, who hovered behind him, her crimson-stained sword hanging by her side.

"Get me one of your clean tops." Tanvir shot a look over his shoulder at his sister.

"You're going to follow *his* orders? I thought you came here to—"

"Now!" Tanvir cut her off impatiently.

Lorcan didn't waste time watching to see what she did or didn't do. Instead, he yanked his own tunic over his head and balled it up to press against Evelayn's throat. Her pale skin, as white as swan feathers, was stained scarlet. Twice now he'd had to do this. Twice in two days he'd been on his knees desperately pressing a piece of fabric against a grisly wound for someone he—

"Do something other than sitting there watching me," Lorcan snapped angrily, cutting off the dangerous turn of his thoughts.

"How deep is it?" Tanvir hesitantly bent closer. "May I look?" His hand trembled a bit as he reached toward the ruined tunic. Lorcan would have mocked him for the show of weakness, except a matching tremor had begun deep within him at the sight of Evelayn motionless on the snowy, cold earth.

Tanvir lifted one corner of the tunic and gently prodded at the skin, trying to gauge the severity of the wound despite the blood that continued to flow so freely. Too freely.

"Well?" Lorcan pressed.

"It's deep. But not life-threatening—*if* we can get it closed off and the bleeding to stop fast enough," Tanvir continued before Lorcan could sigh in relief. "If she had her power, it wouldn't be more than a few hours of healing. But as it is . . ." He trailed off, the unsaid accusation heavy in the air.

Anger rose in Lorcan's body, icy hot and dangerous. Or perhaps it was guilt. "Do either of you have anything we can use to help her? Or did you only bring those useless weapons with you on your quest?"

Tanvir turned to his sister, and when Lorcan looked up at her as well, she glared back at both of them. "Luckily for you, I planned ahead in case things didn't go well." She cut her gaze at Tanvir, but then she swung her pack off her back and yanked it open to withdraw a small leather pouch. She tossed it to Tanvir, who hurriedly undid the leather string and dumped the contents out on Evelayn's chest. It was barely rising and falling with her labored breathing.

There were rolled-up strips of fabric, a small tin, a needle and thread, and a few other items. Tanvir picked up the needle and began to thread it, a process that seemed painstakingly slow.

"Would you hurry up?" Lorcan snarled. "She's going to die before you get that Light-cursed thread through there."

"You think I'm not trying to hurry?" Tanvir snapped back, just as he finally pulled the thread through the eye of the needle.

"Both of you stop it," Letha cut in. "You're like two cocks circling a hen. She's not some animal, nor is she going to survive this if you don't stop pecking at each other and start working together." The female moved to kneel by her brother. "You hold the cloth while I sew," she said to Tanvir. "And you go start a fire—we're going to need to warm her up when I'm finished.

Your Majesty," she added, and then held out one hand toward Tanvir, presumably for the needle and thread.

"You did this to her. You think I would trust you to sew her up?" Lorcan lifted his free hand, ready to bind her with shadow chains if necessary to keep her from harming Evelayn further.

"By *accident*." Letha's expression was fierce, a hint of the pride and courage he'd seen when she'd first been captured rising above the meek creature she'd become under his father's torture— before he'd intervened. "And why should *I* trust that *you* wish to help her live? You, who ripped her stone from her breast and left us all powerless these many years."

Lorcan's lip curled with a low growl of warning. "My life is tied to hers. If she dies, I die."

"Is that the *only* reason?" Tanvir glanced up at him, his expression shuttered. But Lorcan could see in the other male's eyes the burning need to know if that was all—if it was only his oath driving him.

Lorcan cursed loudly. "Of course not, you fool. Now do something!"

Before Tanvir could respond, Letha reached out and took the needle from him. "I will help her. I promise," Letha asserted. "And I will do a much better job than my brother."

Lorcan didn't want to put his trust in her, but there was little choice in the matter. He had no training in binding and sewing wounds. He'd never needed it. It was difficult to tell beneath the coppery tang of Evelayn's blood in the air, but he was fairly certain he scented only honesty on Letha.

"Fine."

Tanvir immediately moved to take his place, holding the cloth over the majority of the wound, leaving just the top exposed for Letha to begin working with the needle and thread.

"It's a mercy she's unconscious," Letha commented as she pierced the soft flesh with the needle, pulling the two grisly edges together.

No longer needed at her side, Lorcan couldn't bear to merely stand and watch. He turned his back to them and paced away, toward the darkened forest, until he remembered the need for a fire. He'd dropped the kindling to defend himself from Tanvir's ridiculous attempt to attack him. *What had the powerless male been thinking?* he wondered as he quickly retraced his steps, passing the smoking remains of the trees he'd obliterated in his halfhearted attempt to frighten Tanvir into submission. If he'd wanted the male dead, he would have been dead.

The question was: Why had Tanvir thought he could possibly succeed at killing *him*?

After he retrieved the timber, Lorcan turned back but slowed his pace. The image of Evelayn lying on the ground, covered in gore, brought back the memories of the time *he'd* been the one to mar her luminous beauty with her own blood. Though that night it had been pristine white feathers stained crimson, rather than her skin.

I did what I had to do. The excuse he'd used over and over again to justify, to explain, to placate. Even to himself.

But it was true, wasn't it? He couldn't have killed his father himself or else he wouldn't have been able to claim the power for his kingdom. And if he hadn't made that oath with Máthair Damhán, Evelayn never would have succeeded in obtaining the silk and defeating his father. But the cost . . . oh, the cost of it all.

A cry of agony roused Lorcan from his thoughts.

She'd woken up.

Lorcan sprinted back to the trio. Darkness had nearly overtaken the forest entirely, but his Dark Draíolon sight allowed him to see them in stark detail—including Evelayn's eyes wide open but glazed with pain as she thrashed on the ground, forcing Tanvir to hold her down while Letha hurried to finish the stitches.

Lorcan tossed the branches down and rushed to her, dropping to his knees on the mud.

"Help me hold her still!"

But he ignored Tanvir and reached out to gently stroke her lavender-streaked hair off her clammy forehead. "Evelayn, listen to me." He spoke quietly but firmly. "You have to hold still."

"You think I didn't try that?" Tanvir growled.

"I know it hurts, but you must be still," Lorcan continued without pausing, keeping his voice low and calm, even though his heart pounded fiercely against his rib cage. Her lips were bloodless and her skin sallow. She shivered violently beneath their hands when she wasn't moaning and thrashing in pain. But as he spoke, her eyes rolled up to meet his. A shudder went through her body. "Find the strength so Letha can sew up this wound. If you lose too much blood, you could die, Evelayn. You can't let that happen. Your Draíolon need you. They need their queen."

She stared at him, her violet eyes two wells of pain and loss and grief, and that's when he realized what was happening. He saw the willpower to fight leaving her. She'd been through so much. Largely because of him, which made him sick. But she wasn't the only one who had suffered, who had bled and hurt and lost. And she couldn't leave him now.

"Your Draíolon need you . . . and . . . and *I* need you," he whispered hoarsely, letting his forehead drop to gently rest on hers. "Please. *Please.* Be still."

And miraculously, she stiffened—and stilled.

"Go, Letha. Hurry," Tanvir urged.

Lorcan didn't have to look to sense the jealousy on Tanvir's face. He could hear it in his voice and scent it on the cold night air. But none of that mattered at that moment. Only Evelayn did. When Letha punctured the skin, Evelayn cried out again, but other than going rigid, she managed to keep from moving.

"Keep . . . talking . . ." she rasped, taking Lorcan by surprise. But he quickly complied.

"The first time I saw you," he whispered, his mouth close to her ear, "running through that forest, so determined to defeat my father, I thought I'd never seen any Draíolon more beautiful and fierce all at once." Lorcan let his eyes close, picturing her as she'd been on that day. Lithe and powerful and so driven to succeed, despite all the odds against her. "And you were so *fast.* I'd never seen any female *or* male your equal."

Evelayn lay still while he spoke, her breathing labored, flinching each time the needle went in and out.

His voice dropped even lower. "And I still feel that way. There is no Draíolon, Light or Dark, who is your equal." Lorcan wasn't sure she could even hear him, but she sighed softly.

"All finished," Letha announced. "It's the best I can do."

Lorcan lifted his head to see a somewhat neat row of stitches running across Evelayn's throat. The wound was barely even seeping blood anymore, but she was still covered in gore, and the cloak beneath her was destroyed, completely drenched.

"If you'll get a fire started, I can collect some snow to melt and boil so we can clean her up a bit. But for now, we've got to get her warm," Letha instructed as she reached for the tin and screwed it open. Inside was a pungent ointment of some sort that she began to slather over the wound.

"Do not presume to order me around. My patience is growing thin with both of you," Lorcan warned coldly.

As Letha finished applying the cream, Evelayn's eyes fluttered and her body softened into unconsciousness once more.

"If you wish for her to survive the night, *Your Majesty*, would you be so kind as to use your power to light a fire?" Letha's sarcasm was thick enough to cut, but Lorcan let it slide. She was right, and they all knew it.

Ignoring the way Tanvir watched him, knowing the other male had likely heard most if not all of what he'd said to Evelayn, Lorcan stood and gathered the wood one final time, arranging it to start the fire. It took only a small blast of shadowflame and the timber caught. Within moments their little grouping was lit by the firelight, and the warmth spread to ward off some of the chill of the night. The tunic he'd been wearing was ruined, soaked with Evelayn's blood. He spread his cloak on the ground beside the fire so they could lay Evelayn somewhere clean and hang her tunic up to dry.

"Let me help," Tanvir offered when Lorcan bent to move her to the makeshift bed by the warmth of the flames.

"You've done enough, I think." Lorcan's voice was as frosty as the breeze that cut through the trees around them. He easily lifted Evelayn into his arms, careful not to jostle her head and pull at the stitches. She was so light—too light. Once she'd been strong, her body tautly muscular, a testament to the hours she had spent training and running every day. But now she was malnourished and weak. A shadow of her former glory. His gut burned with guilt as he gently laid her down next to the fire and brushed her hair back from her face. The scar on her breastbone was covered by the tunic she wore, but he knew exactly where it would be if the fabric was removed. When he'd ripped the conduit stone from her body, he'd taken more than just its light and power. He'd stolen an integral part of who she was—what had made her strong.

Why? Why force me to do that and yet still require so much from us? If only Máthair Damhán could hear his questions, feel his wrath. *Soon,* he vowed as he tucked the fur-lined cape over the top of her body. He would do what it took to keep his oath *and* return Evelayn's stone to her. And then he would make Máthair Damhán pay.

Though it had grown bitterly cold, the night remained free of snow, for which Lothar was intensely grateful. He and Ceren dashed through the forest as quickly as possible, despite their exhaustion. Though it was easier to track the footprints left by the other Draíolon in the snow, it was also much more perilous to run on the slippery stuff in his weakened state. Luckily, he was an excellent tracker and was able to keep following their path without the snow. But neither of them was in the condition necessary to catch Tanvir and Letha. Regardless, they continued to tail them, hoping against hope that they would somehow close the gap and stop them before they reached Lorcan and the queen.

"We have to rest," Ceren panted from beside him.

"We will soon," he replied, the same answer he'd given her for hours. They were slowing, but he hoped that perhaps the other two would stop for the night, and if he and Ceren kept going, they'd finally catch up.

As he'd told her the previous day, his wounds were mostly healed, but there was still a lingering ache deep inside his body, and the skin itself felt taut where they'd sewn him back together, as if it had been pulled too tight. A peculiar weakness infiltrated his muscles, the effects of his power being drawn upon too heavily in order to heal him.

"Can we at least walk for a few minutes?" Ceren grabbed his arm and pulled him to a stop.

Lothar couldn't explain his strange sense of urgency, the deep-rooted feeling that they needed to hurry as quickly as they were able. But when he glanced at her, the female was red-faced and practically gasping for air. "Just for a few minutes. I think we're gaining on them."

"Truly?" Hope lit her face, and he almost felt guilty for the lie. Almost. If it kept her going, then it was worth it. Their only chance of actually gaining on them was to press on.

Taking advantage of the slower pace, Lothar pulled out his waterskin and some food.

"Why did you insist on following them?" Ceren's question took him off guard.

Lothar took a long draft of water to give him a moment to collect his thoughts and decide how to answer.

"You didn't have to—in fact, you probably shouldn't have. You have been gravely injured. And with Lorcan and Evelayn both gone, you are the last royal who could take their place if things . . . go badly."

Lothar stared into the dark forest, his keen eyesight able to pick out the details of the hulking trees and the scraggly undergrowth. But hard as he tried, he couldn't see far enough to make sure they weren't too late. "He's my brother," he finally responded.

"But what kind of brother has he been to you?" Ceren pressed. "I've never really thought of you two as close."

Lothar quickened their pace slightly, though he didn't start running again—yet.

"It's complicated," he finally admitted. "We were close once. When we were younglings. Before . . ."

"Before your father began to train you?"

Lothar shot her a look but saw nothing except sympathy in her expression. "Yes."

"I saw Lorcan's scars . . . He told us it was from his training."

Lothar took a deep breath, trying to calm the visceral reaction of fear that still ensnared him when he thought about the years of terror living under their father's rule. "He mostly ignored us until he deemed us old enough to remove the block on our magic and made us begin to train. That's when we were closer . . . when I wanted nothing more than to be like him."

"Your father?" Ceren sounded shocked, but before he could respond, she corrected herself. "Oh, of course not. You mean Lorcan."

Lothar shrugged, his gaze on the ground and the partially obscured prints of the Draíolon they were trailing.

"Why did it change?"

"Our father didn't believe in love—not between brothers, not between parents and children. Love, connections, loyalty . . . he said they made us weak. If he witnessed any indication of such weakness between me and Lorcan, he did his best to beat it out of us. At first, Lorcan told me to just pretend, to put on a show for Father. That we could still be brothers in private. But he kept slipping up, kept trying to protect me." Lothar couldn't bring himself to continue, the memories he hadn't let himself think of in decades rising to choke him. Memories of Lorcan being brutally beaten by their father over and over again. Of the day Lothar hadn't been fast enough to please the king and he'd lost his temper. But Lorcan had jumped in front of him, saved him from the vicious lashing their father had been about to give him. It was the first time they'd ever seen their father that angry before. He'd been even more furious at Lorcan for risking himself to protect his brother, a sign of the weakness Bain had thought they'd overcome long before. Lothar had never seen him beat someone so viciously; he'd been truly afraid for Lorcan's life. Bain only stopped when Lorcan collapsed on the ground, nearly unconscious, his torso ripped to shreds from the shadow-whip their father preferred to use.

A gentle touch on his arm jerked him back to awareness and

made him realize he'd unknowingly halted, staring blindly into the inky blackness of the cloud-covered night.

"I'm very sorry for what you both went through."

Lothar looked down at her, the fire-haired female who by all accounts should have loathed him entirely for what his family had done to her kingdom, and was shocked to see only concern in her eyes. He hadn't seen anyone look at him like that in a long time, not even his own mother. Not until the attack two nights ago, when he'd gone to Lorcan for help.

"I wondered for so long if he truly had come to hate me, as our father wished. Or if he'd become so accustomed to pretending that he didn't know how to break free of the unseen chains Bain had created. Even after he was gone, Lorcan didn't change. Not really." Lothar began to walk again, more slowly this time. "But I saw it the other night, in the moment before I lost consciousness, when he was afraid I was about to die. I saw fear in his eyes. And I knew, somewhere deep inside, my brother was still there." Lothar hooked his waterskin back onto his waistband. "That's why I insisted on going after them."

Ceren was silent for a long moment. Finally, she merely said, "I've rested long enough. Let's go. We have some ground to make up."

Lothar glanced over at her and then nodded. "Yes, we do," he agreed, and then took off at a sprint.

TWENTY-FOUR

T HEY'D BEEN RUNNING FOR THE BETTER PART OF AN hour when Lothar slowed slightly and then suddenly halted, throwing out his arm to stop Ceren as well—and to keep her from slipping and falling on the muddy earth.

"Did you hear that?" he asked.

Ceren cocked her head, straining to listen beyond the harsh sound of her labored breathing and the noises of nocturnal animals rustling through the woods. Then she heard it, simultaneous with a slight tremor beneath her feet. A distant boom—the sound of power exploding into a large target.

Her gaze flew to his in alarm.

They both turned and sprinted in the direction of the fight. Well, Lothar sprinted. Ceren did her best to keep up with him. But he had access to his power to strengthen his body and give him endurance; she didn't. He kept glancing over his shoulder at her, frustration evident on his face.

"Go! I will follow as quickly as I can."

Lothar nodded and increased his speed, but only for a few steps. Then he slowed slightly once more, allowing her to catch up.

"What are you doing?" Ceren panted. "Just go!"

"No," Lothar said. "We're too far away to get there in time, even if I run full speed. Whatever is going to happen will happen. We're in this together, and I'm not going to leave you behind."

"But . . . he's your brother." She could barely get the words out past the wild thudding of her heart and the burning in her lungs.

"And she's your dearest friend. I'm not going to let you get lost out here." Lothar glanced over at her, his gray eyes earnest. "It's not like Tanvir and Letha really have a chance of hurting him."

Ceren just nodded, no longer able to speak, surprised and grateful for his kindness. She was mostly certain she would have been able to follow his tracks. But it was very dark, and a storm was coming. She wasn't sure how far away the others were. Close enough to barely hear the explosions, but with their acute hearing, that was still quite some distance away.

True to his word, Lothar stayed by her side, urging her along when her muscles felt like they were on fire and she got a cramp in her calf. They had to stop briefly so she could rub it out. Again she insisted he continue ahead, but he again argued that whatever had happened was done. The sounds of fighting had ended some time ago. But she felt guilty—and worried. True, Lorcan could easily defend himself, but Evelayn couldn't. And she wasn't entirely sure who Tanvir and Letha were going after.

Finally, they caught the scent of fire, and soon after saw its flickering light ahead, between the trees and bushes, a beacon in the darkness. Ceren pushed herself through the pain and exhaustion, half running, half limping beside Lothar.

Lothar said, "Someone's lying on the ground. It looks like—"

But Ceren squinted and saw her lavender-streaked hair, stained with blood and spread out beneath her head, at the same moment. "Evelayn!" she cried out hoarsely, and somehow found one more burst of speed to sprint the last few lengths to reach her friend.

Lorcan had been sitting beside her but jumped to his feet, spinning to face them as they burst into the makeshift camp.

"Lorcan, stop, it's us!"

Ceren barely heard Lothar's words past the pounding of her heart in her ears as her gaze immediately went first to her friend's face, to her eyes that were half-open and shiny with pain, then to the wicked gash that bisected Evelayn's throat. Uneven stitches held the inflamed skin together, but blood still seeped out.

"You *hurt* her!" Ceren went hot and cold all at once, a raging inferno of fury. She launched herself at Lorcan, but Lothar grabbed her and held her back. She struggled against him futilely. When she couldn't break free, she spat, "I trusted you!"

"It wasn't me." Lorcan cut off her accusations. "*They* did this to your queen." He gestured to Tanvir and Letha, who sat on the other side of the fire, watching them warily.

"*Tanvir* did this? You tried to kill *Evelayn*?" Lothar had to tighten his grip on Ceren again, this time keeping her from flying at Tanvir. "I thought you were going after the king! Oh, if only I had my power right now—"

"It was me." Letha cut Ceren off this time. "And it was an accident."

"How do you accidentally almost cut someone's head off?" Ceren shrieked.

Lothar snorted from behind her, but she ignored him, too furious and upset to chastise him.

"It wasn't *that* bad," Evelayn rasped, but Ceren just shook her head, sudden tears filling her eyes. Lothar released Ceren when it was obvious she was no longer attempting to lunge at any of the other Draíolon.

"Look at you. You're a . . . a . . ."

"Mess," Evelayn supplied with a weak laugh. "I'm going to be all right. But what are you doing here? Your younglings . . ." The effort just to speak that much sent her into a coughing spasm. Lorcan immediately crouched down once more, carefully lifting her head off the ground with one hand and offering her a water-skin. She winced but took a sip, and he gently laid her back down again.

Ceren glanced at Lothar to see him watching them intently, his expression shadowed in the firelight. What did he think of the tenderness Lorcan was showing the Light Queen? He didn't yet know they were Bound . . . he had been unconscious when they'd made the decision and left his room to complete the ceremony. Ceren hadn't known whether she should tell him or not, and had decided to stay quiet about it, for now at least.

But she was just as disarmed by the way Lorcan hovered over Evelayn as Lothar seemed to be; if she didn't know better, she would have thought he truly cared for the queen, and not just as a means to an end.

Once he made sure she was settled, Lorcan looked up at them. "Now would you like to explain what in the name of Darkness the two of *you* are doing here? Shouldn't you be in bed recovering?" He pinned Lothar with his searing gaze first, then Ceren. "And what of your younglings—and your Mate?"

"You can't keep leaving me behind," Lothar said before Ceren could speak.

"You were unconscious!" Lorcan retorted sharply. "And now you've left the kingdom in *Mother's* hands."

Lothar grimaced at Lorcan's words. Ceren hadn't even thought about the fact that the dowager queen would no doubt wonder what had become of her sons. What would she do when their absence became known?

"Why did you come?" Evelayn's feeble question broke through the sudden tension between the brothers. Ceren went to her friend and knelt down on the cold ground beside her.

"I saw them leaving to follow you"—she nodded toward Tanvir and Letha, who had remained quiet throughout the exchange—"and knew it couldn't be a good thing. Especially since they were fully armed. Lothar had healed enough to come in search of us all, but he only found me, and insisted he was going after them. I was afraid he wouldn't be strong enough, so I went with him. And here we are."

"And now you must return to the castle. We can't all go on," Lorcan announced.

"Evelayn is injured. You can't possibly think of continuing this quest now—let alone just the two of you." Ceren met his challenging gaze across Evelayn's prone body.

"We have to," Evelayn said softly, reminding them that she was still awake. "It's my only hope of ever regaining our power."

"You're in no condition!" Ceren protested, which was only punctuated by yet another bout of coughing that caused Evelayn to stiffen in pain.

"The fire is dying down. I'll go collect some more wood," Letha suddenly offered, rising to her feet.

Lorcan glanced at her speculatively. "Lothar, go with her and make sure she keeps her word—and returns as quickly as possible."

Ceren glanced at the younger of the two brothers to see if he would balk at the order, but he just nodded and gestured for Letha to lead the way.

Mere moments after their departure, snowflakes began to spiral toward them from the darkness above. Lorcan glanced up, inhaling deeply. "It's going to be another blizzard, I'm afraid."

Ceren could scent the incoming storm as well, the biting frost and driving snow blowing toward them on the breeze that lifted her hair and sent a chill through her body, even with the fire and her warm clothing.

"If we don't keep moving, we'll never reach the l—" Lorcan cut himself off with a sharp glance at Tanvir. "The goal," he substituted quickly, "before the end of Athrúfar."

"You most certainly will not reach *any* goal in time if you try to take her by yourself. I will accompany you." Tanvir spoke for the first time.

"There's no chance in all the burning fires of Ifrinn you will," Lorcan bit out in return. "You and your sister are not getting within two body lengths of Evelayn ever again."

"Are you planning on carrying her wherever you are traveling to? Because you might want to take a long hard look at your traveling companion. She's not going anywhere anytime soon."

"And how would letting you assist me change that?"

Both of the males' rising tempers cast a cinders-and-ash scent to mingle with the already potent morass of Evelayn's pain, the oncoming storm, and the smoke from the fire.

"I am not dead yet," Evelayn cut in, albeit weakly. "Ceren, help me." She reached out for her.

"Help you what?"

"Sit up, you ninny." Evelayn grasped her hand and began to attempt to pull herself up. When she lifted her head, she emitted a small yip of pain but quickly schooled her features into a mask of composure again, as she had so many times before when concealing her true emotions.

"Ev, stop this. You need to rest and heal," Ceren argued, even as she reached out to brace her.

"Lorcan is right. There's no time. I will have to heal while we continue on." With more than just a little effort and help, she finally sat up.

Lorcan watched the entire thing silently, a muscle ticking in his jaw. But Ceren knew him well enough now to recognize the dismay in his hooded eyes. He knelt down on her other side and took her other hand in his. Ceren felt a draw of power but nothing happened.

"What are you doing now?" Evelayn asked, sounding exasperated.

"You know what I'm doing," he replied steadily.

"Lorcan, stop it. You're just going to drain yourself. It's one thing to loan me strength, but healing?"

Ceren and Tanvir shared a look of confusion. He apparently had no idea what the king and queen were talking about, either. Despite her protests, Evelayn let her eyes close momentarily, until Tanvir spoke again.

"Look, you've made remarkable time so far," Tanvir admitted. "But she can barely sit up, let alone walk or run. How much farther is your destination? What was so vitally important that you Bound yourself to him and then left the castle in Abarrane's hands—immediately after that terrible attack?"

Ceren watched as Evelayn struggled to control her ragged breathing, to hide the pain that made her violet eyes turn indigo in the flickering firelight. She glanced to Lorcan, who shook his head infinitesimally, but she ignored him and responded, "We're going back to Máthair Damhán's lair."

Tanvir stared at her in open disbelief. "By the Light, you truly do have a death wish, don't you. Why would you ever return there?"

"Evelayn." Her name was a low growl, a warning of sorts from Lorcan.

She squeezed Ceren's hand tightly, to bolster her confidence or because of another wave of pain, she wasn't sure.

"Why are you both going back to the White Peak—and why is it so urgent?" Tanvir repeated. "Why did you return now, after all these years, only to leave again?"

There was a long, breathless pause while they waited for Evelayn to respond—even from Lorcan, which shocked Ceren.

"What in the name of the Light would make you wish to return to Máthair Damhán? And with him?" Tanvir pressed, his gaze slicing toward Lorcan, then back again. "This is another trap, Evelayn, can't you see—"

"No, it's not." She cut him off. "We're going to Máthair Damhán because she has my conduit stone. And we're going to get it back."

TWENTY-FIVE

THE NEXT MORNING DAWNED CLEAR AND BITTERLY cold. It had snowed throughout the night, as Lorcan had predicted, turning the world around them pristine white, hiding the ugliness of the dying forest. Evelayn's breath crystallized on the brisk air, puffing into small clouds every time she exhaled as she forced herself to sit up without assistance, even though it was agony to jar her neck in any way. She'd never realized until now just how much her neck was involved in practically any movement she made. When she reached up to touch the rough stitches, she was happy to realize her skin wasn't as puffy as it had felt hours earlier. Perhaps Lorcan's assistance had helped after all. The swelling and inflammation were going down—a huge relief, as she'd overheard Letha murmuring to Tanvir about the possibility of infection before they'd fallen asleep.

Despite his efforts to assist in her healing, Lorcan had eventually agreed that Evelayn needed to rest if she was going to be in any condition to continue onward, and elected to let them all sleep through the night. Using his power to help her heal must have drained him more than he'd been willing to admit. She'd tried to insist she could push through the pain and exhaustion, but he'd surprisingly taken Tanvir and Ceren's side. When Lothar and Letha had returned with more wood, they'd built up the fire once more, and they'd all dug in for the night, curling into their cloaks, huddling close to the fire for warmth.

It was little more than a pile of smoking embers now—only a small tendril of smoke still curled lazily up toward the blue sky above.

Evelayn's neck throbbed, and she had to fight a bout of dizziness when she rose to her feet, but she was much better than the previous night. When she glanced around at her companions, she wasn't surprised to see Lorcan awake, watching her silently, his silver eyes disconcerting in the iridescent morning light. She was surprised, however, to realize one of their number was gone. A quick look revealed it to be Lothar.

"Where did he go?" she whispered, conscious of the others who were still sleeping.

Lorcan lifted a shoulder. "He left a while ago" was his low response. "But I believe he is coming back as we speak." He jerked his chin toward the forest behind her.

She turned but didn't see anything—at first. Then something moved in the distance. At least she thought she saw something move. Evelayn squinted to sharpen her eyesight, and sure enough she caught the movement again. But whatever it was definitely wasn't a Draíolon. A massive creature, as white as the snow around it, silently stalked toward them. Her heart leapt in her chest, furiously pumping adrenaline into her system alongside her blood. She looked over her shoulder at Lorcan in panic, disregarding the spike of pain that shot from her neck up into her skull from the motion.

But Lorcan remained where he was, an expression almost like amusement making his lips twitch.

Evelayn spun back to the coming beast, unsure why Lorcan was so nonchalant, when the reason suddenly dawned on her. The beast came close enough now for her to see that the massive animal was a snow bear—a powerful, deadly creature carrying a limp deer in his mouth. She watched in awe as he silently worked his way through the trees and ultimately stopped a few lengths from them to set his prey down on the snow. And then, in a whirl of dark smoke and a rush of power that brushed her skin like a long-forgotten song whose melody she could almost remember, the bear was gone and Lothar stood before them, his skin flushed and his gray eyes bright.

A snow bear, a hawk, a leopard. Agile, fierce, swift animals. All fit for royalty. All except her. As much as she loved the swans, she couldn't help but wonder why—why had she imprinted on the swans rather than any of the other, more magnificent options?

"What are we supposed to do with that?" Lorcan asked, looking at the dead deer with one eyebrow raised.

"Eat it." Some of the light went out of Lothar's eyes, but he quickly knelt in the snow, pulling a knife out of his belt. Evelayn swallowed her nausea and turned away as he made the first cut to begin skinning the animal.

"It seems a waste to slaughter such a large animal when we won't be able to consume it all."

Evelayn wondered why Lorcan couldn't scent the bitter tang of Lothar's disappointment on the cold morning air, where moments earlier it had been sweet with his pride.

"I thought we could eat some this morning and cut the rest into strips to cook and take with us. We'll need more food to sustain us on a journey this long." Lothar spoke without looking up.

Lorcan opened his mouth to reply, but Evelayn rushed to cut him off. "I think that is a wonderful idea. Thank you, Lothar."

Lorcan shot her a questioning glance but mercifully didn't contradict her. Though Lothar was only a few years younger than his brother—and quite a few years older than she—he often deferred to his brother as if he were a youngling and not the powerful prince he ought to have been. And if Evelayn wasn't mistaken, it was all in an effort to please Lorcan, to somehow win his approbation or favor. She wasn't entirely sure the reason why, but she was certain that she was close to the mark on her supposition.

"Lorcan, will you help me build the fire back up?" she asked now, drawing his attention away from his brother.

The king of Dorjhalon met her gaze with slightly narrowed eyes, but got to his feet and crossed to stand beside her, bending so his mouth was close to her ear.

"What was that about?" he murmured, his warm breath tickling her ear.

"Can't you see how badly he wishes to please you?" she responded, her voice barely a whisper.

Lorcan straightened to look past her, to where his brother knelt, working diligently on the deer. The coppery smell of blood filled Evelayn's nose and turned her stomach, but she refused to let Lothar realize that she didn't enjoy meat much, if at all. Not when he'd been so pleased with himself for providing for all of them, until his brother's lack of appreciation had deflated him.

"Indeed" was all Lorcan said, and then he bent to pick up the last of the wood he had collected the night before and kept protected underneath a large bush. For the first time, Evelayn noticed he wore no tunic, his muscular torso completely exposed in the cold. The scars she'd seen once before were even more horrifying in the illuminating morning light, the discolored stripes of ruined flesh crisscrossing all over his skin. But somehow, they didn't take away from the beauty of his body or the power he exuded.

"No, I'm not cold," he said before she could say anything, though that wasn't at all what she'd been thinking. Her cheeks heated when she realized she'd been caught staring. But then he shivered slightly, and he added, "Not *very* cold, at least."

"Where's your top? And your cloak?" She forced herself to meet his eyes as he placed the dry wood on the pile of embers and sent a small blast of his power at it, turning the fuel into fire almost immediately.

"The tunic was used to stop your bleeding," he said matter-of-factly. "And I put my cloak on you during the night when you were shivering in your sleep."

"Oh." Evelayn glanced down at the flames, her fingers going to her neck once more, to the wound that ached with each pump of her heart. "I'm sorry."

"There's nothing to apologize for. I gladly would have given up all my clothes to save your life, if necessary."

Evelayn's eyes flew up to meet his again, aghast to realize her cheeks burned with a shocked blush. He smirked at her, one eyebrow raised in amusement. He was . . . *jesting*? Was he even capable of such a thing?

"I'm fairly certain I could have lived my entire life without knowing that." Ceren's sleepy voice jarred Evelayn back to the awareness that they weren't alone.

"I believe we all could have." Tanvir spoke up as well, though he didn't sound nearly as drowsy, making Evelayn's blush intensify, wondering just how long he'd been awake, eavesdropping on them. She glanced over to find Tanvir staring at her, his golden eyes ablaze with jealousy. Her stomach twisted, a gut reaction to feeling as though she was doing something wrong by allowing herself any kind feelings toward Lorcan, especially with Tanvir mere feet away, listening, watching. She'd loved him with her whole heart, had even pledged her body and soul to him.

And now she was suddenly Bound to Lorcan instead, a male she barely knew.

You have nothing to feel guilty about, she reminded herself. Tanvir had lied to her, had manipulated and betrayed her. The male she'd thought she loved, whom she'd made the oath of intent to, didn't exist.

"Here," Lothar said, a welcome intrusion to the sudden tension in the air. "Start cooking this while I prepare the rest of the meat."

He tried to hand the bloodied flesh to Evelayn, but she blanched, her stomach turning in on itself. "I—I think I need to sit down and rest a bit more," she stammered lamely. Luckily, he didn't question her, and turned to Lorcan instead as she slowly lowered herself to the ground again.

The king took the meat without comment, but when Evelayn shot him a look, a muscle ticked in his jaw and he cleared his throat. Then, "Thank you, Loth. This was very . . . thoughtful of you." The words seemed a strain for him to say. But Evelayn didn't miss the smile that broke out across Lothar's face as he ducked his head away from his brother, trying to hide his pleasure.

"Once that finishes cooking, we can eat it while the rest of the meat cooks. Then we should be ready to head out before the sun finishes rising." Lothar picked up his knife and got back to work.

Evelayn watched as Lorcan skewered the meat on some thin, sharp branches that he propped over the fire, using other pieces of wood and rocks to create a makeshift spit.

"You don't have to eat it," Lorcan murmured for her ears only as he sat down beside her.

She was all too aware of Tanvir's sharp gaze on them, but she smiled gratefully at Lorcan, pleased he had been observant enough to recognize her initial distaste. However, as the aroma of sizzling meat wafted through the forest, the fat popping and spitting over the flames, she unexpectedly found her stomach gurgling in hunger.

"Perhaps I will have a little, after all," she admitted. "Just to keep my strength up," she added, feeling the need to justify her decision for some reason.

"Of course," Lorcan agreed.

As the others gathered around the fire, the meat finished

cooking and they all ended up eating it, even Ceren. Evelayn was surprised at how much better she felt with a full stomach.

Not long after, Tanvir strode over and tossed something at Lorcan.

"In case you don't wish to go before Máthair Damhán half-naked."

Lorcan picked up the item and revealed it to be a crumpled-up tunic. Evelayn had to smother a smile when he gave Tanvir a curt nod and pulled it on. He was taller and more broad, so it was a bit of a tight fit, but better than nothing, she supposed.

"We need to leave soon if we have any hope of reaching the lair in time," she said to dispel the sudden tension in the make-shift campsite, while Lothar finished cooking the strips he'd prepared to take with them.

Evelayn glanced up at the brilliant blue sky, toward the sun, which had broken free of the tree line. Its light glinted off the snow, making the forest glisten and sparkle, as if the dying trees and decay-strewn earth had been remade out of diamonds and crystals during the night. Though she didn't enjoy the cold, she had to admit there was an icy beauty to winter. She could see why Dark Draíolon loved it so much, especially since they didn't get cold as easily. But an eternity of it? With no spring or summer? Even diamonds lost their luster if they became too common.

They had to get her stone and her power back.

They were a quiet group when they finally broke camp. Lorcan kept glancing at Evelayn, trying to ascertain if she really was healed enough to withstand the rest of the journey. But other than an occasional wince or sharp intake of breath, she gave no indication of the pain she was in.

He walked over to where she stood, staring to the northeast, as if she could part the forest and see straight to the White Peak. "Are you sure you can run?"

She startled at his voice. "I don't really have a choice, do I?"

"I remember you telling me once that we always have a choice."

Evelayn turned to look at him, her eyebrows raised.

"I listen to you more carefully than you think." Lorcan studied her face, his gaze lingering on her lips for a beat too long to go unnoticed before lifting his eyes to meet hers. This close, he could see the indigo ring rimming the outside of her violet irises. His hands twitched at his side, longing to reach up and brush her hair back from her cheeks, to cup her face and—

He cut off the thoughts before they could progress any further. Already his body had grown warmer, his heartbeat faster. Could she scent his uncertainty and desire? She hadn't turned away . . . and last night, she'd calmed at *his* voice, at *his* touch, when nothing else worked. Was it possible—was there any hope—that she could come to care for him?

"If you wish for us to accompany you on this ill-fated journey, stay away from my queen." Tanvir's angry voice cut through the trance she seemed to put Lorcan under with little to no effort.

Lorcan slowly faced the other male. "I *don't* wish for you to accompany us. In fact, nothing would make me happier than for you to leave immediately."

"Well, since your happiness is the last thing I'm concerned about, I believe I will stay after all."

"I asked you to leave. And I don't ask twice." Lorcan let his power rise in his body, the threat of it audible in his voice, and the scent of it undeniable—a reminder of who held the control between them.

"If you force me to leave now, I will just turn around and follow you as I did before. You don't have time to keep trying to scare me off." Tanvir's hand fell to rest on the hilt of his sword.

"Don't try my patience any further. I have been lenient with you until now." The power he'd summoned simmered icy hot in his veins, demanding release, along with his anger. Tanvir had pushed him one too many times. Perhaps he'd made a mistake in letting him escape last night.

"Lenient?" Tanvir laughed. "You tried to kill me last night."

Now it was Lorcan's turn to laugh, a harsh, barking sound full of derision. "You honestly believe that? If I'd wanted you dead, trust me, you would have been."

"Stop it!" Letha jumped in front of her brother when he moved to yank his sword out of his scabbard.

"We don't have time for this." Evelayn placed a hand on Lorcan's arm, pulling his focus back to her. Her gentle touch and calm voice helped cool his ire, but Lorcan's power still ached to be released. "Let's continue on. If he follows us, so be it. But we're wasting time arguing with him."

It was her use of "us" that broke through. She'd placed herself squarely beside him—a partner at his side, with Tanvir opposing them—in that one seemingly small word.

"Fine," he agreed. "But now that we are no longer alone, I am going to scout ahead. Lothar"—he turned to his brother—"please stay by our queen until I return."

A flicker of confusion crossed his face, but Lothar quickly agreed. "Of course," he said, stepping up to Evelayn's side.

Lorcan looked at Tanvir one last time, making sure to wait until the other male grudgingly met his eyes. "And you stay away from her. Or you will find out what it means to have exhausted my patience."

"I'll make sure of it," Lothar assured him.

Lorcan let his piercing gaze linger for a moment longer on Tanvir, until he was satisfied that the other male understood how serious he was.

Finally, he turned back to Evelayn. "Will you be able to run without my help—at least for a little while?" He asked quietly enough that none of the other Draíolon would have been able to catch what he'd said, even with their acute hearing—except perhaps Lothar, who stood on her other side.

"I hope so."

His gaze dropped to her throat, to the thin red line that curved through her previously unmarred skin. Though the wound had been cleaned off to the best of their ability, her hair, cloak, and tunic were still crusty with dried blood. Despite all the eyes on them, and his own wariness about her feelings toward him, Lorcan lifted his hand and gently pressed his fingers against the line of stitches. She shivered beneath his touch, with a soft gasp of surprise. Lorcan let his eyes close for a moment, directing his power to his hand, letting it flow from him directly into her wound.

"That should help," he said, pulling away, hoping she didn't notice the huskiness of his voice. Then, in the blink of an eye, he shifted into his hawk form and took to the skies, winging away from the group of Draíolon who stared after him in varying degrees of shock.

TWENTY-SIX

L ORCAN HAD FLOWN INTO THE DISTANCE AT AN UNBE-
lievable speed at least an hour before, leaving Evelayn
alone with the rest of the Draíolon, as they ran through
the snowy forest. Her throat still burned with the memory of his
touch—and the surge of power that had rushed into her body,
diminishing the pain in her neck even further. She hadn't begun
to tire yet, despite the injury and her lack of conditioning, and she
could only attribute it to Lorcan and all the power he'd given her.

"You're doing remarkably well," Lothar commented from
beside her, his feet striking the ground stride for stride with hers.

"Yes," she agreed, "but only because your brother keeps sharing
his power with me. You have to tell him to stop it. He's going to—"

But she cut herself off when Lothar stumbled and nearly fell.
"He's doing *what*?"

Evelayn reached out to steady him, but he yanked his arm
away, quickly regaining his footing, and they continued forward.
The rest of the group seemed content to let them lead, running

behind them. She glanced over her shoulder to see if any of the others were close enough to listen in, but Letha and Ceren were next, talking to each other, and Tanvir ran behind them—as far away from her as possible.

"Evelayn?" Lothar prompted. "Are you certain that's what my brother is doing?"

"Yes," she confirmed.

"He's siphoning his power to you?"

"Yes."

This time, Lothar reached out to grab *her* arm, yanking her to a stop. "That would only be possible if . . . By the Dark," he cursed, sudden realization dawning on his face. "You're *Bound* to my *brother*?"

"What's going on—why did we stop?" Ceren looked at Evelayn first, then to Lothar, who stared at her in unadulterated shock.

"Look out!" A sudden shout from Tanvir was all the warning they had before he leapt at Evelayn, slamming into her body and knocking her to the ground.

She cried out in pain, as the stitches in her neck pulled at her skin and her head collided with the cold, hard earth. The snow only softened the impact slightly.

Before Evelayn could open her mouth to yell, something flew through the air right above them. Lothar shouted in alarm but seemed unable to lift his arms. *Spider silk*, she realized. That's what Tanvir had saved her from—but it got Lothar instead. And then a creature, half arachnid, half female, lunged out of the forest at them on her remaining four legs with an unearthly shriek.

ê

As a hawk, Lorcan flew at speeds he could only dream of in his Draíolon body. The wind surged around his wings, lifting him up ever higher into the sky. There were times when he longed to stay in this form, to escape the pressures of being king and the other worries that constantly beset him in exchange for the weightless oblivion of the bird.

But as he dipped his wing and banked sharply to head back the way he'd come, he realized today was not one of those times. He'd needed to escape for a moment, needed the freedom of the wind and sky—and he'd also wanted to make sure no other unexpected visitors awaited them—but he was already eager to return to the Draíolon he'd left far behind. Well, to *one* Draíolon, if he was honest with himself.

One of Máthair Damhán's stipulations had been for him to convince Evelayn to Bind herself to him, and he'd succeeded, despite the curse the Ancient had also required of him—to keep her chained to her swan form every day of the year except the seven of Athrúfar. Until this year. And now, the longer he spent time with Evelayn, the wider the crack in his heart grew, leaving him far too vulnerable to her and the way she made him feel. Was that part of the Ancient's plan as well?

As he soared back, he scanned the forest ahead, his already keen eyesight immensely more powerful in this form. Every tiny detail opened up to him, even from heights far enough above the earth to allow him to fly among the clouds. Winter made it even easier to spot movement of any creatures—large animals, tiny rodents, and Draíolon alike.

Lorcan had recovered more than half the distance back the way he'd come when he finally spied the group of Draíolon running through the forest. They were still quite a distance from him, mere specks on the horizon, but a wave of relief washed over him and he slowed his flight considerably. They were headed in his direction, so he allowed himself the slight break to bolster his strength once more, in preparation to siphon some of his power to Evelayn, as she no doubt would be tiring by now.

He did a lazy loop through the air, taking a few minutes to simply enjoy the sunshine on his back and the wind in his feathers. When he was in his hawk form, it was an interesting mix of animalistic instinct and Draíolon awareness and rationale. When he let himself relax, the instincts grew stronger, pushing away the consciousness. He became more hawk than king.

Some time had passed when he straightened out again to check their progress, expecting the group to be drawing fairly close to him by now. But Lorcan was shocked to realize he'd lost sight of them entirely somehow. He searched futilely for a moment, before a burst of light to his left caught his attention.

There. He spotted them once more, but the tiny heart of the hawk raced in his breast when he realized the light had been an explosion of Lothar's power. Lorcan soared toward them with a burst of speed that turned the woods to a blur far beneath him, all his focus on the figures in the distance, heading the wrong direction, rushing away from something . . . And then he saw it. Or, rather, her.

With his hawk sight, he was able to see her missing legs and her arachnid body. It was the daughter he'd gravely injured and sent back to Máthair Damhán as a message of his own. How had she found them—and why?

Lorcan was closing in on them when something else snagged his attention. From the north, there were more animals moving through the woods toward the group. No, not just animals. More of Máthair Damhán's daughters. A handful of them of varying sizes, scuttling through the snow on their many legs, pincers clacking in anticipation of the fight ahead.

He redoubled his flapping, picking up speed until the wind whistled past him. When he got close enough, he plummeted into a nosedive, barreling through the air with such speed and force that the wind became a shriek in his ears along with a cry he recognized, even as the bird.

"Lorcan!"

The daughter had only a split second to turn her head toward the sky where Evelayn pointed, and then Lorcan was upon the spider, his beak puncturing one of her eyes while he used his sharp talons to destroy as many of the others as possible. The creature screeched in agony, reaching up to claw at him, but he was already gone, taken to flight once more. He headed straight for Evelayn, who had fresh blood running down her neck.

In a swirl of smoke he shifted back mid-flight and landed on his feet beside her, spinning to throw out a shield that blocked all the Draíolon from the creatures that were closing in on them. None of the others realized how many of the enemy surrounded them yet.

"Go!" he shouted, jerking his head to indicate where. "I'll hold them off."

"Them?" Lothar repeated, as Evelayn simultaneously asked, "Go where?"

"There are more coming," Lorcan said, gritting his teeth as the creature threw her ruined body against the shield of swirling darkness he'd created. "We can't make it to the border without fighting all of them, and I'm not risking you getting hurt again. If we retreat into the Undead Forest, they won't follow."

"The Undead Forest?" a female screeched. He wasn't sure if it was Ceren or Letha.

"You can't be serious." Tanvir stepped up beside him, holding a sword dripping black ichor, the creature's blood.

"Do you have a better plan? We can stand and fight, but there are only two of us with power, and the closer we are to the White Peak, the stronger *they* are. And more numerous."

Tanvir ground his teeth in frustration but backed off. "Fine. We retreat. And then what?"

Lorcan scented the others moments before he saw them rushing through the trees toward them. They'd fanned out into a semicircle so that he had to draw upon more power to widen the shield protecting them.

"There's no time—*run!*" Lorcan shouted, even as the creatures split into two groups and rushed to both edges where the shield ended.

Tanvir finally listened, turning and sprinting back to the others. "Go, now! To the Undead Forest!"

"I'll help you." Lothar was suddenly at his side, but Lorcan shook his head.

"No, you go and protect them. I'll hold these creatures off as long as I can."

He could scent Lothar's frustration, but his brother did as he asked, just as Lorcan knew he could always count on him to do.

There were no natural blockades to use, no way to permanently impede the arachnoids' progress. Lorcan could only continue to send the wall of darkness farther and farther away from his body, hoping to stop the creatures long enough for Evelayn, Lothar, and the others to gain the distance they needed to reach the Undead Forest before Máthair Damhán's daughters caught them.

Evelayn's lungs burned, and her neck throbbed with every pounding beat of her heart. She could feel hot, sticky blood on her skin, soaking into the collar of her tunic. The others were all ahead of her, including Ceren. Only Lothar stayed by her side, even as she began to slow, her muscles screaming in protest. Behind them, Máthair Damhán's daughters shrieked, the clacking of their pincers and the pounding of their many legs on the snow-crusted forest floor audible as they tried to outrun Lorcan's shield to reach their prey. She glanced over her shoulder to see the shield still growing, but he couldn't possibly hold it much longer. Even Lorcan had limits to his power—didn't he?

"Hurry, Your Majesty," Lothar urged from beside her.

"Evelayn," she panted. "Just call . . . me Evelayn."

"Evelayn," he amended, "you have to go faster."

"I'm . . . trying . . ." But even as she said it, she stumbled on a half-buried rock and, with a sharp flash of pain through her ankle, nearly crashed to the ground. Evelayn tried to push forward, but each step sent a stab of pain through her left leg. "Give me . . . some power . . ." she gasped to Lothar, holding out her hand as she half ran, half limped forward.

"I can't."

"Please," she begged, wincing with each step. "Just a little."

"That only works with Lorcan because you are Bound to him!"

"What? But . . . I thought . . ."

Lothar looked behind them and his eyes widened, the scent of his concern turning to rancid horror. Evelayn twisted to see what had caused such a reaction and everything in her went cold. Two of the creatures had made it past the shield and were headed right for them.

Lorcan sent a blast at the faster of the two, but she was far enough away that she easily dodged it.

"Go! Just leave me," Evelayn urged, even as her palms turned slick with sweat and her stomach to lead.

Instead, a rush of power washed over them. Lothar was enveloped in a swirl of smoke and emerged the massive snow bear. He planted his paws on the snow and roared ferociously at the daughters, a deafening threat that left Evelayn's ears ringing. They both stopped momentarily, seemingly rethinking the idea of attacking such a massive predator, but then continued toward them.

The terrifying bear looked at her with those same gray eyes she knew and tossed his head toward his back, then bent his front legs to lower his haunches within her reach.

"You want me to *ride* you?"

He gave a short, impatient growl.

There was no time to question him; it was her only hope of escaping oncoming doom. If only she could have shifted as well, she would have taken to the skies, out of reach.

But she couldn't.

Instead, she quickly scrambled on top of Lothar's muscular back and grabbed patches of the thick white fur with both hands. The moment she was settled, he took off, nearly tossing her from his back. Evelayn threw herself forward and wrapped her arms around his neck, squeezing him as tightly as possible with both of her legs. For such a large animal, he moved with incredible speed and grace, loping through the forest and easily catching up to the other Draíolon.

"Evelayn!" Ceren cried in alarm, veering to the right when the bear came up alongside her, but Evelayn quickly called out to her.

"It's fine—it's Lothar! I'm fine!"

Ceren corrected her course, but still looked shaken as she continued running east, toward the Undead Forest.

A bloodcurdling caw sounded from above, and Evelayn glanced up to see a hawk speeding through the air toward them and then circling back around.

Lorcan.

Which meant the shield was gone.

She lifted one arm slightly to look back and saw all six creatures, even the one he'd blinded, racing after them.

TWENTY-SEVEN

H OW MUCH . . . FARTHER?" LETHA WHEEZED, HER lungs and legs on fire. Once she'd been as strong as her brother, able to challenge any Draíolon on the battle-field. But she'd grown weak, and her senses dulled from lack of use. The trees whipped by them so quickly, sometimes she barely had time to avoid them.

"Not far now." Tanvir was the closest to her and barely sounded winded. Although he did have rivulets of sweat running down the sides of his face, so maybe he was just better at hiding it than she.

The huge bear—Lothar—loped along beside them, Evelayn holding on to him for dear life. Letha was rather shocked that he had stooped to helping her, rather than merely leaving the Light Queen behind to be devoured.

Tanvir believed Lorcan and Lothar intended the queen harm, but if they did, why go to such effort to protect her now? Why command Lothar to guard her? And when Lothar had

gone with Letha the night before to collect wood, he'd been nothing but considerate to her. She'd expected far worse from the son
of the male who'd held her hostage and the brother of the male
who'd used her to manipulate Tanvir.

"Are we even sure . . . this will work?" Up ahead, if she
squinted, Letha caught a glimpse of the crumbling stone wall
that had existed for all of recorded time, separating Éadrolan
from the Undead Forest.

"No," Tanvir said as they pushed harder, trying to reach that
wall and the supposed safety beyond it before the daughters reached
them. "But I sure hope Lorcan knows something we don't."

Letha couldn't do anything else besides nod, too winded to
speak, as she lengthened her stride to try to keep up with Tanvir.

Lothar let out a sudden roar and Letha glanced over her
shoulder to see one of the creatures coming up alongside him. His
flank was bleeding—it looked like she'd wounded him with one
of her pincers.

"Lothar!" Evelayn screamed, hanging on for dear life when
he twisted suddenly and slashed one massive paw through the air,
his claws slicing into the arachnoid's torso. She screeched in agony
and scuttled away before he could attack her again.

A shriek from above was the only warning before Lorcan, as
the hawk, plummeted toward them, wings tucked in a dive so
swift, even Letha's acute eyesight could barely track him. The
split second before he would have crashed into the creature's head,
he opened his wings and attacked her face in a flurry of razor-
sharp talons and beak. She tilted her head back to snap at him
with her deadly pincers, but he'd blinded her and she missed.

Lorcan easily swooped out of reach, speeding to Lothar's side, where he shifted back into Draíolon form mid-flight and landed lightly on his feet, only to immediately spin and impale the arachnoid with a massive shard of ice.

The trees had begun to thin out and the wall was now within plain sight, the gray stone so ancient it had cracked and crumbled in places. They only had the length of the castle grounds left before they reached it. But when Letha glanced back again, the creatures hadn't slowed or given up their pursuit. *This isn't going to work*, she realized with a sinking sense of dread. She was on the verge of collapse. There was no chance she could continue to run, let alone maintain such a grueling pace, much longer.

"Go! You're almost there!" Lorcan's shout galvanized her to keep her legs moving, though her muscles shook uncontrollably and it took every ounce of strength she had to keep moving forward.

Then the other female—Ceren—stumbled and fell to the snowy ground with a terrified cry.

"Ceren!" Evelayn screamed. "Go get her! Turn back! *Ceren!*" But Lothar raced right on past Letha and Tanvir, headed for the wall.

Letha's first instinct after the horrors she'd experienced at King Bain's hands was to leave Ceren there also, to save herself.

But once she'd been a commander in the queen's army—once she never would have left someone else to die so she could live.

With a hiss of frustration, she turned and rushed back to the other female's side, as Ceren tried to climb to her feet. But she'd obviously pushed herself past her limits because her legs gave out, sending her to the ground again.

Letha crashed to a halt beside Ceren and, grabbing her arm, yanked her back up onto her feet. "Come on—we're almost there! You can do this. You *have* to!"

Tears filled Ceren's cornflower blue eyes, but she nodded and tried to move forward. Letha knew the signs of total muscular fatigue; she had nearly reached that point herself. Still, she pulled Ceren forward, both of them half limping, half jogging toward the wall and the hope of safety and rest in the Undead Forest, even as the daughters gained on them.

Lorcan was suddenly there on Ceren's other side, helping Letha drag her forward with one arm, and using the other to throw blasts of shadowflame and bolts of ice at the arachnoids, barely keeping them at bay.

"Go! I will hold them off," Lorcan yelled, shoving Ceren toward Letha. His silver eyes were so bright—*too* bright. And the stone in his forehead flashed like a beacon from the sheer amount of power he continued to draw upon.

"You have to stop," Letha warned, even as she and Ceren clutched each other's arms and stumbled toward the wall, neither one able to run. "It's too much! You'll be consumed by it!"

But Lorcan turned away from her and lifted both hands. Rather than the shield made of impenetrable shadows, he summoned a wall of living shadowflame between them and the arachnoids.

"Letha!" Tanvir shouted from where he sat perched on the wall, gesturing for her. "Give me your hand!"

They limped across the last few lengths of Éadrolan, and then she shoved Ceren toward her brother. "Help her first." She turned back to see Lorcan standing like a Dark specter in front of the writhing green-and-black flames, his white hair blowing in the wind, his arms outstretched and his entire body shaking from the sheer amount of power he'd called upon. "Someone has to stop him!"

"I'll go."

Letha turned to see Evelayn climbing back over the wall to Éadrolan, Lothar right behind her.

"Let me—he's my brother, and you can barely walk, let alone run."

She'd reached the frozen ground and stood tall, despite the blood on her neck and the wince of pain when she put weight on her left leg. "I am Bound to him. And I know what it is to nearly lose yourself to the power." Evelayn's tone brooked no argument, and when she turned and began to limp back to Lorcan, no one argued with her.

There were times when Letha couldn't imagine her as queen, this wraith of a female who had been trapped as a swan for so long. But in that moment, Evelayn was every bit the ruler Letha had heard stories about when she'd returned to Éadrolan. The queen who had defeated Bain and brought peace to their kingdom—albeit briefly.

"Lorcan!" Evelayn's voice carried back to them on the wind, along with the screams and shrieks of the creatures on the other side of the shadowflames. "Lorcan, you have to let go!"

Letha watched breathlessly as Evelayn reached him and

gently touched his arm. Lorcan jerked as if he'd been scalded, but the flames continued to burn. Evelayn's mouth moved, but Letha could no longer hear what she said. However, the *look* on the queen's face . . .

Lorcan finally turned to the queen, staring down at Evelayn, his expression too difficult to read from this distance. But slowly, with a shudder that rippled through his body, he lowered his arms and the flames came down with them. Evelayn took his hand and together they ran back to the wall—Evelayn trying to mask her pain with each step—as the creatures shrieked and took up their pursuit again.

"Letha! *Now!*" Tanvir shouted, and she spun and grabbed his hand, letting him drag her up the stones as she scrambled for a foothold to boost herself over the top.

Lorcan and Evelayn reached the wall just as she swung her legs over the stones and found herself staring at Lothar, Ceren, and Tanvir—and, rising behind them, the shadowy depths of the Undead Forest.

Evelayn could practically feel the hot breath of the arachnoids on the back of her neck as she and Lorcan hit the wall and scrambled to climb over the top. He easily reached it first and leaned down to grab her arms and pull her the rest of the way, just as one of the creatures lunged at her, pincers snapping in the air where her legs had been half a second earlier. Together, they swung over the rocks and jumped down to the other side. Pain shot up her left leg at the impact, and she had to smother a cry. Lorcan's head immediately jerked in her direction.

"You're injured." Ice-cold fury laced his voice. "I told you to protect her," he snarled, turning to Lothar.

"It was my *own* fault. He saved me." Evelayn reached out and touched his arm. "Lorcan, he saved me," she repeated quietly as he glared at his brother, teeth bared.

He took a few more seething breaths, but slowly the fight went out of him.

"I can't believe it worked," Letha commented softly, still staring at the wall with wide eyes.

"They're gone?" Ceren's voice wobbled, and Evelayn looked over to see tears in her friend's eyes. Her body trembled, and she seemed barely able to remain upright.

"They won't enter the Undead Forest." Lorcan knelt down and reached for Evelayn's left foot. She reluctantly let him lift it up and carefully pull off her boot. There was quite a bit of swelling, making it much more difficult and painful than it should have been. She sucked in a breath when he gently prodded her ankle with his long fingers, rotating it slightly left, then right. "It's not broken, thankfully. Sit down and I'll help you heal this."

"No," Evelayn said.

His eyes lifted to hers, exasperation flashing across his face. "You intend to try to run the rest of the way suffering from blood loss, with stitches in your neck, *and* a sprained ankle?"

"You can't keep doing this—especially now. You're in no condition to use any power after what you just did, let alone try to siphon it to me." She pulled her foot away. "Perhaps in a few hours after we've all rested." Evelayn shot a meaningful glance toward Ceren and Letha, who had both sat down on the ground, pale and visibly exhausted, now that the immediate danger was gone.

Lorcan sighed but didn't argue. "I suppose we can rest for a little while. There's a faster route to the White Peak, now that we're going this way."

"If it's faster, why didn't we come this way to begin with, especially if it means avoiding those creatures?" Tanvir groused.

"And why do you suppose they refuse to go past the wall?"

Evelayn looked around them, *really* looked, for the first time, and had to suppress a shudder. There was no snow on this side of the wall, but it wasn't warm, either. The forest grew close and heavy, trees and bushes crowding in on one another, their leaves not quite green but not quite brown, either. A creeping gray mist snaked across the forest floor, undulating up the trunks to dissipate into the steely sky. On the other side of the wall, it had been brilliantly sunny. Evelayn glanced up to see that even though there were no clouds, the sun was no longer visible. An involuntary shiver raked down her spine.

"I have been here only once and never wished to repeat the experience. But here we are, so we might as well take advantage of it." Lorcan pulled a piece of the meat they'd cooked that morning out of his pack.

"Can we start a fire if we're going to rest for a while? I could use the heat to warm up," Ceren said.

"Me too," Letha agreed.

"There will be no fires here." Lorcan's response was curt. "You may have noticed the light is different in this forest. A fire would attract notice—and if there's one thing you want to avoid here, it's being noticed."

Letha glanced at Tanvir in alarm, and Ceren pulled her cloak more tightly around her body, her face drawn and pale. Evelayn wished there was some way she could send her friend back to Quinlen and her younglings, but there was no way except forward now. Especially with Máthair Damhán's daughters hunting them on the other side of the wall. Why had Ceren been so foolish as to follow Tanvir and Letha?

They were a silent, somber group, sitting on the mossy earth after Lorcan's warning. Even he was subdued, his conduit stone dulled somehow in the peculiar lighting.

"Are you weaker here?" Evelayn's question was so quiet, she hoped only he could hear her.

"Why would you ask that?"

Her gaze flickered up to his conduit stone and then back to his eyes again. "It's not as bright. And you seem . . . different."

He didn't respond for a moment, looking off toward the shadowed thicket of trees they would soon be entering. "Nothing is quite the same here," he finally answered. "It is not a place for the living."

Evelayn shuddered, feeling suddenly as though they were being watched.

"We would be wise to continue on as quickly as possible," Lorcan added.

But both Letha and Ceren had curled up on the ground, using their cloaks as pillows, and fallen asleep. Tanvir sat with his back against the wall, his head listing to one side as though he'd also dozed off. Even Lothar seemed to be having trouble keeping his eyes open. And now that the danger was past, a pressing drowsiness weighed on Evelayn as well.

"You're going to have to let me help you with your ankle."

She flinched when he reached out and lifted her still-bare left foot into his lap. "You need to rest and regain your own strength."

"I'm stronger than you think" was all he said in return, and then a surge of his power entered her body, turning her ankle warm with his strong healing abilities. Despite herself, Evelayn sighed in relief as the deep, throbbing pain ebbed beneath his touch. And when he stroked the soft skin along her ankle, sending a delicious shiver up her leg, she didn't protest, though she knew she probably should have . . . shouldn't she?

"At least your stitches didn't tear open."

"My stitches?" It took her an extra beat to remember the wound in her neck, with his distracting hands on her bare leg.

"It bled some more, but the stitches look to have held," he confirmed, his voice as steady as ever. She would have believed him utterly unaffected by her, if it weren't for the telling desire she could scent mingling with his fragrance of ice and night. A scent that all the others would also recognize, she realized, her body growing hot.

Evelayn pulled her foot away and grabbed her boot. "Thank you, I believe it's better now," she said rather unsteadily.

"You're welcome." He watched her intently, his silver eyes like iron in the gloomy light of the Undead Forest.

"I've never been told about the ability to do that before. Where did you learn it?" Evelayn asked, partly out of true curiosity and partly to distract herself from the unsettling way he kept making her feel.

A shadow crossed his face, a fleeting expression that bespoke darkness, and she immediately regretted asking. "My parents knew of it, I don't know how. As a youngling, I saw my mother use it to help heal my father."

"Your father needed help healing?" Evelayn couldn't disguise her surprise.

Lorcan nodded, his gaze flickering to Lothar, who had also dozed off now, and then back to her again. "He was extremely powerful, but not infallible. He brought me to watch him train many times when I was a youngling. My mother always came as well, to make sure I didn't get in the way, as I apparently had a habit of getting into trouble."

Evelayn stared at Lorcan as he spoke, finding it difficult to imagine him ever being a mischievous youngling.

"That day, she got distracted talking to a few of the High Lords and Ladies who had also come to the training rooms. Somehow, I entered the training ring and headed for my father just as his opponent attacked. Though you may not believe it, my father dove for me, most likely saving my life. But in his haste, he didn't protect himself and took the entire hit. I don't remember much of that day, other than my mother's scream and watching her run to his side. She told him, 'I can help you. Give me your hand and I will help you.'" Lorcan shook his head, his eyes on

Evelayn, but his gaze far off in the distant past. "She helped him heal. I watched her save his life by gripping his hand and giving him her power when he was too weak to rely on his own."

Evelayn couldn't reconcile his story with the icy, bitter queen she knew. Abarrane was many things, but she'd never thought of her as a loving Mate to Bain. That made her wonder what kind of a mother she had been to Lorcan and Lothar.

"I thought it was something all Draíolon could do—or at least all royals—until the day I tried to help Lothar heal and it didn't work. I asked my mother and she told me it was something you could only do if you were Bound to each other." Lorcan refocused on her face, his gaze searing into hers. "The vow we made did more than just join our lives together."

Before she could say anything, he continued, "Shortly after that day, he made the decision to force the High Priest to remove the block on our magic as soon as he felt we were old enough to train, rather than waiting until eighteen. That is also when he began to make plans to go to war—to try and claim the power of both kingdoms for himself . . . and for us."

Evelayn's eyes widened. "You can't possibly . . . You think this was all *your* fault?"

"My father was faced with his own weakness that day, for the first time. He'd had to save me, and then to rely on my mother to help save him. He was determined to never worry about being too weak again—and he thought that was how he could accomplish it."

She hesitantly reached out and placed her hand over his. "And what started out as a noble cause in theory—"

"Turned him into a monster," Lorcan finished bitterly.

A monster that he had helped her destroy, even though it was his own father. A father who had once had enough heart to save him. After a heavy pause, she whispered, "I'm so sorry."

He shook himself, pulling his hand away from hers. "We've lingered too long. Can you run now?"

Evelayn nodded, trying to ignore the sting of his rejecting her attempt to comfort him. "Yes. Thanks to you."

"Good." Lorcan swiftly stood up. "Help me wake the others. We need to go right now."

He turned away, but not before she saw a mask fall across his face that chilled Evelayn to her core.

TWENTY-EIGHT

THEY RAN SILENTLY THROUGH THE FOREST, NO ONE daring to speak after Lorcan's warning about drawing attention to their presence. The farther in they went, the thicker the mist became, till it was almost corporeal, a choking, climbing entity stretching up their bodies, curling around their torsos and making it hard to breathe.

Lorcan guided them, as he was the only one who had traveled through the Undead Forest before. Evelayn stayed by his side, and Ceren let Lothar, Letha, and Tanvir take up the rear. She felt safer in the middle of the group. Perhaps it was selfish, but she couldn't help the thought that if something attacked them, she wouldn't be the first one it would reach. It also gave her the opportunity to observe Lorcan and Evelayn. Occasionally he'd reach out and grip her hand, rather than letting her run on her own. Ceren wasn't sure how she felt about what seemed to be happening between the two of them—even though she wasn't sure they were aware of it yet, not completely. The longer they ran, the more often Evelayn had to hold Lorcan's hand, as if he were strengthening her, as he had somehow helped her heal her neck and her ankle. She'd never seen or heard of anything like that.

She'd also never run so much in her life, but she didn't have a choice except to continue, even though the excruciating pain and exhaustion she'd experienced trying to escape Máthair Damhán's daughters was still fresh. Her legs had completely given out—one of the most humiliating and terrifying experiences in her life. She'd never been so scared as those moments when she thought she might not make it, that she might leave Saoirse and Clive orphans, that she might never kiss Quinlen again, or hold any of them in her arms. But her relief at climbing over the wall had been short-lived. For the second time, staring into the eerily lit forest, she realized she might not get out of this alive.

In the break Lorcan had allowed them, she had recovered enough physically to continue on, and, thankfully, here their pace was somewhat slower, impeded by the fog and the fear of being discovered. But as the minutes bled into hours, her muscles began to cramp and burn again. As much as she hated to admit it, she wasn't going to be able to keep moving unless they rested again. She pushed forward as long as possible, but sharp pain began to shoot up her legs with each strike of her feet.

"I . . . need . . . a . . . break . . ." she gasped before stumbling to a staggering halt, nearly causing Letha to crash into her.

"Ceren!" Evelayn stopped, pulling Lorcan to a halt with her, and hurried to her side.

Lorcan also came over, though he kept glancing over his shoulder. "What happened?" he asked, his voice low.

"I need to rest, just for a moment." Ceren grabbed her knees, trying to catch her breath.

"We can't stop, not here."

All heads turned to Lorcan.

"Why not? She's obviously in no condition to continue," Tanvir argued, always the first to speak out against the king, as if he had some sort of death wish.

"Which is why she never should have come," Lorcan retorted, but when Evelayn turned beseeching eyes on him, he softened slightly. "There are some ruins ahead. Can you make it that far? I rested there once in peace, I suppose we can try to take shelter there for an hour or two. But then we must keep pressing forward."

Ceren blanched. "I can try."

She attempted to walk forward, but her muscles had already stiffened; her legs buckled and Letha had to grab her arm to hold her up.

"How far away are the ruins?" Evelayn took her other arm, much to Ceren's humiliation.

"Too far if she is unable even to walk." Letha spoke this time.

"I can do it, I just need a minute," Ceren protested, angry tears pricking at the back of her eyes. She was furious with herself for being so weak when Evelayn needed her to be strong. All these years when she'd done what she could to search for her friend, to try and figure out how to help her, she should have been conditioning herself. Training for *anything* that could come, including a trek like this.

"I'll carry her," Lothar volunteered suddenly.

"You do not want to shift here—calling upon that much

power would definitely draw attention to us." Lorcan shook his head.

"Then I will carry her in my arms. How far is it?"

"You are not going to carry her." Lorcan's eyes were flinty.

"What do you suggest instead? Leaving her here by herself?"

Ceren shuddered when the fog grew thicker at his words, as if it had heard him and was anticipating claiming her.

Lorcan regarded his brother for a long moment, then gestured to a spot in the grayness that seemed slightly lighter somehow, the fog possibly not quite as thick. How he had any sense of direction in this cursed place was beyond Ceren. "It's up there. Perhaps a quarter hour at a run. If you wish to carry her, be my guest."

"Excellent." Lothar didn't hesitate to come over and, ignoring Ceren's protests, swoop her into his arms.

"Is everyone else capable of continuing? Or perhaps we should take the time to build stretchers and pray nothing else finds us first?"

Ceren caught Evelayn shooting Lorcan a scathing look as her already warm cheeks burned hot. Without another word, the king turned, his crimson conduit stone flashing in his forehead, and took off once more.

"I'm sorry," Evelayn said softly before turning to dash after him.

No, I'm sorry, Ceren wished to say, knowing she was causing them trouble they didn't need. But there was no chance. Lothar tightened his grip around her and took off after his brother.

ê

"What is your problem?" Evelayn hissed when she caught up to Lorcan. Exhaustion weighed heavily upon her as well, but she wasn't about to seek out his help, not when she was so angry at him.

He glanced over at her and, as if sensing her weakness but also her stubbornness, slowed slightly. Which only made her even more furious. "I'm worried," he finally admitted.

"And you show it by making my dearest friend, and the only Draíolon even remotely like family left in my life, feel as worthless as the mud beneath your boots?" Evelayn hoped he couldn't hear how out of breath she was.

"I did not intend to make her feel that way." He squinted as the mist undulated ahead of them, wrapping around the trees.

"Well, you did!" Evelayn insisted.

Rather than responding, Lorcan reached out and grabbed her hand.

"Stop it," she protested, trying to pull away, but he held on tight. "I don't want your help."

"You don't have room for that infernal pride, not right now. Do you wish to collapse like your friend?"

Evelayn growled angrily but stopped trying to get free of his grip. He was, unfortunately, right. She had to be sensible. Even if she felt like she'd begun to crave his touch almost as much as the strength that flowed into her from him.

"What is it you're so frightened of?" she asked to distract herself before he sensed or scented her tumultuous feelings.

Lorcan glanced over his shoulder, which made her do the same, half expecting a horrifying creature to be right behind them. But there were merely the other Draíolon, Letha and Tanvir running alongside Lothar, who held a very unhappy-looking Ceren in his arms.

"I have a right to know," Evelayn insisted when he didn't respond. Of course she knew a bit about the Undead Forest from her studies years ago. But most of it was legend, stories. No Draíolon ever crossed the wall. None who returned to speak of it, until Bain laid his trap for her mother and then again for her, taking Lorcan with him. Lorcan was the only Draíolon she knew with actual experience in the Undead Forest—the only one who could tell her what was real and what was myth.

"This forest is old." He glanced over at her but quickly away again, keeping his eyes focused ahead of them. "Older than the Draíolon, older than magic itself, they say. There are many things that live here, seen and unseen, that do not wish to be disturbed."

"I've read the tomes, I know the warnings. But what *exactly* lives here? Why don't they wish to be disturbed?" Despite herself, she clutched his hand tightly, telling herself it was only to keep up her strength. "You've been here before . . . what did you see?"

Before he could answer, a horrific scream split the silence of the mist-shrouded forest. Evelayn whirled around mid-stride to see Letha on the ground, a creature as big as a male Draíolon that was half canine, half exposed skeleton, snapping its blackened fangs at her face and neck, while she frantically struggled to hold it back.

A Dheagmadra.

Evelayn hadn't thought the so-called demon dogs existed. Tanvir grabbed his sword and swung it at the creature, but before it impacted, a blast of shadowflame exploded into the Dheagmadra's chest, sending it flying into the mist with an unearthly howl of agony. Letha scrambled to her feet, the right sleeve of her tunic ripped, her bloodied skin visible through the tears and a similar gash on her collarbone.

"Go to the ruins! Now!" Lorcan gestured them forward. *"Run!"*

A bone-chilling sound that was part howl and part unearthly shriek echoed through the mist.

They took off in the direction Lorcan pointed. Renewed energy washed through Evelayn's muscles as terror sent adrenaline coursing into her veins. Another howl sounded, this time much closer than the last, and she kicked up her heels even harder, pushing her body to the edge of her endurance and then past it. The other Draíolon sprinted all around her, their haggard breathing a desperate counterpoint to the incessant pounding of her own heart.

And then she heard other footfalls—the soft beat of padded feet on earth—and breathing that was far less winded than theirs, closing in.

They were being hunted.

"Keep going straight—we're almost there," Lorcan said, squeezing her hand more tightly for a moment. "They won't follow us into the ruins, so lead everyone inside. Do you understand?"

"What are you going to do?" Evelayn asked in alarm.

But he had already let go of her and turned away. "Lothar, put her down and help me," Lorcan ordered, falling to the back of the group.

"I'll take her," Tanvir offered, rushing to Lothar.

"I can run—just put me down!" Ceren protested, but Tanvir grabbed her into his arms, ignoring her protests.

"There's no time to fight about it" was all he said.

"What do we do?" Evelayn heard Lothar ask, even as she pushed herself to go faster, hoping the others followed her lead—and praying the ruins were closer than the Dheagmadra circling in on them. She could smell the pack now, a mixture of burning embers and rotting meat.

Lorcan responded, "They can't be killed, but they do hate fire."

"Even shadowflame?"

Before he could answer, the first Dheagmadra emerged from the mist, loping alongside Lothar and Letha, its massive head turned toward them, red eyes glowing and gray spittle dripping from its black fangs. Letha screamed and veered to avoid it, nearly crashing into Tanvir. Lothar sent a flash of shadowflame at the creature; as if expecting it, the creature attempted to dodge the attack, but the blast still exploded on its hind flank. The Dheagmadra howled and dashed off to the right, disappearing into the mist again.

But then three more burst into view, two behind them and one closer to Lorcan.

Evelayn forced herself to look forward, to focus all her energy on escaping.

"Follow me!" she cried to the others, praying to the Gods somewhere above them in this Light-forsaken place for the energy and strength to flee.

There were more explosions behind her and more howls and snarls, but Evelayn didn't look back. *Please, please, please.* It became her mantra with each desperate pound of her feet on the ground, and the thundering of her heart. Each breath was like fire ripping through her throat and lungs.

Someone behind her shouted in pain at the same moment she felt a burning flash of agony from the scar in her right hand. Evelayn risked glancing over her shoulder and saw Lorcan down on one knee, two Dheagmadra on him.

"*Lorcan!*" she screamed.

His silver eyes met hers for a mere millisecond before he twisted, blasting one of the creatures off him while the other tore into his shoulder.

"Evelayn, *go!*" someone shouted when she hesitated.

It took every bit of willpower for her to turn away from him, to leave him to the creatures and keep going, when all her instincts told her to rush to his aid, to attack the monsters hurting him. But there was nothing she could do—she had no power. None except to lead the others to safety.

A strange desperation washed over her—but somehow separate from her own and tinged with regret. She realized with a sudden stinging in her eyes that it was *Lorcan's* emotions she could feel, whether through her scar or their Binding, she wasn't sure. All she knew was that her chest constricted with grief in response to the realization that he thought he wouldn't survive this.

And then, finally, she saw it, rising out of the trees and mist. The massive, crumbling ruins. The fog seemed to flow around it, not through it, as if even the unnatural mist avoided whatever this place was.

Please. Please. Please. Her mantra was now to save Lorcan somehow, to save them all. Her entire body screamed at her to stop, but stopping meant death; she knew it as well as she knew that her legs were about to give out on her, just as Ceren's had earlier.

Just twenty more steps, she told herself as hot tears slipped down her cheeks. *Nineteen. Eighteen. Seventeen.*

A roar sounded from behind her, and she realized Lothar had shifted, choosing to fight off the Dheagmadra in his bear form rather than using his fire.

Sixteen. Fifteen. Fourteen.

Another scream, this time female. Evelayn glanced back wildly over her shoulder to see Letha being dragged off by her ankle into the forest by one of the creatures. In the space of a breath, Tanvir dumped Ceren to the ground, leaving her to scramble to her feet, and he charged after his sister—but not before the bear got there, grabbing the Dheagmadra with its massive jaws. The Dheagmadra howled and released Letha just as Evelayn heard the snapping sound of Lothar crushing its spine. It went limp and, using his immense strength, Lothar threw the body backward to slam into two Dheagmadra racing toward them. Ceren reached Evelayn's side and grabbed her arm, yanking her forward.

"Keep going!"

Thirteen, twelve, eleven, ten . . .

Tanvir had Letha in his arms now, her ankle a bloody mess. But where was Lorcan?

As Ceren passed her, just a few strides from the steps of the ruins, Evelayn fought the urge to turn back again, to search for him. And then she felt it—the hot breath of a Dheagmadra on the back of her neck. She leaned forward, reaching for her friend—for safety—

Nine, eight—

The hit came like a blast of power, knocking into her and sending her tumbling to the ground, rolling across the dirt with a cry of pain as her shoulder struck a rock. Evelayn tried to launch herself back to her feet—*she was so close*—but the demon dog pounced on her back, slamming her face into the ground.

Everything slowed, narrowing in on that moment, on the brief interlude between life and death. A sob built in her chest, even as Evelayn fought to escape, writhing and twisting beneath the claws that dug into her spine, knowing the fatal blow was coming.

"NO!" A thunderous roar sounded in the instant before she felt the heat of a massive blast of shadowflame explode directly above her, searing her back and legs but sending the Dheagmadra flying, freeing her.

Ignoring everything but that brief flicker of hope, Evelayn jumped to her feet to see Lorcan limping toward her, his left arm hanging unnaturally at his side, his face bloodied, his right pant leg ripped to shreds, with more blood running down his skin. Rather than taking the last few steps to the ruins, she rushed to him and took his unharmed hand in hers.

"You fool!" he choked out, even as more Dheagmadra rushed toward them. *"Go!"*

"Together" was all she said, with a fierce shake of her head.

Was that surge of relief her own or his?

Lorcan somehow managed to lift his injured arm enough to raise a flickering wall of shadowflame between them and the three Dheagmadra as they limped toward the ruins and the others who had managed to reach safety there.

Seven, six . . .

Lothar shifted back into his Draíolon form and blasted at two others that were sprinting through the trees to their left, trying to cut past Lorcan's flames before he and Evelayn reached the ruins.

Five, four, three, two—

Lorcan stumbled and collapsed into Evelayn, his eyes rolling back into his head, sending them both crashing to the ground, inches from safety. His wall of flames flickered and went out, and the three creatures rushed forward, maws gaping, fangs bared—

And then Lothar and Tanvir were there, grabbing both of them and dragging them up onto the steps of the ruins. Evelayn was shocked when the three Dheagmadra skidded to a halt at the edge of the stone steps, snarling and snapping their teeth in fury but remaining on the ground, not stepping even one paw onto the ruins.

Lorcan had been right . . . about many things.

And now he was unconscious.

TWENTY-NINE

WHAT HAPPENED? IS HE—"
"He's alive." Lothar cut Ceren's question off.
"Barely."

Letha watched as Evelayn knelt by Lorcan's side. "He drew too much power for too long." The queen's voice shook. "He's Flared—he is being consumed by the power. If we don't find a way to call him back fast enough, it will kill him."

"What do we do now?" Letha looked around at their haggard group, trying to ignore the horrific creatures still circling the slight clearing around the ruins, waiting for them. She'd never seen anything so terrifying, with their partially exposed skulls and their glowing red eyes and black fangs as long as her fingers. The pain in her foot was nearly unbearable. She was certain the Dheagmadra had crushed the bones with its jaws. And a burning sensation had begun to climb up her leg, making her afraid that there was more than just saliva in their mouths.

"Can you walk?" Tanvir's question was quiet, as if he was still nervous about attracting the attention of the Dheagmadra.

Letha shook her head. "No. Not without help at least."

Lothar glanced over at them from where he crouched beside his brother, his eyebrows drawn together, Evelayn by his side. The young queen's lips were nearly bloodless, her face stark white and tear-streaked as she tried to wake Lorcan. Letha had been certain Evelayn was about to be killed when that Dheagmadra had pounced on her, but somehow they'd all made it—thanks to Lorcan, who had used too much power to save them and now had lost himself to it.

"Should we go inside?" Ceren suggested from behind them. "It looks abandoned. Perhaps we could try to help him in there . . ." She trailed off.

"I don't think we have a choice," Tanvir said, staring out at the Dheagmadra, which had fallen silent but stalked back and forth at the edge of the stone steps, their fangs bared.

"Can you help me carry him?" Lothar looked up at Tanvir, his coppery skin gone pale and his face drawn as he gestured to Lorcan, who hadn't responded to either of them.

"I have to help Letha. She can't walk."

"I'll help her," Ceren quickly offered, coming back down the steps to reach out and pull Letha to her feet—well, her foot. She couldn't put any weight on the injured one. Ceren helped Letha place an arm around her shoulders, and together, they slowly moved toward the darkened doorway of whatever the structure had once been. The outer edges of it had crumbled into ruin, but the main section directly above them seemed to be mostly intact.

Lothar and Tanvir were right behind them, hefting Lorcan off the steps—one lifting him by his torso, careful to avoid his shoulder, and the other lifting his legs. Evelayn trailed behind them, visibly shaken and upset.

Letha and Ceren reached the opening first but paused before entering.

"I hope the reason those things didn't follow us isn't because there's something worse hiding in here." Letha suppressed a shiver of fear as they stared into the shadowed room. It was extremely large, with a ceiling that soared far above them; she could make out vague shapes but nothing definite.

"What's wrong? Why did you stop?"

Letha turned to see Lothar right behind them, straining to hold Lorcan as they climbed the stairs.

"Nothing, sorry," she answered, and hopped forward, Ceren assisting her wordlessly.

It took a moment for her eyes to adjust, but Lothar didn't seem fazed by the darkness one bit. His Dark Draíolon sight was much better suited to low light than hers. He continued confidently right on past them, Tanvir following his lead. The females all trailed behind, Letha trying to ignore the pain that had become excruciating, spiking with each painful hop.

As her eyes grew accustomed to the darkness, she realized where Lothar was headed. In the center of the large room, there was a round cistern full of water, with hulking slabs of marble at evenly spaced intervals encircling it like benches of some sort—or altars. As they got closer, Letha had to blink a few times to make sure she wasn't imagining things.

"Is it just me or is that water . . . glowing?" She was a little afraid that perhaps whatever poison was working its way up her leg was making her delirious.

"I see it, too," Ceren said, her voice shaking slightly as they approached the cistern and Letha let go of the other female to clutch the stone edge with both hands. It wasn't strong, but there was definitely a faint light emitting from the water, or from the cistern holding it. The surface was as smooth as glass, not a ripple to be seen.

"It's as clear as a mountain stream," Tanvir commented, sounding slightly awed. He and Lothar had gently laid Lorcan down on one of the marble slabs. "How is that possible when it has to have been sitting here stagnant for ages?"

"I don't know, but I ran out of water hours ago." Letha's mouth had gone bone dry and her stomach clenched with thirst.

"Letha, don't—"

But she'd already cupped the water and brought it to her mouth. It ran down her throat, cool and delicious. She'd expected it to be warm and to taste of dirt, or at least like the stones it sat in, but she'd never drunk anything so fresh and delicious. When it hit her belly, a wave of energy cascaded over her, revitalizing her so thoroughly, she hadn't realized just how worn down she'd been until the exhaustion was gone. She reached out to get another handful when someone grabbed her arm and yanked her back.

Letha whirled to see Tanvir glaring at her, but before he could say anything, Lothar spoke up.

"Letha, your foot!"

She looked down to see what he was talking about and realized she was standing on both feet with no pain, and the burning sensation that had been traveling up her leg was gone.

"You . . . you're *healed*." Ceren's shock was unmistakable.

Letha looked back up at Lothar, whose dark-gray eyes were wide. Then they both looked to Evelayn, who sat beside Lorcan.

She blinked, and her eyes, which had been frighteningly empty, sparked back to life. "The water healed you?"

Letha took a hesitant step, but again there was no pain whatsoever. "Yes, it did," she confirmed.

"If we can get him to drink some . . ." Evelayn trailed off, and Lothar jumped to action, grabbing his waterskin. He pulled the cap off as he hurried over to the cistern and plunged it in.

The moment he lifted it back out, Evelayn took the waterskin from him. "Can you open his mouth?"

Lothar nodded and reached out to gently pry his brother's lips apart. "His teeth are clenched," he said in frustration, trying and failing to get them to open.

"Maybe if we can even get a tiny bit to go in . . ." Evelayn bent and tipped the waterskin into his mouth. The water ran right back out again, dribbling down his chin and cheek to soak into his blood-streaked hair.

"It's not working!"

"I *know* it's not working," Evelayn snapped while Lothar pushed at Lorcan's teeth, desperately trying to force them apart.

Letha watched, battling internally with herself. She'd dealt with many different kinds of injuries on the battlefront, and she knew a tactic that could possibly work to help open a seemingly stuck jaw. But did she *want* to save him? He wasn't his father, she knew that. He had never hurt her during her imprisonment; however, he *had* used her, manipulated Tanvir and caused him immeasurable suffering . . . but he'd also saved all of them on this trek, more than once.

He'd been completely motionless the entire time, but suddenly the king's whole body began to tremble, his head thrashing.

"What's happening?" Ceren's question was fraught with fear.

"Lorcan, don't you *dare* leave us now. You are stronger than this. Fight it!" Evelayn cried out. "Don't let it take you!" Something inside Letha cracked open at the expression on the queen's pale face, as she frantically tried to get the water into Lorcan, to save him. She didn't understand what was happening, and she didn't hold any affection for the king, but she recognized the look on Evelayn's face, the panic in her eyes as she kept commanding him to fight the pull of the power that was consuming him.

"I might be able to help," she found herself saying as she stepped forward. "If you push on his jaw, there and there, it might release." She pointed, but Lothar moved, turning beseeching eyes to hers. Letha took a deep breath and forced herself to reach out and take the king's face in her hands. His hairline was damp with sweat, yet his skin was as cold as ice when she attempted to find the two trigger points she'd once been shown by a Draíolon gifted with healing, even as he continued to thrash, fighting her efforts.

"There!" she finally announced, pressing down as hard as she could on what she hoped were the right spots. "Do it now!"

Lothar grabbed his chin and pulled. The king's jaw released just enough for Evelayn to pour some of the water into his slightly opened mouth. Letha watched his throat to see if he swallowed any before it came trickling back out, despite their efforts.

"Did any go down?"

Letha could sense the strain in Lothar's body as he stood beside her, his arm crossed over hers to continue trying to keep his brother's mouth open, and she could scent his fear.

"I don't know." Evelayn tipped the waterskin once more, letting the clear, cool liquid run into Lorcan's mouth.

Letha watched it go in and then come back out again, and had a sudden burning urge to grab the waterskin for herself. If he was going to keep wasting it, she deserved it—she *needed* it—

And then Lorcan coughed, a brief choking noise, and Letha saw his throat move. He'd swallowed some. His thrashing stopped as quickly as it had begun. They all stared, waiting and watching in silence.

"Should we give him more?"

Before anyone could answer Lothar, Lorcan gasped and his eyes opened.

"Oh, thank the Light," Evelayn breathed.

And then a voice thundered from behind them:

"You have desecrated the Water of Life."

THIRTY

Evelayn's overwhelming relief when Lorcan's eyes opened shrank at the unfamiliar voice.

At first she could barely see the being, but as she watched, he became more corporeal, taking on a definite form. He looked like a Draíolon in shape—but one composed completely of light and shadow. His hair was made of sunbeams and flowed in an unseen wind, his skin glowed with starlight, and his eyes bore through her—one as bright as day and one as dark as night.

"Why have you come here and defiled sacred ground with your unclean hands?" His voice was the sound of thunder on a summer's night, and it shook Evelayn to her core.

"We didn't know it was sacred, please forgive us," she said when all the others seemed too terrified to respond. "We were attacked by the Dheagmadra and we were told they would not follow us here."

"Knowledge learned only through our previous leniency. He was warned never to return. And now he has not only returned, he has consumed the Water of Life." The being seemed to grow even larger and brighter, so that it was painful to look at him.

"He is not responsible for what has happened. He was nearly Consumed protecting us from the Dheagmadra—we brought him here and gave him the water. The fault is mine." Evelayn bent her head in supplication. "If there is a price to be paid, I will pay it."

"No . . ." The moan came from Lorcan, but she placed her hand on his shoulder—which had healed completely—and hoped he would be silent.

"I drank first. If there is a price to be paid, *I* should pay it."

Evelayn turned in shock to see Letha step forward.

"I asked for them to use it to save my brother. I will pay the price," Lothar said, moving in front of Letha.

"You have no knowledge of the price of which I speak, and yet you so willingly offer yourselves in the stead of others." The being regarded them silently for a long moment. Evelayn tried to hold on to her courage, to keep from quaking before him, but she was certain if Lorcan was still conscious, he could feel her hand trembling. "The price owed a Spirit Harbinger is often steep indeed."

A Spirit Harbinger. Evelayn's stomach dropped. She should have recognized what he was immediately—but she'd thought them no more than a bedtime tale. Yet here he was, undeniably real. A Being of Eternity, one who ferried souls to the Final Light

and guarded the Gateway that could allow the living or the dead
to cross barriers meant to be left alone.

"This is a temple," she breathed, the stories she'd heard as a
youngling coming back to her in sudden realization. "The Temple
of the Living Waters."

"A temple lost to time and memory," the Spirit Harbinger
confirmed, his voice changing to the melodic sound of a river
flowing over rocks made smooth from eons of wear. "Where
Spirit Harbingers rest in this world. A sacred place where demons
may not tread. You are neither sacred nor demon, so you may pass
the threshold, but for drinking the Water of Life without sanc-
tion, the price must be paid."

Lorcan's hand closed over Evelayn's, and she looked down to
see him staring up at her, his silver eyes bright. Then, in one fluid
movement, he sat up and faced the Spirit Harbinger. "No debt
shall be paid by any other than I. I am the one who knew this was
hallowed ground and still led them here. However, I beseech you
for mercy, as I only did so that I might save their lives."

The Spirit Harbinger's burning gaze fell upon Lorcan.
"Never considering that perhaps by so doing, you upset the natural order of life and death." His words boomed through the
temple and yet still held such an infinite amount of sorrow—as if
he knew exactly the desperation that had led them here—that it
nearly brought Evelayn to tears.

"If there is a life to be taken, take mine. They have done no
wrong, except to have had their destinies altered by my actions."
Lorcan stood and walked toward the Spirit Harbinger without

an ounce of fear, his shoulders back and his head high. Evelayn's heart leapt into her throat, and she had to smother the instinct to cry out for him to come back. She already thought she'd lost him once today and she'd been shaken at the sharpness of the grief and fear she'd felt. Had they found a way to save him only to have him taken as payment for that very miracle?

The Spirit Harbinger's unearthly eyes met hers, and she had the uncanny feeling that he'd somehow heard her unspoken thoughts.

"The bonds of loyalty and love among you are complex and yet admirable. They cross boundaries of power and prejudice that have slowly been built up in this world through eons. Power has corrupted some, but there are those among you who have fought back and tried to replace the pain with hope. I *see* you—the *real* you, beneath your flesh and bone. Spirits that shine more brilliantly than you might suppose." The Spirit Harbinger slowly looked at each one of them in turn. When his eyes fell on Evelayn's again, something sparked inside of her—a pull that filled her with warmth, reminding her of drowsy summer evenings, lying in a field of wildflowers with her father and mother, watching clouds drift past on a tapestry of brightest blue above them. When his gaze moved on, taking the sensation with him, she felt desolate, a barrenness of feelings that made her miss them more intensely than she thought possible.

"I have looked on your hearts and agree upon this mercy. One chance will I give you to return that which was stolen in the beginning, that which has led to death and grief in the past and will again if not returned. Choose the right path and you will find help when you need it most. If you do this, your debts will be repaid."

"I don't understand," Evelayn said.

"You may rest here for a night in peace, but then you must leave," the Spirit Harbinger continued. "And remember, if the price is not paid, I must claim the debt owed. The answers you seek can be found here for those who know how to see."

"Here, meaning in this temple?"

But he had already begun to fade from view before he disappeared entirely, leaving them standing in bewilderment, staring at the empty air where he'd hovered only moments before.

Lorcan couldn't bring himself to turn and face the other Draíolon yet, not when he'd failed them so completely. He'd been severely injured and weakened, he'd felt the power overtaking him, but when that Dheagmadra had leapt onto Evelayn, sending her to the ground and preparing to go in for the kill, he hadn't even thought—he'd merely reacted. Holding up the wall of shadow-flame and protecting her had been too much. He'd made it to the steps, but just before he reached them, everything went blank. The well of power he had access to as the king, as the conduit for his entire kingdom—that he risked being consumed by if he called upon too much of it at once—had done exactly that. He'd been trapped, enveloped by the power, slowly being absorbed into it, when he'd dimly heard Evelayn's voice. It had only been enough to pause his descent, though; he'd been too weak to break free.

Until, suddenly, he'd surfaced. The Spirit Harbinger's voice had been audible through the haze of the power still leeching out of his body, gradually releasing its grasp on him. Though he tried to hide it, he was deeply shaken by how close he'd been to succumbing. If they hadn't brought him the Water of Life and forced some into him . . .

"Is anyone here any good at deciphering riddles? Because if not, I have a feeling we're doomed."

Lorcan stifled the urge to send a blast at Tanvir that would knock him to the ground. He scented Evelayn moments before she stopped by his side, sliding her hand into his. He looked into her weary, dirt-and-blood-streaked face and nearly shuddered in relief that the Spirit Harbinger hadn't taken her from him. She squeezed his hand once, softly, then turned with him to face the others.

"We have to return something that was stolen. It can't be the Water of Life," she mused, steadfastly ignoring Tanvir. "So it must be something else equally powerful."

"He said the answers we seek can be found here if we know how to see . . . so maybe we should split up and search the temple?" Ceren suggested.

"I think that's an excellent suggestion," Evelayn said. "Ceren, why don't you come with me and Lorcan. Lothar, you can go with Letha and Tanvir, so there is someone with power in each group?"

Lothar nodded, his gaze immediately going to Letha, then quickly away again. "Of course."

Lorcan's eyes narrowed, but he also agreed.

"We'll take this side." Evelayn gestured behind them to her left. "Meet back here in a few hours?"

"What are we looking for?" Letha asked.

"Anything." Lorcan finally spoke up. "Statues, carvings, tomes, tapestries, anything that has survived all these years and can give us a clue as to what he wants."

"Sounds so simple." The sarcasm in Tanvir's voice earned him scathing looks from both Evelayn and Letha. "Well, best of luck, everyone," he continued on, undeterred. "Our lives apparently depend on this."

Evelayn squeezed Lorcan's hand softly. "Ignore him," she said under her breath. That she'd read his irritation so easily clearly meant he wasn't concealing his emotions nearly well enough.

"I always do," he retorted, making sure he sounded as unconcerned as possible.

"It's quite dark in there," Ceren commented. Though her voice was steady, Lorcan could scent her underlying fear. He forgot that as Light Draíolon, their eyesight in the dark wasn't as acute as his.

"I can help," he offered, lifting his palm and summoning a small shadowflame to hover above his hand. It wasn't the same as the light they could have produced if they had their power—his flames burned greenish black—but at least it offered a bit of extra illumination.

"Should you be using any power right now?"

Lorcan shot her an imperious look. "I'm fine now. You know any youngling can do as much."

"If you insist. I'm merely saying you should be careful. I don't think we should use any more of that water to heal you."

Nothing had ever made Lorcan feel weaker than having Evelayn question his ability to control his power, even for something as ridiculously simple as summoning a bit of shadowflame to help light their way. But he refused to let her know how deeply her worry cut as she let go of his hand to follow Ceren farther into the depths of the temple.

THIRTY-ONE

EVERYTHING IN THE TEMPLE HAD A FINE COATING OF dust, yet it didn't smell stale. In fact, the air was completely clear and fresh, void of the fog that entrenched the forest surrounding it. Their progress was painstakingly slow, as they searched for any hint of the answer the Spirit Harbinger had promised was there for "those who know how to see." Even with the help of Lorcan's shadowflame, Evelayn had to strain to see clearly in the gloom. It wasn't fully dark in the temple, but it was close.

They were quiet at first, as if afraid speaking would bring the Spirit Harbinger back. The three Draíolon wandered through abandoned hallways and rooms. Some were in nearly perfect condition, while others had entire walls that were collapsed. They were methodical in their search, wiping dust from the stones, inspecting every ceiling, floor, and wall for anything that would indicate what they needed to return. There seemed to be nothing to find, however; the stones were smooth, and the entire structure was barren of any furniture, decorations, or other sign of having ever been inhabited.

"What *is* this place?" Ceren finally asked, her voice hushed, when they paused for a break in one of the rooms. She sat on a pile of rubble where the wall between two rooms had partially collapsed. "Why build something so massive and leave it completely empty?"

Evelayn paused in her inspection of the opposite wall for any sign of a possible hidden door or storage area. Lorcan was in the hallway, running his hands over the doorframe. A frame for a door that didn't exist—none of the rooms had any.

"I don't know," Evelayn admitted with a shiver. This room had a thin window with no glass, allowing in some of the gray light from the forest surrounding them, as well as a draft of cool air that still held the scent of the Dheagmadra, which were probably circling the temple, waiting for them to emerge.

If the Draíolon even figured out what the Spirit Harbinger wanted, how would they escape the death that awaited them outside? How would they ever reach the White Peak to reclaim Evelayn's stone and her power? A mounting sense of hopelessness grew heavier with each room they passed through with no answers.

"I'm so sorry, Ceren," Evelayn said softly, facing the wall.

"You have nothing to be sorry for," her friend protested, but Evelayn suddenly had to blink back tears.

"Yes, I do. I failed my parents, I failed my kingdom. And I failed *you*. Because of me, you're trapped in here instead of at home with Quinlen and your younglings. And I don't know how—"

"Ev." Ceren cut her off. "Stop."

Evelayn sensed Ceren rising and coming to where she stood, still turned to the wall. "*I chose to follow you. I chose to stay.* You can't blame yourself." Ceren put an arm around her shoulders, squeezing her tightly. "And you didn't fail any of us."

Evelayn inhaled slowly, trying to rein in her emotions. She didn't want Lorcan to hear her crying and think her any weaker than he most likely already did.

"But I did—I have. Ten years ago I couldn't even protect myself, let alone my kingdom. And look at what's happened to all of us because of that—because of *me.*"

"Ev, you were *poisoned.* No one would have been able to defend themselves if that had happened to them."

You were poisoned. Evelayn's head jerked up suddenly. "Lorcan," she called out, knowing he couldn't help but overhear them with his acute hearing.

The king of Dorjhalon stepped into the doorway, as much a mess as she was, with his ripped, bloody tunic and pants, his dirt-streaked face and hair—and yet everything inside her tightened at the sight of him. She didn't want to admit it, but there was something building between them.

"Who poisoned me?" It was the one detail she hadn't remembered until that moment.

Lorcan shook his head. "It doesn't matter, does it?"

"I have to know."

He sighed with a grimace and said, "The only Draíolon who had access to your drinks that night."

Evelayn thought for a moment and then: "*Tanvir,*" she breathed, her stomach caving in as if he'd punched her. "*No.* He wouldn't have . . . would he?" Tanvir had done much to deceive and manipulate her . . . but to poison her? On the night she made her Oath of Intent to Bind herself to him?

Lorcan remained silent, but his expression said it all.

"*How?* How did he even know to do it—or where to get it?"

"My mother. I sent her a message to have him do it so I could fulfill Máthair Damhán's demands."

"He *knew*? What you were going to do to me?" An awful weakness hit her, making her legs tremble and her heart constrict. "But . . . he fought you. He was so upset. It was all an act?"

Lorcan took a step toward her, but she lifted her hand, palm extended, and he halted again, his mouth twisting. She couldn't bear to have him near her, not right then.

"I didn't expect him to fight me," he said. "But I do think he truly cared for you, and that he felt guilty for what he'd done. And no, he didn't know I was going to take your stone. No one did."

Evelayn stared at him, so many conflicting emotions roiling through her body that she wanted to scream and cry all at once. He'd said something that night to Tanvir about being one to talk about oath breaking. Now she understood. Tanvir had made an oath to love her, to protect her, for her to be as his right arm, flesh of his flesh. And the same night he'd poured poison in her cup and let her drink it, enabling Lorcan to take everything from her.

Ceren suddenly cleared her throat, reminding Evelayn that she was there. "I think maybe you should rest for a minute. I'll keep going and you can catch up."

Evelayn barely acknowledged Ceren's less-than-subtle attempt to give them privacy. Even after she left, Lorcan remained motionless and silent, waiting.

"Why did you do it?" Evelayn couldn't help but ask. "Why did you make me think he'd died?"

His gaze was unwavering, but a flash of chagrin crossed his face. "I didn't really have a chance to think it through. *He* attacked *me*, remember. Perhaps what you *should* be asking is why, when I could have actually killed him, I chose not to."

Evelayn wasn't sure she wanted to know the answer to that question. She wasn't sure about anything anymore. Binding herself to Lorcan, going on this quest to retrieve her stone, now finding herself trapped in a long-forgotten temple with a new threat from the Spirit Harbinger pressing in on them, while bloodthirsty creatures circled the crumbling stone walls . . . The weight of it all felt suddenly unbearable. She jumped to her feet and strode to the window, staring out at the gray forest, into the swirling mist.

"Is there no day or night here?" she demanded angrily. "How do we know when our time is up if the light never changes?"

There was a long silence before Lorcan spoke again, much closer than she'd expected.

"Why did *you* do it? Why risk yourself to save me?"

Evelayn stared out into the fog, her neck growing hot. She felt him drawing even nearer to her, and for some reason she didn't stop him. "You saved me first. I owed you a life debt."

"I don't believe you." It was a low whisper, from directly

behind where she stood, still staring resolutely at the thickening fog. Her heart beat in her throat and deep in her abdomen. When his fingers skimmed the back of her neck, moving her hair to expose the skin, she shivered.

"Why not?" she tried to sound unaffected, but the words came out with a tremble.

"Because." His warm breath brushed her exposed skin, sending another heated shiver through her body. "I can scent your lie."

Neither of them moved; Evelayn could barely breathe for the pounding of her heart. It seemed as though Lorcan was everywhere—the heat of his body emanating mere inches from hers, and the pine-and-frost scent she'd come to know so well filling her senses, now laced with the deeper musk that meant he was as deeply affected by her as she was by him.

"Tell me I'm not the only one feeling this." The words were a hoarse murmur, setting her body aflame. It took all her self-control to remain still, to keep her back to him, even as her heart beat so hard against the cage of her ribs that it stole her breath.

"I . . . I don't know what you mean," she managed.

"Liar." He took her shoulders in his hands and gently turned her to face him.

She stared at his chest, knowing his silver eyes would be her undoing.

"Evelayn, please," Lorcan rasped, "look at me."

Finally, she did as he asked, her gaze traveling up his body to his throat, his strong chin, his full lips and aquiline nose, at last meeting his eyes—and was shocked to see what looked like grief in their silver depths.

He lifted one hand and softly brushed her hair back from her cheek. They stared at each other, neither moving toward the other. Finally, he murmured, "I want you, Evelayn. So much, I can barely stand it. But I don't want to ask anything of you that you aren't willing to give." He let his thumb trail hesitantly across her lip, sending a shock wave of desire through her body.

"You want me?" she asked unsteadily.

"*All* of you," he confirmed, his eyes dropping to her mouth. "Body, heart, and soul."

Yet he still didn't kiss her.

"But . . ."

"But," he continued, at her prompting, "you've been hurt—badly. And I am largely to blame for it. So I understand if you can't ever forgive me, if you can't look past that and—"

She cut him off by pressing her fingers to his lips. "I . . . I do care for you." Evelayn let her hand fall to his chest, where she could feel his heart beating against her palm.

There was a sudden burst of the most exquisite brightness in his scent. It nearly made her want to cry when she realized it was hope—something she'd never seen or scented on him before.

Lorcan cupped her face, his thumb tracing the corner of her mouth as he slowly, slowly leaned toward her. Inch by inch, giving her ample time to stop him, to turn away. Instead, she lifted her chin, raising her face to his. His lips finally brushed hers and sent a jolt through her body as if lightning and ice had met and exploded in her veins. She grabbed his tunic with both hands, curling her fingers into the fabric to pull him closer. His arms came around her, but he was very careful, holding her as though afraid she could break—or might still decide to push him away.

"Please," she groaned, her lips moving against his with her plea. The ache inside—the sudden insatiable need to get closer to him—was nearly unbearable.

Lorcan let loose a deep, guttural growl, and finally pressed her to him, his hands clutching her back. His lips moved on hers, a shockingly tender kiss that stripped away his bravado, his power, the facade that he presented to the world, and left him more vulnerable and open than she ever dreamed possible. And that ache morphed into something *more*, growing stronger but also different, melding into a need to not only care for him and to want him, but to *shield* him somehow . . .

And then it hit her, as he ran his fingers down her spine, and his mouth parted over hers, growing more insistent. She wanted to *love* this fierce, powerful king of Dorjhalon—to whom she was Bound—who had never known true love in his entire existence.

Lorcan claimed to want her body, heart, and soul, and though she was frightened, she believed him. And somehow, despite everything, she wanted all of him, as well. This male who kissed her with such strength and yet such gentleness, who touched her body as if he'd never held anything more precious.

"I found it!" Ceren's shout shattered the stolen moment, and they abruptly broke apart.

She dashed back into the room a moment later, her eyes wide, seemingly too excited to notice how flustered they were as she announced, "I found the answer!"

THIRTY-TWO

CEREN WANDERED DEEPER INTO THE TEMPLE, GIVING Evelayn and Lorcan the time alone that they so obviously needed. She still wasn't sure how she felt about Evelayn Binding herself to him . . . but Ceren was also learning there was much more to Lorcan than she'd originally thought. The longer she spent with him—and with him and Evelayn together—the more she wondered if perhaps there was a possibility of a happy future for them—provided they all survived this ill-fated journey.

Even just the brief memory of what she'd left behind—a flash of Quinlen's face, and Saoirse's downy-soft hair, and Clive's mischievous giggle—hit her like a punch to the gut. Ceren had to force the thought of her family far, far away, or else she would break down entirely. She missed them more fiercely than she thought possible, so much that it was an actual physical pain laced with the fear that she would never see them again.

"Focus," she commanded herself, inhaling slowly and blowing the air back out through her mouth to regain control of her quickly escalating emotions. *Find the answer, and maybe you* will *get back home to them.*

The first three rooms they'd searched had been of normal size and completely empty. But as Ceren continued down the dim hallway, she saw a much wider doorway at the end of it and felt a faint tug, as if something was beckoning her inside. Her heart rate sped up as she hesitantly walked toward it, ignoring the other smaller rooms to her left and right.

The chamber was massive, she realized when she drew close enough, and there seemed to be a faint glow emanating from within. After their experience with the glowing water earlier that day, Ceren was suddenly nervous. But they had found no answers yet, and the pull that bade her enter the room grew stronger the closer she got. Something in there was calling to her . . . and something inside her responded.

Taking a deep breath, she walked in and her mouth parted in awe. It was a circular chamber, the walls made entirely of carvings: scenes of celebration and scenes of death and violence. Some of the figures were familiar—they looked like Draíolon—and some were unfamiliar, creatures and beings she'd never seen before. The room was again barren of any furniture or other items, but in the center, there was a stone structure that looked like a well. Parts of it were broken as if an explosion had blasted through it. That faint glow she'd noticed came from the depths of the well.

Hesitantly, Ceren moved toward it. Did it hold more of the Water of Life? That would certainly explain the glow, and it made sense for a well to have water in it. But when she drew close enough, she bent over to glance down and had to quickly back up again, her heart thumping. It was *deep*. So deep she hadn't been able to see the bottom—just an abyss of darkness, broken only by the strange glow that somehow shone through the darkness without dispelling it.

Ceren turned back to the carvings, inspecting them more closely. They were remarkably detailed. A few on the wall farthest from the doorway were caved in. Something had happened in this room. Maybe all of the rooms. It almost seemed as if . . .

And that's when she realized what she was looking at. Ceren slowly turned in a circle, her eyes growing wider and wider. And then she spun and dashed back the way she'd come, shouting, "I found it!"

She rounded the corner to the room where Evelayn and Lorcan stood only a few feet apart. Ceren ignored the obvious signs that she'd interrupted a private moment to announce, "I found the answer!"

"Where? What is it?" Lorcan was quicker than Evelayn to regain his composure.

"I'll show you."

They followed her into the chamber and she gestured at the walls.

"The carvings?" Evelayn sounded confused.

"I thought that's all they were at first, too. But step back. Look at them as a whole."

Ceren waited while Evelayn and Lorcan slowly turned in a circle, taking in the entire room—all except the section that was broken.

"It's a story." Evelayn's eyes were wide.

"I think it's more than a story," Lorcan commented quietly.

"What do you mean?"

"I think it's a depiction of history. Of how the Ancients stole the original power from this temple." He pointed at the well. "From right there."

Their entire group was gathered in the round chamber, trying to piece together all the elements of the carvings and the history they detailed.

"I think it starts here, with these males and females guarding the well. It looks like they lived here, in the temple?" Letha pointed and Evelayn came over to look at the same section. "See how the building is intact? And there *was* furniture here then, it looks like."

Evelayn nodded beside her. "I think you're right. The forest also looks like it was beautiful back then." The carvings weren't in color, but the forest was depicted with flowers and sunshine, birds and trees lush with life. There was no sign of the encroaching mist, the constant gray light, or the Dheagmadra.

"But this—here—that's an attack, don't you agree?" Ceren stood to their right. Letha shuddered at the depiction of massive creatures from myth and legend tearing through the walls of the temple, and tunneling up through the ground into this very room. Some Letha recognized from stories she'd heard as a youngling, such as the serpent with two heads—one that of a snake and one that of a Draíolon—but others she'd never seen before. Such as the creature that was larger than a horse with wings, and talons on its feet, and a mouth sharpened into the deadly point of an eagle's beak.

"Those are *all* of the Ancients," Lorcan commented quietly. "And that tunnel came from the Sliabán Mountains." He suddenly turned and began inspecting the ground around them. Letha ignored his odd behavior to continue following the carvings around the room. She'd heard about the Ancients as a youngling—the creatures that had supposedly inhabited Lachalonia before all others, even Draíolon. But she'd never known there were so many. The Ancients had broken into the temple and fought the males and females who lived there—they looked like Draíolon to her—to reach the well. It seemed as though they'd been trying to get to something inside it; in fact, the next panel of carvings showed a massive half spider, half female using her sticky legs and spider silk to drop herself into it and then coming back out with something gripped in her hands.

"That's Máthair Damhán," Evelayn gasped. "And what is she holding?"

"Those lines coming out from her hands . . . is that supposed to be Light?" Lothar leaned in closer.

"I think you're right," Letha agreed excitedly. "And that looks like clouds . . . Maybe it's supposed to be Darkness?"

"It's power," Evelayn whispered. "This is where the power originated from. By the Light, *they* stole it."

There was a caw from above them and Letha glanced up, realizing Lorcan had shifted into his hawk form and was hovering near the domed ceiling of the massive room.

He swooped toward them and shifted back into his Draíolon form.

"I found it," Lorcan said triumphantly.

"Found what?" Tanvir asked.

He strode over to a section of floor and bent down to grab the massive stone slab.

"What are you doing?" Ceren shared a confused look with Letha.

"Lothar, come help me."

The brothers worked together while the rest looked on for several long moments. Just when Letha was about to suggest they quit, the slab of stone came loose with a low grinding sound that echoed strangely. Rather than the dirt she'd expected to see, there appeared to be a gaping opening beneath it.

"You want us to dig our way to the White Peak?" Tanvir groused.

"No, I want us to walk. Maybe even jog." He grinned at their confusion. "It's a tunnel. *The* tunnel. Come look."

Sure enough, there was a path leading down into the dark depths of the earth.

"How did you find this? And how do you know where it leads?" Tanvir sounded as baffled and concerned as the rest of them.

"Sometimes all you need is a little perspective." Lorcan

pointed at the lines that ran all across the ground. "From here it looks like a normal floor, but from above, I realized it was a map of this temple, including the tunnel the Ancients used to attack them." He gestured to the dark opening. "This will take us to the Sliabán Mountains and the White Peak, hopefully far enough to avoid the Dheagmadra."

"I'm not sure I want to trust lines on a floor to guide us," Tanvir hedged. "Especially when we don't know who—or what—made these carvings. For all we know, this could be a trap."

"Then stay here or take your chances with the Dheagmadra." Evelayn stepped up beside Lorcan, the musty scent of disuse and the loamy fragrance of earth rising from the tunnel. "But the Spirit Harbinger said we would find the answer, and the only one we've found is right here. I'm going down there."

"So am I," Ceren agreed.

Lothar also stepped toward his brother. That left Tanvir and Letha.

"I can't face those . . . *things* . . . again. Maybe the Spirit Harbinger is the one who made the carvings. Either way, I'd rather risk the tunnel." Letha looked pleadingly at Tanvir.

He regarded her stubbornly for a few long moments, but eventually sighed. "All right."

"We should still try to be as silent as possible," Lorcan warned before descending, "so we don't attract the attention of the Dheagmadra. They might be able to dig down to us if they realize we're in the earth beneath them."

Evelayn shuddered at the thought of not only being beneath the earth but also having those creatures digging through it to devour them. Accordingly, they were completely silent as they descended the steps onto the earthen floor of the tunnel. It was just large enough to accommodate them—all except Lorcan, who was the tallest and had to stoop to avoid hitting his head.

He and Lothar both summoned a bit of shadowflame, the dark fire barely enough to dispel the blackness, so they could see where to step. The group stayed close together. Evelayn couldn't let herself think about what had happened between her and Lorcan, knowing it would raise emotions the others would no doubt be able to scent, giving away the tumult within her.

But it was incredibly difficult when her lips still burned from his kiss and the rest of her burned from how badly she wanted more.

Lorcan abruptly glanced back at her. Evelayn quickly looked away, her cheeks hot, forcing her thoughts to safer avenues . . . such as avoiding being eaten alive by Dheagmadra and the coming confrontation with Máthair Damhán.

Time seemed to drag by, a slow, interminable march, made worse by the never-ending blackness and the tightness of the tunnel. It wound up and down, left and right, leaving them no way of knowing if they were headed in the correct direction or not. Evelayn prayed Lorcan had interpreted the map correctly. If only she had the ability to shift, she, too, could have flown above them and studied the markings. But instead, they had to trust him.

Which, no matter how foolish it might make her, Evelayn realized suddenly that she did.

She'd been walking a step behind Lorcan, but she quickened her pace just enough to come alongside him. He looked over at her questioningly, but since she couldn't speak, for fear of being heard by the Dheagmadra or by the others, she merely reached for his hand, weaving her fingers through his. A smile unlike any she'd ever seen changed his face entirely. He'd always been blindingly attractive, but in a commanding, severe way. As he squeezed her hand back, this smile softened his entire face and made his eyes glow. The shadowflame that floated above his other hand even brightened slightly as they continued their seemingly endless march toward the White Peak.

At one point they heard an unearthly howl above them, through the soil and tree roots that tangled in the earthen walls all around them, and Evelayn's heart jumped up into her throat. Lorcan motioned for them to speed up slightly.

Not long after, Evelayn started to notice something . . . different. Something she hadn't felt in so very, very long that it took her a moment to recognize the sensation surrounding them.

It was *power*. Gradually at first but steadily increasing in strength as they pressed forward. It flowed through and around them, a river that she could sense but couldn't access.

She didn't even realize her grip had tightened on Lorcan's hand until he squeezed hers back and murmured, "I feel it, too. We're getting close."

Sure enough, it was only a few minutes later that the pathway ended at a ladder.

"We made it?" Lothar whispered.

"We have no choice but up," Tanvir replied, his voice hushed, "so we will soon find out."

"I'll go first." Lorcan had already released Evelayn's hand and grabbed on to the rungs in front of him. "Wait a moment and I'll make sure it's safe."

They all watched as he quickly ascended the ladder and strained to push aside the stone at the top, stuck from centuries of disuse. Finally, it gave way, and he disappeared.

When he didn't immediately return, Evelayn refused to allow herself to worry. After all, there were no sounds of a struggle. But as the seconds turned to minutes, her stomach twisted into a knot of fear.

"I'm going to go up there," she finally said.

"And do what?" Ceren whispered sharply, grabbing her arm. "If Lorcan can't handle whatever is up there, what could you possibly do?"

Her friend's words were like an icy blast, reminding her of how she was so utterly helpless. The power surging all around them had almost made her forget she couldn't access it.

"I'll go," Lothar offered.

"No." Letha's response was immediate, and she quickly added, "That would leave us without anyone to defend us."

Lothar's eyebrows raised, but he nodded. "That's a good point."

Evelayn couldn't be sure in the uncertain light from Lothar's shadowflame, but it looked like Letha was blushing. That was an interesting development. If they all somehow managed to survive this, Evelayn was very curious to see if anything came of what seemed to be a burgeoning connection.

And then they heard the sound of Lorcan coming back.

Evelayn looked up with a smile, but her relief turned to terror when, rather than Lorcan's face, she found herself staring up at Máthair Damhán herself.

THIRTY-THREE

D O COME UP. I DON'T APPRECIATE BEING KEPT
waiting."

Ceren stared at the Ancient, frozen in fear. Máthair
Damhán's voice was vaguely feminine, but her words were
clipped and accompanied by a faint clicking of the sharp pincers
that curled over her ink-black lips.

"Where's Lorcan?" Evelayn's voice was admirably steady.

"He's waiting up here. I suggest you hurry before I grow
impatient."

Ceren couldn't tear her eyes away from Máthair Damhán,
from the monstrously stunning sight of her. The lower half of
her face was almost that of a Draíolon, except for the pincers,
and her main eyes were larger than Ceren's and entirely black.
But the arachnid portion of her head sent a shiver down Ceren's
spine—the two other pairs of smaller eyes, the ropes of black hair
growing from the ridges that made up her skull.

"Why didn't *he* come back?" Evelayn demanded, still refusing to climb the ladder.

The trapdoor opened wider and a sudden blast of light tore through the air, exploding into the soil at Ceren's feet, knocking her to the ground.

"Ceren!"

Ceren vaguely heard Evelayn's cry over the ringing in her ears. Gradually she became aware of a sharp pain in her right leg. When the residual flash of light cleared from her eyes, she saw Evelayn kneeling beside her, staring down at her legs. Ceren was afraid to look, based on the expression twisting the queen's features. She must have been burned—and badly. The stinging pain grew worse with every labored breath she took.

"I did warn you."

Evelayn's eyes flashed when she looked up at the Ancient again. "How did you do that?"

"Quite a bit has changed since we last met, Little Queen. *You* are powerless, and I . . . Well, thanks to years of studying your stone, I am not."

Evelayn stiffened with anger beside her, but Ceren was overcome by a terrible sense of hopelessness. If the Ancient had captured *Lorcan*, there really would be no escaping their doom this time.

"Now come out of that pit before I strike to kill."

"If only we had some of that magic water with us . . . We should have all filled our skins with it. Since we're obviously not going to survive this, that Harbinger's threat doesn't seem very valid anymore." Letha's humorless comment made Ceren smile despite the tears that pricked her eyes. She'd escaped death too many times on this quest. Letha was right—they weren't going to be able to do it again. Though she valiantly tried to hold them back, a few tears slipped out, sliding down her cheeks as her thoughts inevitably turned to Quinlen and their younglings again.

"Here, I'll help you." Evelayn climbed to her feet and then bent to grab Ceren's arms as Letha stepped up to the ladder and began to climb. "This isn't over yet," she murmured as she leaned in close. "Don't lose hope."

Ceren nodded, even though she knew Evelayn was only saying it to try to make her feel better. "You're right," she lied in return. She finally looked down and had to fight a surge of nausea at the sight of her legs. Her pants were burned almost completely away, exposing the charred flesh beneath.

"Put as much of your weight on me as you can," Evelayn instructed as she helped pull Ceren up to her feet. Ceren swallowed the cry of agony that threatened to escape when she tried to walk. *I can do this. I can be as strong as Evelayn.*

Together, they moved forward, right behind Tanvir and Lothar.

"One rung at a time. I'll be right behind you if you need help." Evelayn stepped back for Ceren to go first.

She gritted her teeth together and reached for the rung. *One at a time,* she repeated with each painful movement that took her closer to the Ancient who had done this to her. Evelayn had to help push her over the top edge, and then they were suddenly both free of the tunnel, only to find themselves surrounded by a dozen of Máthair Damhán's daughters.

Evelayn helped Ceren to her feet once more while she frantically scanned the cavern for Lorcan. The daughters surrounding them were of various sizes but looked every bit as dangerous as their creator. A couple were nearly as large as Máthair Damhán herself and had similarly Draíolon features and arms and hands. But most of the others were somewhat smaller and almost entirely arachnid. Lorcan, however, was nowhere to be seen.

"Where is he?" Evelayn demanded again.

Máthair Damhán's gaze pierced her from where she rose above them on her eight massive legs. "I have to admit, I wasn't sure he could do it," the Ancient said.

Evelayn remembered her scent from their last encounter— the malice and darkness and perhaps even a little bit of decay. "Where. Is. He."

Máthair Damhán moved, revealing Lorcan lying on the ground, bound entirely by spider silk, even his mouth. His head was turned to her, his silver eyes wide and full of regret. His conduit stoned burned crimson in his forehead.

"Lorcan!" Evelayn cried, lunging forward only to have Máthair Damhán step over the king, her bulbous body directly above him.

"Swans are such loyal creatures, wouldn't you say?"

"Excuse me?"

"Of all the creatures you could have imprinted on, it was a swan. Docile, useless . . . but loyal. So very loyal." Máthair

Damhán made a terrible noise that was part screech and part clicking of her pincers, and her daughters moved toward them. All at once, they sent silk flying from their spinnerets at all the Draíolon except Evelayn.

Lothar shot a massive blast of shadowflame in defense, his abilities bolstered from being so close to the Immortal Tree, where all the power in Lachalonia originated, burning away the silk before it could bind him and forcing daughters to scuttle out of its way. Máthair Damhán made another noise and then lifted one leg. Evelayn realized what she was going to do an instant before the Ancient stabbed Lorcan with it.

"Lorcan!" Evelayn's scream was drowned out by his muffled howl of pain.

"Do that again and he suffers." Máthair Damhán leveled her unnerving gaze on Lothar.

He slowly lowered his hand, and the daughter launched more silk at him; this time he allowed himself to be bound, his gaze on the blood soaking through the white spider silk encasing Lorcan's body.

Evelayn was shaking inside but valiantly tried to hide it by clenching her hands into fists.

"Now"—Máthair Damhán turned to Evelayn—"it's time for you to do me that favor you promised."

THIRTY-FOUR

E VELAYN STARED INTO LORCAN'S EYES, REFUSING TO meet Máthair Damhán's gaze. She couldn't bear to see him—the powerful king of Dorjhalon—so helpless and injured.

And then it hit her. "Wait . . . how did you entrap him?" The only thing that stopped Lothar from continuing to blast away at her daughters was Máthair Damhán's threat to hurt his brother further. She remembered how instantaneous and strong her power had been when she'd come to the White Peak before . . . and Lorcan was already incredibly powerful. This close to the Immortal Tree, he should have been as close to invincible as possible.

"It would seem the Dark King cares for you, Little Queen, enough to offer himself as a sacrifice to protect you."

"I don't understand." Evelayn couldn't fathom it—if he *wasn't* powerful enough to defeat Máthair Damhán, he could have shifted into his hawk form and at least escaped. He, who always touted his duty as king to do what he must as most important. Surrendering without a fight—leaving himself vulnerable—didn't make any sense.

"You aren't required to understand."

"Then what *do* you require?" Anger warred with helplessness within her. Evelayn could sense the power all around her, felt it pulsing under her feet, in the air, trying to enter her body; but without a conduit, she had no access to it. She *had* to get her stone back . . . somehow.

"Ah, that is the question. The one that has haunted you ever since our first meeting." Máthair Damhán's pincers clicked, and her daughters moved closer to Tanvir, Letha, Ceren, and Lothar. They all remained on their feet, wrapped in spider silk. "That's why you've returned, is it not? To fulfill the debt you owe me in return for my gift to you."

"I have come to reclaim my conduit stone." Evelayn lifted her chin, despite the fear that coursed through her body.

The Ancient hissed. "No, Little Queen, you will not be taking this back." Máthair Damhán reached up and unclasped a thin chain, which Evelayn hadn't noticed before, from around her neck. She held it aloft, and there it was—her diamond conduit stone, dangling in the air, winking in the wavering light that illuminated the cave. "*You* are going to give *me* its mate." She pointed at Lorcan, lying beneath her on the dank floor, his conduit stone flashing scarlet from the power flowing through his veins, woven into the very marrow of his bones.

"*No,*" Evelayn breathed, even as muffled sounds of protest were quickly cut off from behind her.

Lorcan closed his eyes, but the defeat she'd seen in their silver depths before he did turned her cold. Why did he lie there—why didn't he break free and kill Máthair Damhán? He was directly beneath her belly, the most vulnerable part of her body.

"The swan queen . . . so very loyal. And now you will prove it." Máthair Damhán scuttled back so that Lorcan was exposed, then she bent all eight of her legs and lowered her bulbous body to reach down and slice away the silk over his mouth with one long, sharp talon. "Tell her to carve out your stone and give it to me—as you did to her."

"No," Evelayn whispered.

"I need him alive to be able to access the power in his conduit stone once you remove it from him—but that doesn't mean I can't make him writhe in agony." Máthair Damhán lifted one leg and let it hover over his abdomen, the threat clear with the blood still drying on his leg where she'd already stabbed him once. "Being this close to the Immortal Tree will enable his body to heal so quickly, I can get very creative if necessary. Shall we see if we can make him scream?"

"This won't work," Lorcan said roughly. "We are Bound, but she doesn't care for me that way. And she knows better than to give you control of all the power in Lachalonia."

"Your lies are not befitting a king. The female reeks of her fear for you—and of her affection." Máthair Damhán lowered her sharp claws until they punctured through the silk, and then pressed a bit harder so that they pierced Lorcan's stomach, agonizingly slowly. His head flung back, his back arching in pain, but the muscles in his jaw flexed and he didn't so much as utter a noise. "You will remove his stone and give it to me . . . Or shall I continue?"

"Don't . . . do . . . it . . ." he panted as the arachnoid withdrew her talons, now dripping with his blood.

"I forgot to mention: Since you were so kind as to bring extra targets with you, every time you force me to ask again, one of them dies."

The Ancient made another horrific noise. Time seemed to slow as Evelayn whirled around with a cry. Lorcan shouted—there was a blast of shadowflame from behind Evelayn that exploded into one of the daughters, throwing the creature against the stone wall—but it was too late. Two other daughters attacked at once. One slit Lothar's throat while the other stabbed him through the gut with her massive, razor-sharp pincers. And then a blast of light ripped through his chest for good measure. Even this close to the Tree, there was no chance of his survival.

A scream tore from Evelayn's throat. Letha lunged toward Lothar but stumbled and fell to her knees with a half-broken sob when he crumpled to the ground.

There was a bellow of fury from behind her, and Evelayn twisted back to see Lorcan lying on his stomach now, having broken the top half of his body free of the spider silk, struggling against Máthair Damhán, who pushed him down with four of her legs. She lowered her body to grab his long white hair, the talons she had in place of nails digging into his scalp as she yanked his head up. "*Stop.* I need you both alive, but the Little Queen won't heal as nicely as you."

To Evelayn's dismay, Lorcan immediately stopped struggling. She was still reeling from Lothar's sudden, violent death. Letha had bent over him, letting her forehead drop to rest on his, unable to touch him any other way. The others were in visible shock; Ceren had begun to cry.

Evelayn's chest was tight with the tears she refused to allow to the surface. They had made a promise to the Spirit Harbinger to return that which was taken—which meant they somehow had to return their power.

Perhaps this was the only way.

"Do you wish to lose another of—"

"I'll do it," Evelayn said.

"What was that, Little Queen?"

"NO!"

Evelayn ignored Lorcan and raised her voice: "I'll cut out his stone."

THIRTY-FIVE

ÁTHAIR DAMHÁN FLIPPED LORCAN OVER, AND THE king let her, still not fighting back. She had claimed she needed him alive, but there was a deadness in his eyes that hit Evelayn like a punch to the stomach. She'd pushed through crippling grief before, she could do it again. Somehow, she would figure out a way to save the rest of them. She just needed a bit of time.

"I will do it," Evelayn repeated, "but first I have some questions for you."

"You dare to make a demand of me?"

"You can't take his stone yourself, or you would have done it by now. You need me for some reason. Just as you needed him to take mine. And I want to know why."

Máthair Damhán moved toward her, but Evelayn held her ground, even though she was shaking inside.

"Do not try my patience, Little Queen." The Ancient stared down at her with all six of her inky black eyes.

"Somehow, you have accessed my power through my stone. Once I give you his, you'll have complete control and all the Draíolon will be powerless against you." Evelayn spoke quickly, hoping to keep her distracted long enough to come up with some sort of plan. "I know I am not going to be allowed to leave this cave alive. What harm is there in answering my questions first?"

Máthair Damhán's pincers clicked together again, but this time she seemed to be considering, not giving a signal. After several tense moments of silence while Evelayn waited with bated breath, the Ancient responded, "We've attempted to get our power back from the Draíolon before. But we were unsuccessful. When other Ancients tried to do it themselves, the living stones of a royal killed them. And we learned that a common Draíolon wasn't enough. He did as we bade; he tried to get to the royals for us, but he failed."

"Are you speaking of Drystan?" Evelayn's eyebrows raised; that wasn't at all what she'd expected. "The first Draíolon to kill another?"

"Wasted millennia," Máthair Damhán spat. "The Choíche moon rises only once every thousand years. We waited and planned and found an impressionable young male to do our bidding. And all for *nothing*. The others who remained gave up, but not me. I came here and waited. For thousands of years, conserving my strength, prolonging my life by staying near the Tree. It was only too easy to convince Bain of what he had to do when he came seeking the Immortal Tree for more power and found me instead. And what fortuitous timing, with the Choíche moon approaching again in just over two decades. I only had to be patient a little longer."

Evelayn felt Lorcan's shock reverberate through her, echoing her own, but she couldn't afford to focus on that—on the realization that perhaps Máthair Damhán had been the one to put the idea of war in Bain's head. That she had been behind *all* of it.

"What does the moon have to do with it?" Evelayn asked instead.

"You Draíolon think yourselves so wise, so knowledgeable. But you don't even know your own history."

Evelayn could scent the others' terror and confusion—their grief. It threatened to distract her, but she forced herself to stay focused. To keep thinking as the Ancient spoke. "Then tell me. What is it we have forgotten?"

"In the beginning of all things, there was only Light and Darkness. Infinite power from which came day and night, summer and winter, this world and all the creatures in it. The Choíche moon is the one time when the seeds of that power can be stolen—and claimed—by another race. Your ancestors attacked us on a night just like the one coming tomorrow and stole our power. You were weaker than we, but you outnumbered us like ants swarming from their hole. You came in never-ending waves, dying in droves, but two slipped past us—a male and a female. They stole the Seeds of Power that belonged to us and planted them here. The Immortal Tree was born and we were left powerless while the male and female hunted down as many of us as they could and slaughtered those who weren't able to escape them."

"You say we are ignorant, but we know more than you think." Evelayn knew she was risking the Ancient's wrath but pressed on anyway. "You act as though you always had claim on the power before it was stolen by the Draíolon, but *you* are lying. You stole it first. It never should have belonged to *any* of us."

Máthair Damhán hissed at her and lunged forward as if to attack but abruptly stopped, her clawed hand inches from Evelayn's face. Her heart galloped beneath her ribs, but Evelayn held her ground.

Lorcan lurched up, watching her warily, the bitter tang of grief mixed with fear so strong it burned Evelayn's nose. If *he* was frightened, she should have been immobilized by terror.

But she had finally come up with a plan. She needed these answers.

"You know nothing of which you speak!" said Máthair Damhán. "That power was ours to wield—until the Guardians cut us off from it. They had access to endless strength, immortality, and power beyond what you can possibly imagine, and they never touched it. They didn't deserve it and they shouldn't have kept it from us."

"The Guardians?"

"Weak, pathetic Draíolon, such as yourselves, who discovered the location of the source of power in our world, hidden in the Water of Life. They built a temple around it, cutting us off from the water and the seeds. They appointed themselves Guardians and lived there. We could have overtaken them and continued to partake of the Water of Life as we had before they came. But instead, we bided our time, waiting for the Choíche moon so that my brothers and sisters—the other Ancients who should have existed forever—could *claim* the power that was rightfully ours.

We never wanted to be reliant on the Water, but nor should any living thing cut us off from it, ever again."

Evelayn focused on her fear, hoping the scent of it drowned out any other emotions Máthair Damhán might notice. "Were the seeds from a tree, too, then? How did you steal it?"

"It was the *original* source, deep in the earth, you fool. There was no Tree until the Draíolon stole the seeds and thoughtlessly planted them."

Evelayn thought of the well they'd found, of the glow coming from somewhere deep, deep beneath them. Of the healing power of the Water of Life they'd used to save Lorcan. Of the depiction of Máthair Damhán herself going down into that well and emerging with Light and Darkness gripped in her hands. "But if you only took seeds . . . does that mean there is still more power there—at the original source?"

"Of course." Máthair Damhán was growing visibly irritated, and Evelayn knew her time was nearly up. But she still needed more. "The Seeds of Power are the source of all the power in our world. We only took one of each—Light and Dark. That was all that was needed."

"If that wasn't all there was, why didn't you go back and steal more after the Draíolon took yours? Or find some other way to access it?"

"Because the Guardians were somehow transformed after we attacked the temple and stole the seeds, and the entire forest surrounding it was cursed. They became the Spirit Harbingers whose power far exceeds any other beings' in this world. They can take the soul right out of your body. If any of us had tried to access the temple again, they would have killed us immediately."

As the pieces finally fell into place, Evelayn shivered. "Only the Gods could have given them such power."

"If *the Gods* even exist, they left the original power to the Ancients," Máthair Damhán snarled. "And they should have left it—and us—alone!"

Evelayn shuddered but pressed on, despite the Ancient's rising temper. Only the knowledge that Máthair Damhán needed them alive gave her the courage to speak once more. "What if we found a way to share the power with everything in our world? What if we tried returning it to the source—where it was intended to be?"

Máthair Damhán's hand lashed out, and this time she grabbed Evelayn by the throat, choking her as she lifted her off her feet, up into the air toward her head, so that the Ancient's foul breath hit her when she hissed, "Don't think I don't know what you are trying to do. *We* made that tunnel—we used it to break into the temple and steal the power. The Spirit Harbingers have more than enough power; they will not be getting any more back." Evelayn clawed at the fingers wrapped around her neck, desperate for air. Then, mere seconds before Evelayn would have lost consciousness, Máthair Damhán threw her toward Lorcan; her body slammed into the stone floor with a sickening crunch and a blinding flash of pain in her left shoulder.

"Evelayn!"

Ignoring Lorcan's shout and the excruciating pain that made

her think she'd probably broken at least a bone or two, Evelayn forced herself to rise up onto her good hand and her knees. Something clattered beside her and she glanced over to see a knife on the ground, the bone-white handle and blade gleaming in the incandescent light from the opening to her right.

"Why?" Her voice was unsteady, and the room spun dizzily around her when she looked at the Ancient once more. But she had to know this one last thing. "Why do you want the power back so badly?"

Máthair Damhán bared her sharp black teeth. "With that power, we were immortal. But after you stole it from us, the first of all creations, my brothers and sisters, have slowly died off, all of them except me. I am the last. And I will not be taken like they were. I *will* have my power—my immortality—back."

"You're afraid to die? That's what this was all for? You have killed so many—you've driven wars that slaughtered thousands— all so *you* didn't have to die?" Beyond Máthair Damhán, Evelayn could see Lothar's lifeless body on the ground, the others standing there, watching her with terror in their red-rimmed eyes.

"What care have I for your worthless lives? You stole my entire family from me. You all deserve to suffer as I do."

"But . . . don't you wish to be with them again? Because of you and the war you started with Bain, I lost my family, too. Of course I want to live a full life here; I want to wear my body out with years of love and laughter and work, but someday I want to be with them again in the Final Light." Despite herself, tears gathered in her eyes as she thought of her mother and father, taken from her by a mad king, driven to desperation by his misguided wish to protect his family and pushed by the avarice of the creature in front of her.

"A fool's wish. There is nothing beyond this sphere. We simply cease to be. And I will not go quietly."

"You're wrong. I know they are there. I know it," Evelayn repeated. But a terrible schism of doubt cracked open in her heart. Máthair Damhán had existed for millennia. If she didn't believe in the Final Light, was Evelayn a fool to do so?

"Take the stone now or another one dies!" Máthair Damhán suddenly shrieked.

Evelayn cringed away from her, almost expecting another blow. When one didn't immediately come, she grabbed the dagger in her good hand, her left arm hanging limp and useless at her side, every movement causing it to throb with pain.

Mother, she prayed silently as she turned to Lorcan, *if you are truly there somewhere, help me. Help me right now. Help* us . . . *somehow.*

She took a deep breath and crawled over to where Lorcan lay waiting for her. The defeat on his face wrenched at her heart. She gripped the dagger tightly, lifting it slightly, but then paused. Lorcan flinched in anticipation but did nothing else to try and stop her.

"Let them go," she said without turning.

"*What?*"

"Let them all go—give them a chance to live and I will give you the stone."

"I will have them *all* killed!" Máthair Damhán roared, and Evelayn flinched—but she didn't back down.

"Fine—then kill them. And I will never carve out his stone for you. You can kill both of us, too. Because there *is* a Final Light, and my mother and father are there waiting for me. If you kill all of them, then I have no more reason to wish to live. Or to give you what you want." Evelayn took the dagger and, rather than lifting it over Lorcan's head, turned it on herself, holding it above her heart.

"Stop!" Máthair Damhán lunged at her, but Evelayn pressed it into her skin, just hard enough to draw blood, and the Ancient skidded to a halt.

"For some reason, you need me alive—and you need me to do this. So let them go—safely. *Now*."

Máthair Damhán clicked and screeched in that otherworldly language of hers, and the daughters cut away the spider silk binding Tanvir, Letha, and Ceren, then backed away.

"The exit is through there." Máthair Damhán pointed to a different tunnel Evelayn hadn't noticed until then, across from the one with the light.

"Ev, no. You can't do this." Ceren was weeping as she limped toward Evelayn on her burned legs.

"Go now before I change my mind!" Máthair Damhán bellowed, her fury twisting any similarity to the Draíolon out of her monstrous face entirely.

"Go, Ceren. Go back to Quinlen and your younglings. *Please*," Evelayn pleaded, tears burning the backs of her eyes.

"I love you, Ev." Ceren's words were almost indecipherable through her sobs.

"I love you, too," Evelayn choked out. "Thank you for being the sister I never had."

Lorcan lifted his head toward Ceren. "Find my mother for me. Find her and tell her I'm sorry—that I never meant for Lothar to"—his voice broke before continuing—"that this wasn't how it was supposed to end."

Ceren looked to him, to the male whom Evelayn knew she'd spent so many years hating and plotting against, and nodded. "I will. I promise."

Tanvir had to drag Letha away from Lothar's body. "We have to go," he urged her, glancing at the murderous expressions on the daughters' faces. He paused to take Ceren's arm, then pulled her toward the exit. His eyes met Evelayn's and her heart constricted. She'd truly loved him once, and even though he'd hurt and betrayed her, she still didn't want him to die here, like Lothar had. He nodded, as if he understood the feelings in her heart.

I'm sorry, he mouthed, and she knew he truly did mean it.

Once they'd gone, Máthair Damhán turned back to her, and Evelayn lowered the dagger.

"I did what you asked. Now do what you said you would, Little Swan Queen. It's not too late for me to send my daughters after them."

Evelayn nodded and turned to Lorcan. "I'm sorry," she whispered, and then she lifted the dagger.

THIRTY-SIX

L ORCAN STARED UP AT EVELAYN AND WAITED FOR THE pain. She bent closer to him and murmured something so quietly he almost wasn't sure he'd heard her correctly. But it sounded like she said, "Take down the Tree."

And then she cut the stone he'd been born with out of his forehead.

The pain was excruciating—as bad as being stabbed by Máthair Damhán. But the realization that he'd failed so entirely, coupled with the immediate loss of his power as Evelayn lifted the stone from his skin, was nearly unbearable. He almost wished for her to plunge the dagger into his chest as hot blood ran down his face. As she'd said, Máthair Damhán was surely going to kill them both once she got what she wanted—or keep them prisoners here, as she'd done to him ten years ago, but this time forever.

Evelayn lifted the stone above her head. Máthair Damhán scuttled toward them, triumph lighting her black eyes, her inky lips stretched open in a disturbing imitation of a grin.

And then Evelayn threw it as hard as she could at the opening that glowed with light.

"RUN!" she shouted, jumping to her feet.

Lorcan stared at her for a split second in shock, then he, too, launched to his feet and sprinted after the wild and brilliant queen he'd Bound himself to. Máthair Damhán screeched, an unearthly sound of fury. He could hear all eight of her legs slapping the ground as she raced after them.

Take down the Tree, she'd said . . . What was Evelayn hoping to do?

They barreled down the tunnel, the light growing ever brighter as the power all around them increased until he felt as though he could breathe it in, snatch it from the very air, and use it, even without his stone. His body still healed rapidly, perhaps just from being so close to the source of their power. When he saw his stone winking ahead of them, he stooped and grabbed it up off the ground mid-stride. Once before he'd come here, to the Immortal Tree, to reclaim his power. But it had taken time— time they didn't have.

"Help me destroy it!" she called over her shoulder.

"Destroy what?" But Lorcan had a sinking feeling he suddenly knew what her plan was.

"The Tree! If we cut it down, maybe that will return the power to its original source."

"What about Máthair Damhán?" Lorcan glanced over his shoulder, but the Ancient was gone.

"The tunnel is too narrow. She can't follow us."

"There's more than one way to reach the Tree . . ." Lorcan

warned, but then they rounded the corner and Evelayn skidded to a halt, her mouth hanging slightly open in awe.

Before them rose the Immortal Tree.

It was taller even than Máthair Damhán, part blinding daylight and part shimmering night. Flashes of lightning and lashes of shadow surged out of it in random bursts of power. Its beauty was beyond Lorcan's power of description, so he'd never even tried to explain it to any male or female. When he tore his eyes away to look at Evelayn, he saw the same reverence and awe in her face he'd experienced when he first saw it—but hers was tempered by grief. Her stunning violet eyes were bloodshot from the tears she wouldn't let herself shed. But he felt it, scented it. The sorrow, the desperation. Emotions that echoed through the gaping wound within him following Lothar's senseless death. They'd already lost so much; destroying the tree would be akin to destroying a piece of themselves—no different from cutting off a limb, or gouging out a piece of their hearts. Perhaps even worse. The power they'd been born to wield surrounded them, filling every space of the cavern where the Immortal Tree had grown without sunlight or water for millennia.

"Quickly," Evelayn finally said, squaring her shoulders and brushing furiously at the tears that finally had escaped, slipping down her cheeks. But Lorcan grabbed her hand and pulled her toward him. She looked up at him and he couldn't help but remember the kiss they'd shared—the hope he'd felt, something he'd given up on long ago as a youngling. He brushed her hair back from her face, trying to memorize the way she looked, the way she felt. Because Máthair Damhán was coming, he felt it. And if Evelayn was determined to do this, then he would help her.

"I want you to know one thing first," he whispered, running his thumb along her lips, wishing he had time to kiss her, to hold her, "that I love you, Evelayn, queen of Éadrolan. And I would do anything for you if you asked it. Even this."

And then he handed her the sword he'd grabbed from the ground where Tanvir had tossed it, pushed her toward the Tree, and shifted into his hawk form, just as Máthair Damhán burst into the cavern from the other side.

Evelayn could scarcely see through her tears, could barely breathe past the tightness in her chest as Lorcan's words pounded through her skull—words she'd been stunned to hear and hadn't been given time to respond to.

She didn't know how he shifted with his stone gone and his power stripped, but there was no time to question it as Máthair Damhán hurtled a blast of Light at her. She flung herself forward and barely avoided being struck.

"What are you *doing?*" Máthair Damhán bellowed, her monstrous voice echoing through the cavern.

Evelayn heard the hawk above, a sharp sound that she recognized as a battle cry, and then Máthair Damhán's screech of agony, but she ignored both as she lifted the sword and swung it toward the trunk of the Immortal Tree. It sliced partway into it with a blow that felt as though *she* had been hit by a blast of power. It wasn't until that moment that she realized she'd used both hands to wield the sword. Her bones were no longer broken—she was healed entirely. One last gift from the Tree she continued to hack at, intent on destroying, while Lorcan dove at Máthair Damhán again and again, keeping her from advancing on Evelayn. Black blood ran down the Ancient's face; almost all of her eyes were gouged out.

Every strike into the Tree sent a shock of pain through Evelayn, as if by destroying it, she was destroying part of herself. The surges and waves of power grew larger, and more unpredictable, as she gouged the trunk, deeper and deeper. She had to jump back to avoid an eruption of lightning from the spot directly above where she'd just cut.

The hawk screamed at her, the only warning before a different blast of lightning struck her from *behind*, sending her flying forward, to crash into the Tree. The already damaged trunk cracked even further at the impact, and a massive blaze of shadowflame burst out from the Tree in all directions. The hawk soared high enough to avoid it, but Máthair Damhán was too large. She was thrown onto her back by the impact with a shriek, all eight of her legs up in the air, her belly exposed.

The agony of Evelayn's charred back had already begun to diminish, as her body was still trying to heal itself, despite the injuries to the Immortal Tree. She climbed back to her feet. The hawk dove toward Máthair Damhán, but only Evelayn saw her lift her hand, summoning more power.

"Lorcan—*NO!*"

But it was too late.

The lightning struck him in the breast. A horrific sound ripped through the hawk's throat and out his beak as he careened through the air and slammed into the stone wall across from them, then dropped to the ground and was still.

"*LORCAN!*" Evelayn screamed, sudden tears nearly blinding her.

There was no time. Already, Evelayn felt the draw of power and threw herself to the side to avoid the next blast of lightning that Máthair Damhán summoned, this time aimed at her. The Ancient had begun to rock back and forth, trying to flip over onto her feet. Evelayn knew she only had moments.

With tears running down her cheeks, and her entire body hurting inside and out, she grabbed the sword from where it had fallen to the ground and sprinted at the Ancient who had caused all this—all for fear of dying. Well, Evelayn wasn't afraid to die. Not anymore. Only Ceren remained of all those she loved, and she had Quinlen and her younglings.

At the last second, Evelayn lifted the sword over her head and jumped, leaping through the air to land on top of Máthair Damhán's bulbous body. In the same fluid motion, she sliced the sword down, carving it through the Ancient's belly.

Máthair Damhán screamed, an unearthly howl that spoke of all the terror of her ultimate end that the creature had harbored for so long.

Evelayn stabbed her again, and then again, as the Ancient rocked her body back and forth, trying to throw her off. Yet another blast of lightning struck Evelayn, this time in the chest. She went flying and landed with a loud crunch as her legs crumpled beneath her and the sword clattered against the stones.

"You . . . horrible . . . little . . . swan . . . queen . . ." Máthair

Damhán panted, her head turned toward Evelayn, her two remaining eyes locked on to her. Her words were a gurgle through the blood that filled her throat and dripped out the corner of her ink-black lips. "If . . . I . . . die . . . so . . . shall . . . you . . ."

And with her last breath, the Ancient blasted Evelayn one last time. She tried to heave herself out of reach, but it still hit Evelayn in the hip and leg, launching her across the ground and slamming her into the severed tree trunk. There was a sharp snap and the Tree groaned behind her.

The pain was unimaginable. Evelayn gasped, each attempt to breathe agony. There were more snaps and cracks from the Tree behind her, and she felt it quake. Evelayn tried to move—but she couldn't. Her legs wouldn't respond to her at all. She realized the first crack she'd heard wasn't the Tree at all—it had been her spine snapping. Tears ran down her cheeks as she tilted her head back and stared up at the white-and-black branches, at the surges of power that winked and shuddered. Then she turned her head toward the hawk that hadn't moved, not so much as a flinch. He'd died trying to help her.

"I failed," Evelayn whispered, to herself, to Lorcan, to the Immortal Tree, to the Spirit Harbinger, to her parents, if they really were out there somewhere. "I'm sorry." Her lungs felt wrong, sort of sticky and . . . viscous. Each inhale grew harder to suck in, and each exhale began to feel as though she were drowning from the inside. "So . . . sorry . . ."

Another shudder went through the Tree, and there were more sounds of it snapping. Then with one final shudder, there was a deafening crack and the trunk gave way. The Immortal

Tree crashed toward the ground. Power that had emanated from it for thousands of years exploded out of it in every direction. Evelayn felt it go through her body, filling it so completely that she seemed to be made of it, every cell and fiber of her expanded with it. In that moment, she could have done anything—she felt every possibility she'd never explored, every ability she'd never mastered . . . she even realized how amazingly simple shifting should have been for her, had she ever learned to do it on her own.

Lorcan had died as a hawk; perhaps it was only fitting that she die as the swan, Evelayn thought suddenly. To shift just *once* on her own, before she was gone.

She let her eyes fall shut as the power began to ebb out of her, to be absorbed back into the earth, where it belonged. Evelayn saw the swans in her mind—her swans. She visualized her skin becoming feathers, her elongated neck, felt the water beneath her breast, and the wind beneath her extended wings. And finally, after all that time and her many failures, Evelayn shifted into the swan.

Then the power was gone and the cave fell into utter and complete darkness.

THIRTY-SEVEN

*S*EVERAL MOMENTS PASSED BEFORE SHE REALIZED SHE *wasn't dead yet. In fact, all the pain had gone and she could breathe easily once more. But it was completely dark in the cavern with the Tree destroyed and the power gone. Though she'd spent so long as a swan, it still took her a moment to grow used to this shape again. She tried walking forward, and much to her surprise, her legs responded. Had she been healed in that last explosion of power? Or did her injuries only last in her other form?*

The swan extended her wings and gingerly attempted to flap them. No pain whatsoever.

If only she'd managed to destroy the Tree in time to heal Lorcan. She carefully moved toward him, using her senses of smell and touch to feel her way across the cavern to where he lay, his wings open and his charred breast feathers completely still.

She couldn't cry as a swan, but she was able to voice her grief in another way, in a long, sorrowful trumpet that echoed back to her. She couldn't leave him here to rot beside Máthair Damhán's massive corpse. Instead, she tenderly scooped him toward her feet with her wings and tried to pick him up. But the webbing made it impossible. Her only option was her beak. He was much lighter than she, and it was easier than she'd anticipated to gingerly clamp her beak around his limp neck and lift him off the ground.

The swan spread her wings and flapped, taking flight. She turned her head in the darkness, smelling for fresh air, feeling for a breeze that would guide her out of the claustrophobic cavern. Finally she felt it—a draft.

It was a cumbersome flight with the hawk in her mouth, but she refused to drop him or leave him behind. He deserved better for what he'd done. She flew slowly, carefully through twisting tunnels and massive caverns. Everywhere was the scent of the monsters who inhabited the White Peak, and her instincts begged her to go faster, to flee, to drop the extra weight that slowed her down.

But she refused.

And then finally, ahead, there was light and a strong breeze that smelled of pine and fresh soil, free from the decay of Máthair Damhán and her daughters.

She soared out of the mountain and spread her wings more fully, flapping hard to rise up, up, up, toward the white clouds that raced past. Even though it was still cold, and winter was still coming, she felt the difference in the earth. It was no longer dying, it was merely slumbering, preparing to return to full life in the spring. The spring that was surely coming now that they'd succeeded in returning the power to where it had always belonged.

And that's when she banked and changed course, winging her way back the way they'd come, only this time, to give the Spirit

Harbinger the sacrifice he had demanded, even though they'd ful-
filled their promise.

It took all day, but as the sun set and a huge, luminous moon slowly
rose in the east, the swan finally saw the temple ruins rising through
a forest no longer encased in fog. The trees were emerald and jeweled
flowers bloomed, glistening with dew. She swooped lower and lower,
the hawk's body limp in her beak, careful not to drop too low, remembering the skeletal monsters with razor-sharp teeth that surrounded
the temple.

But as the swan circled the temple, she saw not demon dogs but
a pack of white wolves watching her somberly with eyes that gleamed
as golden as the sun at dawn. She felt no malice from them—in fact,
they dropped their heads toward the earth when she approached, as if
bowing to her.

Finally, she found the entrance to the temple where the pool of
water sat, as still as ever, with that ethereal glow still emanating from
it. The room where the Spirit Harbinger had come to them.

Carefully, she laid the hawk's body on the stone wall surrounding
the water. And then she filled her beak with the water—not for herself, but for him. If ever a creature was deserving of a miracle, it was
the hawk who had died to help her keep their promise.

But when she tried to dribble it into his beak, using her webbed
foot to pry it open, the liquid merely pooled and then ran out, to soak
into the stone beneath his head.

The swan tucked in her wings and lowered her head in defeat.
There was nothing she could do then. He was truly gone.

She felt the presence before she saw the Spirit Harbinger taking *form across the pool. It was the same one as before, but this time he was not alone. Behind him, others also formed, males and females, all looking at the swan and the hawk in silence.*

Finally, the first one spoke.

"I misjudged you, Queen of Éadrolan. You and your Mate. I set you a task I did not expect you to complete."

The swan lifted her head, confused at his words.

"But you proved yourself. You both put aside the desire for power and kept your promise, returning true balance to our world and the one beyond our shores. For this great deed, you shall be granted a boon. But first . . ."

The Spirit Harbinger waved his hands as if summoning power, but rather than from below, the Light came down from above, encompassing both her and the hawk. Warmth unlike anything she'd ever known filled her body, every cell, every fiber. It was Light and Dark, day and night, it was the most pure love she'd ever experienced. More powerful than anything she'd ever wielded.

When the shift came, it wasn't painful; it was as easy as breathing. And she knew that this time, when she left the swan behind, it was forever.

THIRTY-EIGHT

I N THE BLINK OF AN EYE, THE WARMTH DISSIPATED AND Evelayn stood before the Spirit Harbingers in her Draíolon form, completely healed. All except the grief in her heart.

"Evelayn?"

She went rigid with shock, unable to believe it. But then he was there, standing before her, every bit as alive and healed as she.

"Lorcan!" She sobbed and threw herself into his arms. They came around her, holding her so tightly, he seemed afraid she wasn't real, either.

"For your sacrifices, you have been gifted with healing and life," the Spirit Harbinger spoke again, his voice gentle. "But you may each request one further boon of your own choosing."

Evelayn inhaled the scent of Lorcan as deeply as she could— the familiar blend of ice, pine, and velvet night, even without his power—relishing the feel of his body against hers. He was alive, Ceren had escaped to return to her family, balance had been restored to the world, and Máthair Damhán was gone—the last of the Ancients who might try to steal the power again. What more could she want that was in their ability to give?

"You have power over life and death." Lorcan spoke hesitantly, his voice gruff with emotion. "Can you bring back my brother?"

Evelayn turned in his arms, her eyes wide and her breath held as she looked to the Spirit Harbinger. *Was that possible?*

He smiled benevolently. "You gave your life, a sacrifice above all others. For this deed, life shall be returned to your brother, if that is your wish."

"It is," Lorcan replied immediately. Evelayn felt the way he trembled, scented the hope that sprang up at the Spirit Harbinger's words.

"Then it is done." He nodded at the female behind him, and she disappeared. "And you, Queen of Éadrolan?" The Spirit Harbinger looked to Evelayn.

She hardly dared speak her request. "My parents . . . I know I didn't give my life, but is there any way . . . ?"

The look the Spirit Harbinger gave her was so tender, so full of understanding, it made tears prick her eyes.

"Your parents have been gone too long to return to this world. Lothar's spirit hadn't been taken to the Final Light yet. I am very sorry. However," he continued, when the tears slipped out and ran down Evelayn's cheeks, "you may see them if you wish. That is within our power to do."

Evelayn nearly choked on the sob that rose in her chest. *"Yes,"* she whispered. "Yes, please."

"Then it is done." This time, he himself disappeared, along with all the other Spirit Harbingers.

Lorcan and Evelayn stood together, completely alone and silent. Her heart thudded beneath the cage of her ribs as she breathlessly waited. That same light suddenly shone down from above, but this time it landed on the ground in front of them. The Spirit Harbinger materialized first, but he quickly stepped aside. And then, there they were.

Her mother and father stood in front her.

They glowed with the same light as the Spirit Harbinger, but other than that, they looked just as she remembered.

"My beautiful daughter." Her mother spoke first, and Evelayn choked on a sob.

"I can't believe you're here." Evelayn lurched forward, but her father held up his hand.

"I'm so sorry, my sweet girl, but you can't touch us." His voice was gentle but firm. "Not yet. But one day, when your time here is finished, we *will* be truly reunited, I promise."

"It's real, then? The Final Light?"

"Of course it is." Her mother smiled. "And it is wonderful beyond anything you could imagine. But your time to join us has not come yet."

"I thought I was dying . . . I thought I'd failed . . ."

"No matter if you had succeeded in restoring true balance or not, you would never have been a failure, my darling Evelayn. We are so proud of you." It looked as though a tear slid down her mother's ethereal cheek.

Evelayn had never longed for a touch more than she did at that moment, wanting to embrace them both. But it was enough for now to know they were proud of her, that they were still there, waiting for her to join them—someday. It was enough to tuck away into her heart and hold her through the many years to come without them.

"And you, Lorcan"—her father's gaze rose above her head to meet her Mate's—"we are proud of you as well. When we were alive, we had no knowledge of the depth of suffering you endured in your life, but we have watched you learn—we have witnessed you overcome and change in so many ways. You are truly a worthy Mate for our daughter. And together, the two of you will be able to rejoin our kingdoms in true peace."

"At last," her mother sighed, as if saying a benediction or a prayer.

"Will I ever see you again?" Evelayn asked, sensing that their time was coming to a close.

"Not in this world." Her mother smiled again, but it was tinged with sadness. "But know, Evelayn, that we are with you *always*. When you experience joy or sorrow, we will be with you. When you give birth to your sons and daughters, I will be there beside you. And when your time has ended, we will be there to welcome you home."

Evelayn could barely see through the tears that filled her eyes. "I love you both so much."

"And we love you." Her father smiled gently. "Don't grieve our loss any longer, my daughter. If we had not been taken when we were, you would not have become queen and accomplished what you did. Everything happens for a reason. And we *will* all be together again."

"Until then, hold our love in your hearts. Both of you." Her mother looked to Lorcan, too, and Evelayn felt the gratitude emanating from him. He'd never known love like theirs, she realized. And that made her understand how truly blessed she was, even though she'd lost her parents so early in her life. At least she'd known their love for the time they'd had together. That truly was a gift.

"We will," she said.

"Until we meet again," her father echoed as the light descended one final time, encompassing both of them, growing brighter and brighter until she could no longer see them. And then, from one blink to the next, the light was gone and so were they.

Lorcan wrapped his arms around her from behind, holding her tightly as silent tears slid down her cheeks. Even with the warmth of their love still fresh in her heart, she felt their absence acutely.

But then another voice sounded from behind them, a broken cry that made her and Lorcan both spin around, to see Lothar sprinting toward them, well and whole.

"Lorcan!"

Evelayn had no idea how he'd not only been brought back to life but brought here, to the temple, so quickly. But she was unspeakably grateful to the Spirit Harbingers for it when she felt Lorcan's joy.

"Lothar!" Lorcan's voice broke and he released Evelayn to meet his brother halfway, grabbing him into his arms in a tight embrace. "I'm so sorry," she heard him say, his voice muffled. "For everything."

"You are my brother," Lothar said simply. "There is nothing

to forgive. I saw what you did—and I heard you wish for me to be brought back. But even if you hadn't done any of that, I still would have forgiven you. You are my brother," he repeated.

They embraced tightly again, and then the brothers turned to face her. Her family, she realized with a tightening in her chest. They were her *family.*

"Let's go home," Lorcan said, holding his hand out toward her.

Evelayn nodded through her tears and stepped toward him— her Mate, her family, and her future.

BRIGHT
BURNS
THE NIGHT

ACKNOWLEDGMENTS

As ALWAYS AT THE COMPLETION OF ANOTHER BOOK—ANOTHER *series*—I owe a debt of gratitude to many. The longer I've been published, the more I've realized writing never really gets any easier. But all of you certainly help!

Thank you a million times over to my agent, Josh Adams. You, Tracey, and the entire Adams Lit family have been such a blessing. Thank you for always being in my corner and never giving up on me, even when I'm stuck on bedrest without a single ounce of creative juice left. We made it to the other side, and you were right, I did it!

To my brilliant editor, Lisa Sandell—I am so honored to be able to continue on this publication journey with you. Thank you for your patience with the aforementioned bedrest saga, and for your unending championing of my work. I am so grateful for you in my life!

Thank you to my fantastic publicist, Brooke Shearouse, for your dedication on my behalf. The marketing team: Rachel Feld,

Isa Caban, and Vaishali Nayak—you are all amazing. So much gratitude to Mindy Stockfield, Tracy van Straaten, and Lauren Donovan, as well as Rachel Gluckstern, Lori Benton, and Olivia Valcarce. Big squishy hugs to Lizette Serrano and Emily Heddleson for all you both do. And my eternal gratitude to Elizabeth Parisi and Chris Gibbs for the jaw-dropping cover designs. I wouldn't be where I am without the incomparable David Levithan—thank you. And I can't forget the lovely Ellie Berger. Thank you all for EVERYTHING! To the sales team and everyone at Scholastic who work so tirelessly to put books into readers' hands—thank you!!

For always being there for me, for being willing to read different versions of this story on such short notice, giving needed advice, and talking me off ledges: Lynne Matson and Anne Blankman. I'm so grateful to have you both in my life.

Thank you to Erin Summerill for always making me laugh, and for your unflagging support and friendship. I'm so grateful for you!

Kathryn Purdie—you know how much you mean to me. Thank you for everything. I wouldn't be able to keep my head above water without you.

To all the booksellers, bloggers, bookstagrammers, teachers, librarians, and others who have championed my work and continue to do so—I will forever be in your debt. I wish I could name you all individually, but there are too many incredible people who have touched my life, helped spread the word for my books, and been generally AWESOME on all fronts to include without needing an extra book to do you all justice. I am able to do what I do because you of what *you* do. "Thank you" will never be enough for your tireless efforts to get books into the hands of readers. With a special thanks to Rockstar Book Tours, Storygram Tours, Jenn Kelly, and to The King's English here in Utah—my favorite bookstore in the world.

Music is my muse, and this time my thanks go out to Jessica Rotter, Rupert Gregson-Williams, Craig Armstrong, X Ambassadors with Erich Lee, Fleurie, Henry Jackman, Rob Simonsen, and One Republic.

To my mom and dad, my eternal gratitude, as always, for all your support, love, and excitement. And my sisters—you know that cheesy saying "Sisters by blood, best friends by choice"? Yeah, that. I love you all so much. Special thank-you to Kerstin for pushing me to write this book—for wanting the sequel so desperately, for reading it so quickly and loving it so much, and doing more than your share to support this series (and me!), and to Elisse for always being my number one beta reader, no matter how busy you are.

Thank you to my other parents, the ones I was blessed to gain through marriage, for all your support and excitement, as always. This year has been a battle, but cancer doesn't have ANYTHING on you and by the time this book comes out, it will be behind us. I just know it! Much love to you both.

And last on this list, but first in my life and heart, my family— my four beautiful children and my incredible husband. None of this would mean a thing without the five of you by my side. Brad, Gavin, Kynlee, and now Adeline—this is your first true acknowledgment, because you joined our family during the creation of this book. What a special year 2017 has been because of you. Travis, thank you for being my everything and the most supportive husband on earth. If I had to choose between never writing or reading another book again and you, I would choose you. And that's really saying something.

SARA B. LARSON is the author of *Dark Breaks the Dawn* and the acclaimed Defy trilogy: *Defy*, *Ignite*, and *Endure*. She can't remember a time when she didn't write books—although she now uses a computer instead of a Little Mermaid notebook. Sara lives in Utah with her husband and four children, and their Maltese, Loki. She writes in brief snippets throughout the day and the quiet hours when most people are sleeping. Her husband claims she should have a degree in "the art of multitasking." When she's not mothering or writing, you can often find her at the gym repenting of her sugar addiction. You can visit her at SaraBLarson.com.